I have enjoyed  ık

Grace to Save may

~ Katy C.

Reading a new book by Carol Moncado is like getting together again with a bunch of old friends to find out what's new in their lives. Her newest release, *Grace to Save*, fits right in there…Get ready for a good read as you find out more about old friends. Now I need to get back to the housework I neglected to finish reading, Travis, Cassie, & Abi's story!

~ **Margaret N.**

I love a good romance and this one is good with a whole lot more...I loved the story and how the author weaves Serenity Landing into all her stories. Her characters are old friends who pop in for a visit now and then. We see God's redemption and love throughout the book.

- Linda R.

What a read! Moncado brought a lot of emotions into *Grace to Save*...trauma of 9/11, bad decisions, inability to forgive, abandonment, romance, and then soooo many consequences. I sooooo love the way that this author is so great at weaving Serenity Landing and the people that we know and love from other stories into each of her books!

- R. H.

Carol Moncado

USA Today Bestselling Author

This is a work of fiction set in a fictionalized southwest Missouri and a redrawn, fictionalized Europe. Any resemblance to real events or to actual persons, living or dead, is coincidental. Any reference to historical figures, places, or events, whether fictional or actual, is a fictional representation.

Scripture taken from the Holy Bible, King James Version.

Cover photos:
Couple/boy: CANDID Publications
Girl: Rohappy/depositphotos.com
Yarn pops(courtesy of Show Me Yarn): CANDID Publications, 2016
Author photo: Captivating by Keli, 2010

First edition, CANDID Publications, 2017
ISBN-10: 1-944408-95-9
ISBN-13: 978-1-944408-95-4

For Amy -

one of my oldest (well, longest - because we can't be old!) friends.
You inspire me daily with your courage, your strength, your faith, and the hope you never give up.
I am in awe of your perseverance and overwhelmingly positive outlook. I know you have your moments, but even in those, you inspire.
Thank you for letting me borrow your daughter's name. And her ladybugs.

And Jeremy -

who is Amy's other half. Her partner in life, in love, in music, in hope. Thank you for taking care of my friend, being the strength she needs, the leader of your household.

And to both of you for making us roll our eyes with your sappy, over the top, everso beautiful, posts that show us all that Happily Ever After doesn't only exist in fairy tales.

For Bailey who touched so many during her short life.

For Fiona - who loves her brother so much and is so very talented.

And Liam - for showing all of us what unconditional love really looks like.

Chapter One

May 2017

"I'll pay for them to fly commercial." Christopher Bayfield crossed his arms over his chest and stared down the duke. He could do that because the duke was also his twin brother. No one else would understand why he wanted to avoid this flight.

Alexander tugged on the bottom of his tuxedo jacket and frowned into the mirror. "Someday I'll figure out how to make this look right with the sash on the first try."

"It's your own fault for marrying a queen, Ander, but don't think you're getting out of this. I'll pay for them to fly back, first class."

Alexander turned away from the mirror to face Christopher. "Christiana, your pregnant sister-in-law, asked you to fly them back on the family plane. You're really going to turn her down?"

"If you won't let me pay for them to go back first class, I'll rent a plane for them."

"You get to tell the queen you don't want to do the one thing she asked you to do for the woman who saved her life, and the life of your niece or nephew."

Christopher hated it when his brother was right. "Then they can take the plane home, and I'll rent one of my own. Or buy my own first class ticket."

"Don't be ridiculous, Topher." Alexander limped to the door of Christopher's room, his leg still recovering from the recent shoot out with the man who tried to kill his wife. Alexander had come to Christopher's room to guilt trip him into doing this. Help fixing his tie was just an excuse. "Just ride home in the plane with them. Sit at the table and work the whole time or take the couch and sleep. I'm not saying you have to become busom buddies with the gal, just make sure she and her son don't die in a horrid plane crash on the way back. Once you land, put them in the car Jonathan will provide and go on your merry way."

Before his brother could open the door, someone knocked. Alexander opened it, and in walked the queen.

Christopher was tempted to bow, but knew that was just his inner snark. It wasn't Christiana's fault her uncle was nuts, had set up Julia to make it look like she was having an affair with Alexander, and then tried to kill Christiana when it all went wrong. The uncle had already killed Christiana's family and beloved nanny many years earlier. Christiana had only survived because she was sick and hadn't been in the car.

"Is there something wrong, Christopher?" The queen came to stand in front of him. "You look quite perturbed."

He quirked a brow at her. "You don't know me that well."

"No, but I know what your identical twin looks like when he's perturbed." The smile on her face told Christopher all he really needed to know. He would do whatever she asked. She made his brother so incredibly happy and was giving Alexander the family he'd longed for.

The family Christopher doubted he'd ever have. Not with his history.

He could do the doting uncle thing, though. Prince Harry pulled it off. Christopher wasn't a prince, but surely he could do the same. Bring cool presents. Take them to polo matches. Except he'd never played polo in his life.

"Is there a problem with the flight?"

His sister-in-law was intuitive, too. Or Alexander had warned her this might be an issue. "No. No problem."

Alexander mouthed a thank you.

"It is too bad you will not be able to stay for the ball." Christiana glanced at her husband. "You would look almost as dashing as Alexander. There will be plenty of eligible young women for you to dance with."

Christopher reached for her hand and bowed low over it, kissing the back. "There's only one woman I would want to dance with, Your Majesty, but I fear my brother will keep her all to himself." He knew how to be gallant when he wanted to be.

His brother stepped closer until Christopher moved back. "I'm pretty sure she's going to spend most of the evening sitting out. She's still not back to normal yet, and neither am

I."

"Julia and Alex are ready to go home when you are," she told him. "But it is time for us to leave. Tony is waiting." The head of security was attending the ball as a guest this time.

Christopher watched as they walked away. Alexander rested his hand on his wife's lower back. Christiana leaned toward him, just a bit. They had been through so much to get to this point.

He envied them.

Not enough to get entangled again.

But he did envy his brother the happiness anyone could see.

Just a glimpse of the hope he could, even should, have had for himself.

It would never be more than a glimpse.

With a sigh, he grabbed his bag and headed down the hall. The sooner they left, the sooner this whole thing would be over.

Julia Quisenberry had very little patience left.

"Mom, are we really flying home in our own plane?" Alex asked for the thousandth time.

"Not quite." The car had nearly arrived at the airport. "Mr. Bayfield is letting us fly home with him when he goes back to Serenity Landing."

"Duke Alexander is flying to Serenity Landing?"

"No, sweetheart. His brother, Christopher, is flying to Serenity Landing. The queen asked him to fly us back with him." She'd explained it to him more than once.

"Oh. Yeah." He would have said something else, but the car glided to a stop next to a building on the airport property.

A man waited there to open the door. "This way please."

The small room held only one other person.

Christopher Bayfield.

He was doing an excellent job of ignoring them. Just like she'd figured.

After a few minutes talking with an official of some sort, Julia and Alex found seats across the room from Christopher. She kept her seven-year-old son occupied with a new coloring book and crayons. The queen had given them a travel gift basket, complete with iPads for both of them. Alex's was preloaded with games and apps he'd enjoy. She'd break it out mid-flight when he grew antsy.

Ten minutes later, a woman in a stewardess uniform came into the room and spoke with Christopher for a moment. She left, and he began to pack up his things. "We take off in fifteen minutes. You'll need to be on board in five."

He didn't actually look at them as he spoke. If he said five more words to her before the plane landed, Julia would be shocked. She didn't know why exactly he seemed to despise her so much. All of the things she supposedly did were fabricated. He knew that. Everyone knew that. Except for running into him and Alexander at the hospital in Serenity Landing, where someone took the picture that started the whole mess, none of this was her fault.

"Pack up your things," she told Alex quietly.

Her son stared at Christopher as he slung the messenger bag over his shoulder and walked out of the building. Alex didn't say anything, though, and in a minute, they followed in

Christopher's footsteps.

With Alex's hand tucked securely in her own, they crossed a few feet of tarmac to the steps of the only plane in the vicinity. She urged him in front of her, knowing his eyes would be as wide as hers. Once on board, the interior was as nice as she would have expected based on the television shows and movies where they had planes like this.

It still took all of her self-control not to gawk.

"Over here, ma'am." The stewardess stood next to a couch with seat belts protruding from the crack.

Julia stowed her carry-on bags in the cabinet next to the couch and then helped Alex tighten the seat belt. The stewardess brought them each a bottle of water and asked them to remain seated with their seat belts on until the captain said they could remove off.

Alex looked through a guest packet of information about this particular kind of plane. Julia stared at the back of Christopher's head.

He sat at a table with room for four. His paperwork was already spread out much as it had been in the waiting room. The stewardess spoke quietly to him once again. He nodded, and she took a seat near the door to the cockpit. Once she was buckled in, the plane began to taxi slowly toward the runway.

Alex didn't say it, but she knew he was disappointed he couldn't see better. The back of the couch was too high for him to see much out the window behind them. The window across the plane was too far away to gawk like she wished he could.

After sitting still for a couple of minutes, the engine revved, and g-forces pressed them slightly toward the back of the plane. It wasn't as bad as she would have expected it to be since they sat sideways.

Christopher barely seemed to notice. His pen scratched on the paper in front of him, writing something long-hand.

It didn't take but a few seconds for the wheels to leave the runway as they soared into the air.

The first two hours of the flight were uneventful. Alex dozed as he lay on the couch. Julia read a book on her new iPad. The queen had thoughtfully loaded it with books she thought Julia would enjoy. Or rather, she'd probably had an employee do it.

"Mama?"

Julia set the iPad down, a frown already in place. Alex rarely called her that. "What is it, sweetie?"

"My tummy doesn't feel good."

Great. She looked around to see the stewardess in her seat reading a book. "Ma'am?"

The woman looked up, setting her book to the side. "How can I help you?" By the time she finished the question, she was at their side.

"Do you have a trash bag?" Julia didn't trust Alex's stomach when he said it didn't feel good.

"Of course." In less than a minute, there was a bag in a small can for Alex to use if he felt the need. "Now, how about some crackers or Sprite?"

Julia shook her head. "Not just yet. I'm afraid it'll all come back up."

The stewardess looked concerned. "Has he been sick?"

"No, but it always seems like there's a bug going around, doesn't it?"

After nodding her agreement, the woman went back to her seat.

Christopher glanced at them, at the same moment Julia happened to look at him. Their eyes locked, but all she could see in them was his disapproval. Of her. Of her son. Of her entire life.

Probably of her baby, too.

With one hand protectively covering her abdomen, Julia encouraged Alex to lean against her and brushed his hair back with the fingertips of her other hand.

Ten minutes later, it happened.

Christopher didn't look, but dug frantically through his bag searching for his earbuds before he needed the trash bag the stewardess had already slipped to him.

Just in case.

Because she knew he was a sympathetic puker.

He could handle just about anything, but not that. It was one of many reasons he was okay with never having kids, even if his friends told him it was different when the kid puking belonged to you. He didn't buy it.

With his earbuds firmly in place, the next order of business had to be music. Rather than the rock and roll he might choose another time, he went with some old school Michael W. Smith for now. With Go West Young Man filling his ears, he was able to concentrate on the paperwork before him.

Alexander had been running their family's wedding facility in Ravenzario for years. Christopher had taken over some of it since Ander married the queen. They were in the throes of planning a wedding that would never happen, for Princess Yvette of Mevendia and the deceased Prince Nicklaus of Ravenzario. It needed to be perfect, even if the planning was futile. Ander would help some when he wasn't busy doing all of his Duke-ish stuff, but most of it would fall on Topher. He'd be back every two weeks for the next six weeks and then spend the last couple weeks there.

He didn't know what the backup plan could possibly be. Christiana's younger brother had been killed in the same car accident that took her parents' lives as well as the life of her nanny. But Nicklaus had been betrothed to Princess Yvette of Mevendia since they were small children and the wedding had to be planned regardless of the prince's death.

Ander was keeping a big secret from him about it, though. Topher couldn't figure out what it was, but eventually it would come out.

Meanwhile, Topher finished writing out some contingency plans for the media. His secretary would type it up for him later. He hated typing, preferring pen on paper for this kind of thing. Maybe he should call Mady and see if he could get some acting work again. Then he wouldn't be doing this kind of work anyway.

After another hour of work on several different projects, he debated changing seats to one of the captain's chairs where he could stretch out better. He looked up and motioned to Serena.

She put her book down and walked over.

"How's the kid?" he asked quietly.

Serena glanced toward the couch. "Sleeping. He threw up

three times, but it seems to have settled down for now."

"Good."

"How are you?"

"Thank you for the warning. I appreciate it."

She smirked at him. "I know how you react."

Topher grimaced. She'd cleaned up after him more than once. "Thanks. I'm going to move to the other chairs. Would you stow my bag for me?"

Serena took it from him and went to the back to store it in a closet. Topher moved to a seat on the same side of the plane as the couch, but sort of separated by a shelving unit that also held refreshments. He put his seatbelt on more out of habit than anything and stretched his legs out before deciding to grab a pillow and blanket from the cabinet next to him.

A nice long nap and this flight would be nearly over.

Instead of restful sleep, his dreams were filled with Julia and her son. He couldn't remember the dreams when he woke up, but he knew they hadn't been pleasant. Was there some sort of fight between them? But why would there be? Once they climbed in the car Jonathan would send, he'd never see them again.

"Mister?"

Topher looked up to see the kid standing there. "Can I help you?"

"My mom's asleep, but I need to go to the bathroom. Where is it?"

Shouldn't he be asking Serena? Topher looked to her seat, but she wasn't in it. A glance at his watch told him she was likely getting something to eat. It was about that time for her.

"It's in the back. It's the only door with a little slot that tells you if someone's in there or not."

The kid stared at him for a minute then turned away.

Serena walked by a second later. "You could have been nicer to him. He didn't ask to be here."

"And I didn't ask for them to be here." But he never would have told Ander and Christiana no, even if he had tried to convince them of alternatives. He'd known they wouldn't agree, but had to try.

He wouldn't go back to sleep. Instead, he pulled out a paperback and started to read. It was a political thriller by a local guy his dad recommended. Jeremiah something. Topher didn't bother to look at the front cover to remember the last name.

About the time he flipped to the last page, the plane started to descend. He glanced outside and saw lights of a small town. Not Springfield, not yet.

He used the plane's Wi-Fi to send a message to Jonathan to make sure the car would be there. Ander had arranged for Julia and her son to have security for a few weeks until they were sure the whole mess had blown over. Topher had thought about getting some for his property, though probably not for himself. He still hadn't gotten used to word being out about his past life, and his stint as one of America's twin teen heartthrobs on 2 Cool 4 School. Sometimes he dreamed about going back to acting. Maybe someday.

Twenty minutes later, the wheels thumped down, and Topher breathed a sigh of relief. It was over.

He stayed in his seat until Julia and Alex were off the plane and on their way. His bags had already been loaded into his SUV sitting nearby.

On the drive home, he used an earbud and microphone to dictate an email to his assistant outlining what he needed her to do the next day.

With his car parked in front of the house, Topher headed inside and collapsed, still fully clothed, onto his bed. It had been a long few weeks, and he needed sleep.

Lots of sleep.

If only the pretty woman with the dirty blonde hair and sick son would stay out of his dreams, it would all be okay.

Chapter Two

August 2017

Julia propped her feet up on the ottoman. Late August in Southwest Missouri was too hot, too humid, and she was too pregnant to be comfortable ever again.

And she wasn't even that pregnant yet.

With a sigh, she picked up the yarn and crochet hook determined to figure out this pattern as soon as possible. The patterns, along with the online classes she taught, were the only things keeping food on her table. The classes would end in just a couple of days, and she hadn't set up any more. She hadn't had the time and energy.

After arriving back in Serenity Landing, with no job to go back to, she had increased the number of classes she was teaching each week, both crocheting and knitting. She would have helped Kenzie more with her friend's yarn dyeing business and earned some income there, but because of the baby, she couldn't.

Between the classes, being able to increase the number of patterns she had for sale in her Etsy site, and the custom bags she made, they were staying afloat. Barely. If she could have afforded to break her lease, she would have done so already and moved to a cheaper apartment, possibly even a one bedroom. Kenzie had offered her a small place on the property she now shared with her new husband, who was rolling in dough, but Julia wasn't quite that desperate.

Yet.

She'd made some significant progress when it was time to get Alex off the bus. Fortunately, she didn't have to walk far, but she didn't like letting him walk all by himself. Leaning against the wall at the end of the breezeway, she rubbed her stomach, already tightening with Braxton-Hicks contractions, though she wasn't due until December.

"Mom!" Alex ran toward her. "We're going to Fantastic Caverns for our field trip this year!"

She gave him a big hug. "That's great." He'd wanted to go to the cave with its ride-through tram for years, but it had never been in her budget. Her parents had talked about taking him, but their move to Florida two months earlier meant it would have to happen when they came for a visit.

The evening went well, though she was a bit anxious about the text she'd gotten from Kenzie asking her to call after Alex was in bed. She didn't say what about which made Julia even more nervous. And after the week her friend had, with her daughter going missing and everything else, Julia was almost scared to ask what was going on.

Later, when Kenzie didn't answer the call, Julia turned on the television. One of the weekly news magazines was on, carrying her friend's story from the weekend before, but with a twist Julia hadn't heard about yet.

"But that wasn't what surprised news crews most. Our own camera crew were sent to the Langley-Cranston Estate to follow searchers there." The scene switched to a couple in the distance, clearly holding hands. And then a close-up. Julia didn't recognize them. "Many of you will remember the multiple stories we've done on Philip Langley-Cranston, who disappeared without a trace two years ago. Close friends had even said the family had all but admitted he was likely dead. Instead, he'd used an assumed name, checked into rehab, got clean, got married, and reappeared the week before his new niece disappeared."

Julia just stared at the screen. She remembered the entire county of Pond Creek searching for him, and the news stories saying he'd most likely died in the lake nearby, though it was never dragged.

That had to be part of what Kenzie wanted to talk about, right?

Her phone buzzed as the show ended, and Julia glanced at it to make sure it was Kenzie. "Hey. That show was crazy."

"You saw it, huh?" Kenzie sounded tired. "I'm not sure how Jonathan got them to keep the Philip thing quiet until tonight, but they did. That's not why I wanted to talk to you, though."

"What's up?" Julia shifted so her legs were stretched out on the couch.

"I need help. I know there's a lot you can't do because you're pregnant, but I could use your help with what you can do. Because I got a call today." Kenzie paused. "We got a booth at the Serenity Landing Yarn and Fiber Show!" she squealed.

Julia sat straight up, her mouth hanging open. "We did?" She'd forgotten they'd even applied together.

"We did! So we'll need a bunch of your stuff, patterns and yarn to go with them, some of your bags and order forms, things like that. Just like the other shows, but more."

"Of course." This show was one of the biggest yarn and fiber conventions in the western half of the country. Thousands of people would be passing through every day. If she could hang on until then, she just might be able to make a name for herself.

"They did ask us to share a big booth with the Show Me Yarn girls, but I didn't think we'd be able to fill one up by ourselves anyway."

"The Show Me Yarn girls are good. Their stuff is good quality. It'll be a good match."

"And we tend toward different styles of colors, so there shouldn't be too much overlap."

"With five of us working the booth, we should all be able to break away for classes some, too. At least I'd guess we'll be selling each other's stuff."

"Yes, but we also agreed that at least one of each would be there as much as possible." Kenzie paused again, but this time seemed to be hesitant rather than expectant. "I know you've fallen on super hard times the last six months. Please let me help you get ready for the show. Jonathan is richer than Midas, and therefore I have plenty to help you with."

Julia didn't know what to say. She had never wanted a

handout. "I don't know, Kenz."

"A loan," her friend promised. "After the show, we'll settle up. But I think your patterns will do well, and so will your bags, but you need inventory."

"Okay. A loan." She really didn't have a choice. Alex would love a trip to the fabric outlet store the next day. Not really.

"Why don't you bring Alex over here tomorrow? Lorelai would be thrilled, and Jonathan won't mind at all. We can go shop and what we don't find, we can order from here."

"We haven't been over since you moved into the house," Julia mused. "I'm sure Alex would think it's super cool."

"I'm sure he will. How about 9:30? I'll give you the grand tour after we get back, so you don't have to be up too early. We should still miss the lunch crowds."

"Sounds good." They talked for another minute then hung up.

For the first time in a very long time, Julia fell asleep feeling like she'd finally caught a glimpse of hope for their future.

Christopher leaned back, a sense of satisfaction settling over him. The last few months had been busy with more trips back and forth to Ravenzario than he would have preferred, but he'd had to for the wedding of Princess Yvette to the not-dead Prince Nicklaus. Ander had been keeping from him that the young royal could well be alive somewhere. They finally hired a manager to run the facility there. Ander would keep an eye on things, but only interfere if he had to.

The only trip Christopher planned to make this fall was

when his sister-in-law finally gave birth. Then Christmas.

It had taken another month, but his schedule stateside had finally cleared, too. Could he actually think about a real vacation?

Before he could change his mind, Topher pulled up his favorite travel website and booked a trip to San Majoria in two weeks. School would be back in session, and September was a down time for tourism, which suited him just fine.

Should he find a friend to go with him? His first thought would have been his brother, but with a new wife, an anniversary coming up, and a baby on the way, Ander wouldn't be able to. His neighbor across the lake had spent a fair bit of time in San Majoria lately, but Jonathan had also married in the last couple of months.

Was he really the last single guy in his orbit?

Topher scrolled through his mental Rolodex. All of his close friends were now married. The few he could think of quickly that weren't had never been close friends and likely wouldn't be able to take a week off at a moment's notice anyway.

It had been a while since he'd been to the Caribbean island, but he didn't want to think about his last trip. Too many painful memories. This visit would be to a different part of the island than the secluded huts from the last time.

He shook his head to rid himself of the memories. A glance at the clock told him he would crash soon. After a quick shower, he prayed for a good night's sleep, something that had become increasingly rare.

This night proved to be no different. Julia and Alex appeared in his dreams as they often did. He woke in a cold sweat sometime before dawn and knew he wouldn't be able to get any more shut eye.

A long run to the lake and back helped clear his head. Another hour in the gym in his basement, and he finally felt like he'd chased away whatever haunted him in the night.

As he ate breakfast, his phone buzzed.

The agent he and Ander still shared.

"Hey, Mady. What's up?"

"I had an interesting offer for you."

"I'm not doing a magazine."

Mady chuckled. "No magazine. I know better than that. This is something else. It's super short notice, though. I don't know the details, but I do know they're trying for a *quick* turnaround. Like Christmas quick."

"It'll be September in less than a week, and they want a Christmas show?"

"Not a show. A Happily Ever After TV movie. With Claire Cruz Cartwright."

Topher let out a long, low whistle. "That's pretty impressive. But why me?"

"You're back in the news, but you've been out of the business so there's no chance you're booked up. You're still considered a heartthrob. And your brother married a stinkin' queen. It's a royalty flick, too. You're a prince. She doesn't know it. Thinks you work in the stables or something."

"What happened to get it to this point? Why not put it off until next year?"

"I don't know the details, Topher." His agent sounded both old and annoyed. "All I know is they're offering you a lot of money for three long weeks on set."

"Three weeks? Seriously?" He'd done enough tweenager movies to know that was quick. "Send me the details." He'd look it over. It did sound kind of fun. He'd worked with Claire Cruz Cartwright when they were younger, and she had been fun to be around. It could be the break he'd been looking for.

By three in the afternoon, he'd told his agent to do what she needed to do. He would have to leave on Sunday. The original actor apparently had a motorcycle accident that meant he wouldn't be acting anytime soon. In a few clicks, he'd changed his reservations in San Majoria to after he returned. He'd want a vacation then.

Upstairs, he packed everything he thought he'd need into a couple of suitcases. It had been far too long since he'd done anything like this. Was he crazy?

His phone beeped at him, and he frowned when he looked at it. Who could be pulling up to his front door? His parents were on a month-long second honeymoon ending in Ravenzario in time for their first grandchild to be born. None of his very limited staff should be arriving at this time on a Saturday.

Topher went downstairs and waited for someone to ring the bell. It seemed an eternity before a small knock sounded. He opened the door to see...nothing. Then he glanced down.

A little girl stood there, maybe four years old if his little girl age guessing was any good. She looked up at him with big blue eyes.

He knelt in front of her. "Hi. Can I help you?"

She handed him an envelope.

Topher turned it over a couple of times. His name was written on the front, but had no other identifying marks on it.

The handwriting wasn't familiar either.

Part of his mind noticed a car pulling out of the circle drive to head back down to the road. He ripped open the envelope and unfolded the paper.

He felt the blood drain from his face as he read it.

My name is Bailey Bayfield. My mother was Martha. I'm your daughter.

Chapter Three

"Do you think this is too much?" Julia eyed the huge pile of fabrics.

"How many bags can you make a week?" Kenzie asked, tapping a credit card on the counter as they talked.

"If I work full time on them, a couple of dozen? I don't really know. I've never really tried to focus on them."

Kenzie shrugged. "If it's too much then you'll have it to put on Etsy later."

Julia told the employee how much she wanted of each fabric. In her mind, she was already making bags in different sizes and styles out of each of them. This could be really, really good for her.

The day had started much later than they'd wanted since Kenzie woke up not feeling well. By afternoon, she felt much better and confided in Julia that she and Jonathan were expecting another baby.

Julia was ecstatic for her friend, but had rubbed a hand over her own expanding waistline. Just once she'd like to have a baby without a deadbeat dad. Fine. It wasn't Alex's father's fault he'd gotten drunk and decided to go cow tipping in January, tripped, hit his head, and froze to death. She didn't relish explaining that to her son someday.

And she didn't even want to think about the origins of this child at the moment.

It took half of forever, but eventually, they made it back to Kenzie's new car. Jealousy fought to rear its ugly head. The huge house. The doting husband. The baby on the way. Never having to worry about finances again. All of those things were so fantastic for Kenzie, but only served to remind Julia of what she didn't have.

"You guys should stay for dinner." Kenzie didn't seem to have noticed Julia's sudden reticence.

"I don't think so. I need to get started on all of this."

"Oh, come on. You're not going to work on any of it tonight. Besides, I was thinking you might want to set up a workshop in one of the rooms at the house. You don't have the kind of room you need for this sort of undertaking. There's a big room in the basement that's not being used. You could set up your sewing machine and your embroidery machine and not have to take them down every time you're not using them. You'd have tables to lay everything out on and be more assembly line-ish if you want."

Reluctantly, Julia decided to take a look at the room. It did sound pretty fabulous. Much better than working out of the cramped dining area while they ate in the living room.

By the time she and Alex headed home, she'd agreed to move her things over the next day. Jonathan would let them use his truck to load everything in and would even provide the muscle. His brother and sister-in-law had been there as well, and Philip would help, too. They'd come back after buying property in Spring Meadow. Close enough to be close, but not too close, Kenzie had confided later. An hour away was just about right, though Julia didn't understand all of the reasons why.

Alex woke up in the middle of the night not feeling well. It was all Julia could do to keep her own supper down as he lost his. Normally, she did fine with that sort of thing, but the further along she got in this pregnancy, the worse it had become.

Rather than moving her factory to Kenzie's house, Julia continued work on some patterns at home. There would be time enough to move Monday while Alex was, hopefully, at school.

She was about to put him to bed early, when her phone rang.

Julia didn't recognize the number. It didn't appear someone in her contacts list, but she decided to answer it anyway since it came from Serenity Landing.

"Hello?"

"Is this Julia?" The voice sounded vaguely familiar, but she couldn't place it.

"Yes."

"This is Christopher Bayfield. We flew home from Ravenzario together."

Julia caught herself blinking rapidly. "How can I help you,

Mr. Bayfield?" And how had he gotten her number? He probably had resources she could only dream of.

"Can you come over to the house? I need help, and I don't know where else to turn." He sounded desperate. He'd have to be if he resorted to calling her.

"My son isn't feeling well, and I don't have a babysitter. Can I come over in the morning?"

After a slight hesitation, he spoke. "It really needs to be tonight. I'm going out of town at the crack of dawn. Please?"

Something about his tone called to her. She was familiar with that kind of desperation. "Fine. We'll be there as soon as we can. Text me directions at this number?"

"Of course. Thank you." He clicked off before she could reciprocate.

She quickly changed into something more presentable and made Alex do the same. He hadn't eaten much, but he hadn't thrown up since dawn either, so hopefully he'd be okay.

Julia followed the directions on her phone - southwest of Springfield, and around Serenity Lake. The house was very nice, though not quite on the scale of Kenzie's new home.

"Mr. Bayfield lives here?" Alex asked from the back.

"Guess so." She pulled to the bottom of the stairs leading to the front door and parked. Before she could knock, it opened.

"Come on in." Christopher looked more harried than she'd seen anyone look in a long time. "Thanks for coming."

"What was so urgent?"

Christopher looked at Alex. "Um, would you mind playing on your iPad in the office over there, buddy? We won't be far."

Alex shrugged and took the device into the other room.

"Sorry. I don't know how to deal with all of this yet." As he spoke, they walked through the entryway and into a living area.

A little girl slept on the couch.

Christopher waved a hand her direction. "I have no idea what to do with her."

"Okay." Julia failed to see how this had anything to do with her.

"My parents are out of the country. My brother doesn't know anything about little girls. You used to be a little girl, and you're great with your son, so I called you."

She cocked an eyebrow at him. "I used to be a little girl and have a son so that makes me qualified to take care of some random girl child?"

"More qualified than I am."

Julia asked the question he'd already seemed to avoid answering. "So who is she?"

Of course she wanted to know who the girl was. But Topher hadn't told anyone about her yet. That Julia should be the first one seemed wrong on many levels.

"Her name is Bailey," he finally told her. "Bailey Bayfield."

"Bailey...Bayfield?" Julia repeated, sounding about like he'd felt for the last twenty-four hours.

"Yeah. My daughter I didn't know I had until last night."

"And you're sure she's your kid?"

"I haven't had a DNA test done, but she looks like pictures of my mom when she was that age, and I knew her mother at the right time." He pointed to a collage of pictures, including his parents when they were young. She could see the resemblance.

Julia crossed her arms and turned to stare at him through narrowed eyes. "Aren't you the twin who made a huge deal about not sleeping with your girlfriend ten years ago or whenever it was?"

Topher ran a hand through his hair. "I was. And her mother wasn't my girlfriend."

"Ah, random fan. Even better."

"No." He grabbed Julia by the upper arm and pulled her further away from Bailey. "Very few people know this. *No one* knows this, not even Ander, but I was married. Briefly. She left, and I never heard another word from her until yesterday when Bailey showed up. My ex-wife had my baby, never told me, then died, and the boyfriend she ran off with dropped Bailey off here without so much as a backwards glance."

Julia looked like she might pass out at the sudden influx of information. "Wow."

"Wow is right."

She grasped the edge of the credenza. "That still doesn't explain why you need me."

"I'm headed to Canada to film a HEA TV Christmas movie. I was supposed to be there already, but I hadn't figured out what to do with Bailey yet. She really can't go with me, because I don't have her passport or anything. I Googled. She couldn't get back in the country without one, but I signed the contract already so I have to go."

He wasn't above begging. "Could you please be her nanny for the next few weeks? I'll pay you an exorbitant amount of money to look after her while I'm gone. As soon as I get back,

I'll figure out the dad thing, but I'm stuck. Production on this movie is already way behind because the prior actor was in an accident. They put huge financial penalties in the contract if I break it for any reason not related to my personal health basically." Like more than he could afford. Far more than they were paying him. "Please?"

Julia walked back into the living area. "Fine. Only because she clearly needs someone else in her life for the moment. But why me?"

Topher really didn't want to tell her, but had no choice. "Because you're pretty much the only person I could think of that I knew had experience with kids and might be willing to do it." Because he knew she had no job, one kid, and one on the way. "And I've already got a trip booked to San Majoria after I get back. I've got someone working on getting Bailey's paperwork so she can go." A private investigator would find her birth records and get her birth certificate. And the death certificate. And anything else he needed to get her a passport. "I'll pay to expedite passports for you and Alex, if you'll go with me and help me get to know my daughter."

"Alex has school," she pointed out, arms crossed in front of her. "And we already have passports. We met in Ravenzario, remember?"

Right. He knew that. When he wasn't sleep deprived. "Serenity Landing has two days off that week. I checked."

"Alex doesn't go to school in Serenity Landing."

How had he not figured on that? Topher knew he had to think quickly. He had to get her help not just for while he was out of town, but long term. He'd need a nanny regardless, wouldn't he? "So move out here. Change his school. Be the nanny permanently. You can stay in the house at least for the time being, then find a place close by when you're not needed here 24/7." Or he could turn the top floor of the shop into an apartment. He'd already thought about it so Ander and Christiana and their little family would have a place of their own to stay when they came to visit.

He could see Julia turning it over in her head. "Exactly how much do you mean by exorbitant amounts of money?"

That's when he knew she'd say yes. He named an amount he thought would be enough to pay her bills for at least several months if she decided to quit after the trip to San Majoria. It would get her set up in a new apartment of her own if she needed it to.

"Fine..."

He breathed a sigh of relief.

"...but I need workspace, too."

"For what?"

"I own my own business. I have a big show coming up in about three months, and I need to get stuff done. I won't neglect your daughter to do it, but I do need to work."

"How much room?"

"Enough for three or four six-foot or eight-foot tables, room to move around both sides of them, and electricity."

"I have a partially finished walk-out basement with not much of anything in the finished side except a pool table."

"That should work."

He hesitated. "Listen. I am having a DNA test done. Just to be sure, though I don't think the ex-boyfriend would lie about this. I've sent off for the kit. I'll need you to send the samples as soon as it gets here."

"Of course."

"My assistant will be here tomorrow. She can help you with anything else you need to figure out. I haven't told her about Bailey yet, though." He needed to call her, but he tried really hard not to disturb her on the weekends. She had a life of her own, after all. "Bailey can have the room across from the master suite. You and your son can have the suite in the basement when I get back, but if you'd stay upstairs closer to her for now, I'd appreciate it."

"You've thought this all through, haven't you? What if I'd said no?"

"I've had nothing to do but think it over since she showed up. She wouldn't sleep at all last night. I called you as soon as she dozed off. I don't know what I would have done if you'd said no."

"She misses her mom." Julia nodded like she knew what she talked about.

"Probably. She hasn't said a word to me, though."

They talked for a few more minutes before Julia left, promising to be back in a few hours with enough of her clothes and things to get started. His assistant would keep an eye on Bailey while Julia moved her work stuff and anything else they needed.

Now all he had to do was wake up his new daughter and tell her he was leaving.

Maybe that could wait until Julia got back.

Topher stretched out on the couch opposite Bailey.

Coward.

Chapter Four

"Why are we moving there, Mom?" Alex stubbornly refused to pack any of his clothes.

"Because Mr. Bayfield asked for our help. It's a much nicer place and better schools. You'll still be able to talk to your friends and come visit, but it's for the best." And Mr. Bayfield was paying to break her lease. Even better.

"I don't want to go to a different school!"

"We'll talk about it more later," Julia promised. "But right now it's time to get ready to go."

Still grumbling, Alex finally packed some of his things into a suitcase.

Three hours after they left, Julia pulled the car back into the drive of their new temporary home. She didn't know where to park, though. Before thinking it through too much further, she just parked in the same spot she had before. This time she had to knock on the door for it to open. Christopher opened it, looking even more tired than he had earlier.

"Bailey woke up while you were gone. She still hasn't said anything, though." Christopher opened the door further. "She's watching old episodes of *Blue's Clues* in the living room. Somehow, she managed to tell me that was her favorite without ever actually saying a word. Come on upstairs, and I'll show you where you can stay for the next few weeks."

Julia started to pick her suitcase up, but Christopher beat her to it. He carried their suitcases up the gorgeous, curved staircase.

At the top, he pointed to the left. "The master suite and Bailey's suite are over there. For now, or later if I'm out of town, you two can be over here."

He walked into an open doorway. Julia followed with Alex trailing behind. Christopher set the suitcases on the floor next to the bed. A far nicer bed then Julia had ever slept in, except for when they were staying at the palace.

"There's a bathroom through here." Christopher opened the door and walked through. "And another room Alex can stay in."

Julia followed him with Alex finally catching up. She ran a hand over his hair. "Isn't this nice, bud?"

"I guess."

She closed her eyes and prayed for patience. "Why don't you go downstairs and watch *Blue's Clues* with Bailey?"

He glared at her, but did as she asked.

"Is he okay?" Christopher watched as Alex walked away.

Julia shrugged. "He will be. He doesn't like the thought of leaving his friends from school. Eventually, he'll see this is for the best. Serenity Landing schools are better than the ones where we were."

He led her from Alex's room to the hallway and then on a tour of the house, including a big room in the basement where she could set up her tables and machines, as well as the two bedrooms down there for her to live in with Alex in a few weeks. Julia planned to find her own place as soon as she could, though. Living here, with its reliable hot water and soaker tub, would be nice, but not realistic in the long run. Surely she could find an apartment in Serenity Landing with what he'd be paying her, and Kenzie would give her room to work.

Christopher was even going to pay movers for her. She said he didn't have to, but he said he wanted to so it would be less for her to worry about her first week of work.

They went back upstairs just as an episode was ending. Christopher turned off the television and held his arms out to Bailey. She came to him willingly, wrapping her arms around his neck.

"I need to talk to you, punkin." He sat back down in the chair where she'd been sitting, with her on his lap. "I'm so glad you're here to live with me, but I've got a bit of a problem." He sighed. "I have a job where I'm an actor like you see on TV." She nodded. "Well, I have to go to another country for a couple weeks." Another nod. "But the thing is, I don't have a passport for you, so you can't go with me. And I can't not go."

Julia watched as he rested his cheek against her head. "I'll call you every day, and we can Skype or FaceTime as much as you want. Do you know what those are?"

Bailey nodded and snuggled closer to him.

"It's for about three weeks. Miss Julia and Alex are going

to stay here with you to make sure you're taken care of. When I get back, all of us are going to go on vacation together. We'll stay right near the beach, and swim in the ocean, and maybe see if we can go swim with dolphins or sting rays or something else super cool. How's that sound?"

She gave him a small thumbs up. Julia breathed a sigh of relief. At least the little girl wasn't throwing a fit.

"Would you like to help me make something for dinner?" Christopher asked Bailey.

She nodded again and scrambled down.

Christopher stood and turned to Julia. "Why don't you two get settled? Dinner in about an hour?"

"Sounds good." Julia had to ask Alex twice to head upstairs.

"Why are we unpacking up here? Didn't you say we're moving into the basement?" he asked as she took his suitcase into his temporary room.

"Because he asked us to live up here while he's out of town for the next three weeks," she explained for about the fifth time. "So unpack your things into the drawers, neatly, and then come into my room."

It didn't take long for Julia to stash her things in the dresser. She'd already decided that as soon as the kids were asleep, she would take a long bubble bath. How long had it been since she'd taken one?

Before she knew it, the hour had passed, and she took Alex downstairs for dinner.

Time to figure this new quasi-family thing out.

Christopher pulled the door most of the way shut behind him and went downstairs. "She's asleep," he whispered to Julia who sat in one of the chairs reading a book.

"So is Alex."

"I have a car coming to pick me up so I don't have to leave mine at the airport. I *will* call every day, but I won't know what time each day until I get a schedule, and even then it could vary depending on how long shooting takes." He hated everything about this. Not the movie itself, per se - it would be fun being on set again - but the timing was atrocious. He should have made his agent fight them over the penalties, but hadn't bothered before signing, because he hadn't thought there would be any reason for them to be enforced. What could happen in 24 hours?

"Why don't you text me every morning, and let me know what you think it'll be like? I won't tell Bailey so she won't get her hopes up for a specific time. I know how Alex would be if I said I'd call at five and couldn't until six. He'd go crazy. Then you can text me updates as needed. If you can give me a ten minute warning, that would be great. I can wrap up whatever it is we're doing and have her ready."

He breathed a sigh of relief. "That sounds perfect. I'm thinking some sort of video chat at least until she starts talking. Otherwise, it's just me talking to dead air or you interpreting her facial expressions for me."

Christopher started to turn, but Julia winced. "I don't have a smart phone. Just so you know."

Several thoughts ran through his head, but he stopped on the most logical one. "I'll have my assistant get you an iPhone tomorrow then Bailey and I can use it to FaceTime."

She perked up. Because of course she did at the thought of a free iPhone. "Queen Christiana gave me an iPad. It has service. You could call it, right?"

He thought it over, a bit ashamed of the conclusion he'd jumped to. "I'll have Ida Mae get you an iPhone anyway, but yes. The iPad is bigger so Bailey can see a bit better."

A few minutes later, he was notified the car had arrived. When he took his suitcase out the front door, he noticed Julia's car still parked in front. He needed to make sure she had access to the garage.

The car pulled to a stop on the other side of hers. Once in the back seat, he pulled out his phone. It was incredibly late on the other side of the world, but he didn't want to wait any longer. He called his brother's cell phone.

"Hello?" Ander's voice was quiet, and Topher could hear him moving, probably away from his sleeping wife.

"It's me."

"Who's dead?"

Topher blinked. "What?"

"The only reason you better be calling me at this time of night is because someone's dead. Better yet, deathly ill so I could still have time to come say goodbye, because if someone's dead that information will wait until morning."

Christopher closed his eyes and pinched the bridge of his nose. "It's Martha."

"Martha?" Ander's voice reflected the confusion Christopher had felt for the last twenty-four hours. "Your ex-girlfriend? What about her?"

"She died a few days ago." Did he *know* that? "I think. I really don't know when, but recently."

"Okay. That stinks for her family, but you guys ended years ago."

Topher ran a hand through his hair. "There's something I never told you."

"You slept with her?" Ander's sarcastic tone sliced through Topher.

"I married her first."

Silence met his pronouncement. "You what?"

"We eloped." He leaned his head back. "She wanted to get married, but didn't want to have a big wedding. I wanted to get married, too. So we ran off."

"And why am I just now finding out about this?"

"I was going to tell you about it, but after two weeks on a beach in San Majoria and two more weeks skiing and holed up in a cottage on Eyjania, we came home. The next day, her ex-boyfriend from a couple years earlier showed up, and they ran off together. I got the divorce papers a few weeks later."

"Wow. That's tough." His brother's voice filled with compassion. "I'm sorry to hear that."

"I haven't heard from her in over four years. I'm not that upset about it. God's honest truth, I'm not."

"Then why are you calling me in the middle of the night?"

Topher had no idea how to even say it. "Because you're an uncle."

He could almost see the wheels turning in Ander's head. "You mean you and Martha...? Did you know?"

"Of course I didn't know! The ex-boyfriend showed up yesterday, dropped Bailey off with a note, and left without a word."

"Wow." Ander let it sink in. "How old is she?"

"Four, I think. I don't know her birthday, and she won't say anything, but she looks a lot like Mom."

"Are you having her tested? Are you sure she's not this other guy's kid?"

"I'm having us tested, but there's more."

"What else could there be? Twins?"

"Not quite. I accepted an offer for a HEA TV movie. I'm on my way to the airport now to film in Canada for the next three weeks. I can't get out of it." An idea occurred to him. "Unless you want to do it for me."

"I'm not leaving my very pregnant wife to film a movie." Ander didn't even fake indignation. He knew Topher hadn't been serious. "Are you taking her with you?"

"I can't. I don't have a passport for her."

"Don't tell me Ida Mae's watching her."

Topher cringed. His assistant was many things, but not the mothering type. She liked kids. In small doses. "No. I hired a nanny."

"How'd you find a nanny on such short notice?"

He had no idea how to explain this one, either. "I hired Julia."

"Julia?" Shock colored Ander's voice. "Like Julia who you flew home with? Who you swore never to talk to again? Especially after her kid puked the whole way home."

"I didn't know who else to call. She still doesn't have a job. So I figured she might be interested. She has a kid. She is a girl. She saved Christiana's life. So while I'd never in a million years *date* her, she'll make a decent nanny."

"Famous last words," Ander snorted.

"What?"

"Nothing. Bring all three of them with you when you come meet the baby?"

"If at all possible. I found her birth certificate in her things, so I can order her passport. Otherwise she won't be able to get back in the country."

"Right. Well, we want to meet her as soon as possible. And I want to give you a hard time about starring in a... What did you call the first one we were offered after *2 Cool 4 School* ended? 'A froo froo girly Christmas TV movie-like thing.'"

Topher winced. "You're right. I did say that. But the money's good as long as I don't back out on them. But since I don't actually *need* the money, it would have been a lot of fun with Claire Cruz Cartwright if not for this stuff with Bailey hanging over my head."

"You didn't say that's who you're costarring with. She's one of the few I wouldn't have minded staying in touch with." Topher heard him yawn. "But now I'm going back to bed. Keep me posted and send me pictures."

"I took a few selfies with Bailey this afternoon," Topher admitted. "I'll send them before I take off."

"Talk to you soon." His brother hung up before he could say goodbye, but that wasn't uncommon when they spoke to each other.

The car pulled up to the airport. Time to get this show on the road.

Chapter Five

I'll be home in a few hours, okay?"

Bailey nodded, but Julia noticed she didn't smile. Could she be apprehensive? It had been nearly three weeks since Christopher took off for Canada. He'd hoped to come home on weekends, but the timing hadn't worked out. If he'd left as soon as he could and returned as late as possible, he would have been in Serenity Landing for less than twelve hours, most of which would be overnight.

Julia knew she was nervous. It wouldn't be surprising for Bailey to be, too.

"I'm going to go, but I'll call Miss Julia when I'm on my way from the airport, okay?"

Bailey nodded again, waved, then hopped down off the chair, and ran to play with Alex. Christopher had already hung up on the iPad, but her new iPhone rang a minute later.

"Hey." It had become their routine to talk for a few minutes after Bailey was done. "When's your flight leave?"

"About fifteen minutes after I get to the airport, so in about half an hour, I think. I should be home about six."

"Sounds good. Dinner will be ready to go in the oven if you want to text me when you land. That'll make it done about ten minutes after you get home."

"I'll let you know." He hesitated, but Julia sensed he wanted to say more. "How is she? Is she excited that I'm coming home?"

Julia sank into the seat Bailey had vacated. "I think she's more worried or anxious, honestly. Her mother died. From what you said, her step-dad dropped her off here a week later, she finds out you're her father, and then you dump her with me." She hurried on. "I'm not saying that's what you did, just how I think she might see it. She just needs to get to know you. That's all."

"Right." He sounded weary. "Hopefully, the trip to San Majoria will fix it. Is everything ready to go tonight?"

"It will be. Almost everything is packed."

"Okay. Slight change of travel plans, though. Overnight on Thursday, we're going to fly to Ravenzario. The baby will be here this week. That's not public yet, though."

"I don't think anyone even knows when she's due."

"She was due yesterday, I think. She'll be able to deliver the baby at the palace. They can be rushed to a nearby hospital in case of desperate emergency, but most things can be handled there, or so I'm told. If we fly overnight, the kids should be able to sleep and, if we keep them more or less on a normal schedule, that should mitigate some of the jet lag. We'll be there all of Friday and Saturday then fly home overnight on

Saturday. I know it's a lot, but I'd like to meet my new niece or nephew soon."

Julia hesitated. "Why don't Alex and I get a commercial flight back here? I'm sure the queen and duke don't need anyone extra hanging around."

"Not a chance. Not unless I'm sure my daughter and I are on better standing. Or she starts talking again."

Julia had taken her to several specialists in the last few weeks. She confirmed to all of them she knew how to talk, she just didn't want to. Stalking Bailey's mother's Facebook page revealed multiple videos of the little girl talking. The specialists all believed it was related to the recent trauma, and she'd talk again when she was ready.

"I'll see you in a couple of hours. Thanks again for all your help."

"My pleasure."

He hung up before she could say anything else, though she didn't know what else she might have said.

Alex asked if they could play on the deck. Since she could see them from the kitchen while she got the baked spaghetti ready to go in the oven, she let them. When it was ready, Julia called them back in, and they all went downstairs. They watched Blue's Clues, something even her son found himself enjoying, while she worked on some more of the purses she needed to sell in a few weeks.

Her phone rang as she prepared to start sewing. "Hello?"

"Hey, it's me." Kenzie sounded out of breath.

"What's up?"

"I just got a call from the organizer of the Serenity Landing show. I'm not sure why she's asking us, but she is. They want us to help take care of Lady Margaret of Aquitaine Toulouse while she's here. Make sure she's where she's supposed to be when she's supposed to be there, get her more water if she needs it during her classes. Things like that. They asked all five of us in our booth to help so we can rotate."

Julia's breath caught in her throat. "For real?" She hoped to just take the class the woman was offering, a nearly lost form of spinning fiber into incredibly fine yarn.

"Yes. I told them we could and figured we'd sort it out later. I didn't think any one of us would turn down the opportunity."

"Definitely not." Julia could barely contain her excitement. "That's incredible."

"Even more incredible? Somehow, the organizer found out about Jonathan's security company and wants her to stay with us." Kenzie's pitch rose until it was nearly a squeal.

Julia laughed. "If you're not careful, the only one who will be able to hear you is Mr. Benny Hercules." The little dog had been rescued by Jonathan the night he met Kenzie for the second time.

"I can't help it. I'm excited." Her voice lowered in volume. "I think Jonathan may have pulled some strings. I've told him so many times, I want to do this yarn thing on my own, but even I can't complain about this."

"I wouldn't. Let me know if I can help at all."

"I will, but you'll have your hands full with that new job, two kids, and being about ready to pop. You don't think you'll have the baby before then, do you?" Kenzie's sudden concern echoed Julia's.

"I don't think so. The baby would have to be early. I'm not due until December. Alex was two days early. I don't see this baby being that early unless something weird happens."

"Well, let's not borrow trouble."

"Amen." Julia's phone buzzed in her hand. She looked at it. "I've got to go. Christopher just landed. I'll talk to you later."

Kenzie said goodbye, and Julia took the kids upstairs.

Bailey wasn't the only one who was anxious.

"Change of plans." Topher spoke into the phone as he walked toward the car waiting to take him home.

"Okay." Julia sounded guarded.

"We're going to Ravenzario tonight. The baby should be here by the time we get there. My parents will be there. They don't know about Bailey yet. They had no cell phone service where they were, but already planned to arrive tomorrow afternoon. Also, the kids won't have the huge time change on the way back. We'll head to San Majoria overnight on Sunday or Monday, then home overnight Friday or Saturday."

"Makes sense. When do we leave?"

"As soon as we can after dinner. The kids can sleep on board, and we'll get there in the morning."

He heard something slide into the oven. "I'll work on getting the rest of their things packed. I presume you can handle your own packing?"

"I left my bags on the plane. Most of it's clean anyway."

"Okay. We should be about ready to go by the time you get home then."

He hung up and stared out the window at the passing landscape.

Julia had said his daughter was anxious about this reunion, but so was he. He'd known his daughter for all of twenty-four hours and a few weeks' worth of one-sided video chats.

But every revolution of the tires brought him closer to being a full-time father. He didn't know how to do that.

Before he had time to prepare adequately, the car pulled up the drive to the house. No one waited outside to greet him, but he guessed that might have been too much to ask for.

Topher trotted up the steps and let himself in. "I'm home!"

"In here!" Julia called from the kitchen.

Footsteps seemed to be running toward him. Around the corner came his little girl, auburn hair flying behind her. With her hands outstretched, she practically jumped into his arms.

Topher lifted her up and held her tight as she wrapped her arms and legs around him. No other child had ever clung to him so tightly. "Hi, punkin. I missed you," he whispered.

Bailey's only response was to hold on tighter.

Another voice piped up. "I had the kids start eating as soon as dinner was ready."

Topher shifted Bailey to his hip. "Good idea." He looked at his daughter. "What are you eating?"

If he'd hoped she'd answer, he was disappointed. She just pointed to the kitchen. Once in there, she wiggled down and climbed onto one of the barstools.

"It's baked spaghetti," Julia explained. "I thought it would be quicker and easier just to eat at the bar with paper plates. I'll put the rest in the fridge for Ida Mae, if she'll be here, or see if Kenzie wants to come over and get it." Her nose wrinkled. "If you don't mind, of course. She's always had a key to my place. She said she'd drop some stuff off if it was okay with you."

Topher shrugged. "That's fine with me." He took a paper plate and filled it with spaghetti from the pan. "This looks good."

Julia slid onto one of the other barstools. "Thanks." She went back to eating as Topher sat next to Bailey.

He took a piece of garlic bread off the pan and used it to help scoop noodles onto his fork. It didn't take long for them to finish eating. Julia was done first and cleaned up while the rest of them finished.

She left the kitchen after admonishing Alex to put his dishes in the trash and wash his hands and face well. Topher didn't know where she went, but a minute later, she returned with three suitcases. She went back upstairs and came back with several other bags. She looked at all of it and sighed. "We're ready to go when you are. I hope." He barely heard the last two words.

Topher wiped his mouth with his napkin. "We can buy anything we're missing, or Ander already has it at the palace."

"We're going to see Duke Alexander?" Alex asked as he dried his hands off.

"We're going to Ravenzario for a couple of days," Julia told him. "I don't know that we'll see the duke or queen at all."

Topher tried to figure that out. She and Alex were going with him and Bailey. Why wouldn't they see Ander and Christiana?

He was distracted from his thoughts by Bailey climbing down from her barstool and throwing her things away. Without being told to, she climbed on the step stool to wash her hands. Topher followed suit. "Everyone ready?"

"As we'll ever be," Julia replied, picking up two of the bags and slinging them over her shoulder then reaching for two suitcases. Alex picked up two of the other bags before Topher realized what was going on.

Together the two of them manhandled their loads toward the door.

"I got it, Mom." Alex put one of the bags down and opened the front door.

When Bailey picked up the last bag, Topher shook himself. He should be helping, but something about Julia and Alex intrigued him. If only he could put his finger on what it was he was trying to figure out.

He grabbed the last suitcase and went out the door, locking it as he did. The driver had been waiting outside for them, but now packed the bags into the trunk of the car. After setting his bag down, Topher went to the other side of the car and let himself in. Julia fastened Bailey into the car seat the driver must have installed while they ate. Julia backed out and talked to Alex for a second before the boy climbed in on the other side of Bailey. The driver looked at him a bit odd as he took his place in the driver's seat.

Less than thirty minutes later, they were at the airport, and soon after they were on the runway speeding toward flight.

Bailey's eyes were wide as she stared out the window at the terrain picking up speed.

The apprehension that had been building in his gut slowly bled away. Maybe this would actually be okay.

•

Chapter Six

Julia motioned for Alex to come over. He unbuckled his seatbelt and came to sit on her lap.

"It's time to lay down and get some rest, sweetheart." She rested her head against his. "I'll get your blanket and pillow and turn the lights off, okay?"

"What about brushing my teeth?"

"You can do that in the bathroom while I get a space set up for you."

He hopped down, and Julia went to one of the small couches. She pulled his blanket and pillow out from where she'd stashed it. As soon as Alex came back out of the bathroom, she helped him lay down, buckled a seat belt around him, and covered him up. After a whispered prayer, she kissed his forehead.

Now for Bailey. Or should she let Christopher take care of

it? He seemed engrossed in his tablet, though Bailey was in the seat next to him with her head on his shoulder. His hand played with her hair as she watched a movie on her iPad.

It was a start, but Bailey did need to go to bed.

And since Julia was the nanny, getting her to bed was probably her job.

Julia knelt next to Bailey and touched her hand, waiting for her to take her headphones off. "Sweetie, it's time to get ready for bed."

Bailey looked over at Alex, who had his eyes closed already and nodded. She turned her iPad off on her own and set it on the table.

"Get your toothbrush out of your bag, and I'll get a bed for you, okay?"

Bailey nodded and undid her seatbelt, heading for the lavatory in the back of plane. Julia got her blanket and pillow situated on the other couch, across from Alex, but with their heads at opposite ends. In just a few minutes, she'd followed the same routine with the little girl.

As soon as Bailey snuggled down with her favorite teddy bear, Julia decided it was time to get herself ready to sleep. She'd worn comfortable clothes so she could curl up in whatever space she could find. With her hair pulled back in a ponytail, her teeth brushed, and makeup removed, Julia pulled her own favorite blanket out.

"Going to sleep?" Christopher's voice sounded louder than it should have in the space.

"Figure it's about time." Julia tried to get comfortable enough to sleep in one of the chairs.

"Can we talk for a few minutes first?" He put his tablet

down and came to sit in the chair closest to her.

Julia straightened up a little bit. "Sure. What's up?"

Christopher looked toward the back of the plane and the sleeping kids. "How is she? Really?"

Julia fiddled with the edge of her blanket. "I think she's doing okay. She's sad a lot, which is understandable, but she seems to be adjusting well. I think having you home will help, too. She hated the days you two didn't get to talk."

"I did, too." He blew out a breath. "I really hated leaving. I'm hoping this week will help."

"I'm sure it will."

Christopher looked like he wanted to say something else, but it took him a minute. "Is everything acceptable at the house? Your rooms, the work room, that kind of thing?"

"It's all fantastic." Julia tried not to gush. Even just the two rooms and shared bathroom were far nicer than any place she'd lived for a very long time.

"And Ida Mae has been helpful?"

"Very helpful. I like her." The older woman was fiercely devoted to her employer, and that now extended to Bailey, Alex, and Julia, but Julia had no doubt she could be just as great an enemy as she had been an ally.

Christopher chuckled. "She told me she likes you, too."

"Good."

The silence began to stretch long enough to be uncomfortable, but Christopher stood before it got too bad. "I'm going to read for a bit before trying to get some sleep myself. Good night."

Julia leaned her chair back as far as it would go and snuggled down under her blanket. She tried to steel herself for the visit to Ravenzario. She'd been working to do so for weeks, but hadn't expected it quite so soon. Hopefully, they'd be able to stay under the radar. Christopher and Bailey might not be able to but surely she and Alex could. No one needed to even know they'd come for a visit. She had no intention of seeing the queen or duke if it could be avoided.

She didn't know how many miles passed, but eventually Julia settled into a restless sleep, knowing that when she awoke, it would be time to get ready - just in case she had to face the cameras again.

Christopher was very aware of the cameras on the other side of the arrival area. Hopefully, no one else would notice them, but rumors would be flying in the next hour. He walked down the steps of a private plane, carrying a little girl they'd never seen, and followed by his brother's former, alleged mistress and the son tabloids had claimed belonged to the prince consort.

He'd hoped to avoid all of this, but if he didn't talk to his parents soon, they'd find out about their granddaughter from the tabloid press, or even the regular press when they reported the arrival of the duke's brother and what it might mean about the impending birth of the new heir to the throne.

According to the text from his brother as they taxied to their final spot, the baby had yet to make an appearance, but should soon.

The waiting car was too far away, but at least the chauffeur held the back door open. Topher set Bailey down so she could get in, turned to get the bag Julia held, then stepped to the side so she and Alex could follow. The kids faced the front while he and Julia sat across from them.

"Is that the paparazzi?" she whispered as the car began to move.

"Probably, but the regular media is on baby watch, too, so it's probably some of both."

"Glad I changed clothes and did my make-up," she muttered.

"I would have warned you if you hadn't."

She didn't reply, and Topher wondered if he'd somehow offended her.

The drive to the palace didn't take long, but when they arrived a small-to-medium-ish sized crowd was gathered around the gate. Word must have gotten out that his parents had arrived an hour earlier.

They were greeted by Justin and Diana, Ander and Christiana's assistants.

"Welcome back to Ravenzario," Diana said with a smile. "We'll have good news before you know it." She turned to Bailey as she climbed out of the car. "And you must be Bailey-bug." Diana held out her hand. "It is such a pleasure to meet you, young lady."

Bailey stared at her then grabbed Topher's leg. He reached down to pick her up. "Bailey, this is Diana. She's your aunt Christiana's assistant, like Ida Mae is mine." He turned a bit. "And this is Justin. He helps my brother."

His little girl nodded her head against him and gave them a small wave.

He turned slightly. "I'm sure you both remember Julia and Alex. She's been taking care of Bailey for me while I was out of town."

After handshakes, the two assistants led them to a different set of rooms than Topher had used when he visited before, probably because it wasn't just him anymore. Justin showed him to one room with a connecting room for Bailey. Julia and Alex kept walking with Diana.

"The duke asked for us to escort you to your parents as soon as you've freshened up." Justin headed for the door. "I'll be outside."

Topher didn't feel the need to freshen up but turned to Bailey and asked if she needed to go to the bathroom. A few minutes later, they left the room to find everyone else waiting for them.

"Mr. Bayfield?" Julia said as they all started for the main door.

He frowned at the formal name. What had she been calling him the last few weeks? Anything? "Yes?"

"I don't think Alex and I need to go. We'll just hang out here."

Topher stifled a sigh. Hadn't they already gone over this? "Christiana wants to see you both."

Julia cocked an eyebrow at him. "Right after she gives birth to her first child?"

"She said when you got here."

"But we weren't supposed to get here until well after the baby was born."

He let out an exasperated sigh. "Just come on. If she doesn't want to see you, they won't let you in."

"I don't want to make your parents uncomfortable either," she insisted.

With a whispered prayer for patience, Topher reached out and grasped her arm. Not tightly - she could get away if she really wanted to - but firm enough to encourage her to move. "Come on. It'll be fine."

But he didn't want her to think he was actually forcing her to come along, so he let go and reached for her hand instead, tucking it inside his elbow. "Besides, I may need your help with Bailey while I talk to my parents."

The kids had walked ahead with Justin and Diana, though they stayed in sight.

"Believe me," he admitted aloud. "I'm almost as nervous about introducing my parents to Bailey as Ander is about being a father for the first time. Maybe even more. At least they know he's married."

"And you're not." She shrugged. "Not like I'm going to judge you."

Topher hesitated. "I was married. Briefly. But had no idea she was pregnant when she left me. I told you that."

Before she could ask any other questions, they walked into a sitting room. He dropped his arm, but put his hand in the middle of her back, to urge her forward. "Mom, Dad, I know you remember us talking about Julia and her son, Alex. Julia, Alex, these are my parents, James and Leigh Ann Bayfield." He dropped his hand as someone closed the door behind them. His brother-in-law, Prince Nicklaus, and his wife, Princess Yvette, stayed on the other side of the room. Did they already know and were trying to give them some privacy? Had Ander told them about Bailey?

Julia just sort of nodded at them. "It's nice to meet you."

His mom started to say something, but was distracted by

Bailey tugging on his shirt. He picked her up. "And there's someone else I'd like you to meet."

"Who's this pretty girl?" Mom asked.

Topher took a deep breath. "As much as I hate stealing Ander's thunder, this is..."

The door to the medical suite burst open, and his brother came out, a big grin on his face. "The baby's here!"

Mom and Dad glanced at each other then back at Ander, the anticipation on their faces mirrored everyone else's.

"And?" Mom finally asked.

Ander just grinned. "Come on in." He looked around the room quickly. "*All* of you." The emphasis made it clear he included everyone in the statement.

Topher glanced back to make sure Julia and Alex came, too.

Once in the spacious suite, Ander took the baby from a very tired-looking Christiana. "As of an hour ago, Ravenzario has a new heir. Everyone, I'd like you to meet Prince Nicklaus Richard Jedidiah James.".

Chapter Seven

Julia hung back, holding Alex by the shoulders so they wouldn't intrude more than they already were. She heard a gasp and saw the queen's sister-in-law covering her face with her hands and the not-dead Prince Nicklaus seemed to be struggling to hold back tears.

"So there's going to be a King Nicklaus anyway, someday?" the princess asked, her arm going around her husband's waist.

Despite the uncertainty about how the family really felt about her, Julia had watched the wedding. She couldn't help it. She'd been as surprised as everyone when the prince showed up alive.

Queen Christiana nodded. "We'd already decided to name him Nicklaus if he were a boy, in memory. But you should have been king, Nicky, so this way, even though you're not, your namesake will be someday."

Prince Nicklaus moved to the side of the bed and leaned over to kiss his sister's forehead. "That better not be for a very, very long time."

"Amen," Duke Alexander added.

The princess squealed a bit. "Can I hold him? Please?"

Julia reminded herself that the girl was just that, barely more than a girl. The wedding had taken place immediately after she turned eighteen. Prince Nicklaus wasn't much older.

Julia slid her hands forward so she was hugging her son's upper body rather than holding his shoulders, while the rest of those in the room ooh'd and ahh'd over the baby. This was definitely what it felt like to be an intruder in some other family's private moment.

She watched Christopher whisper something to Bailey then set her down. The little girl came to stand in front of Alex, clearly uncomfortable as well.

"Julia?"

She looked up to see the queen motioning to her. "Yes, Your Majesty?"

"I thought we did away with that nonsense the last time you were here." The tired smile reminded Julia of what it was like to give birth. This would be her before she knew it.

"Yes, ma'am." Julia knew she'd never be as casual as the queen had told her to be.

"Who is this lovely girl you have with you? Is this Miss Bailey?"

"Yes, ma'am." Julia stepped away from Alex and urged Bailey forward.

The queen patted the side of her bed. "Can you come sit by me, Miss Bailey?"

Bailey looked up at Julia with those big eyes of hers, waiting for permission. Julia nodded, and Bailey walked the few steps before climbing up onto the side of the bed and perching carefully.

Queen Christiana held out a hand. "Hello, Miss Bailey. I'm your Aunt Christiana."

Bailey shook her hand then jumped back down and ran to Julia who picked her up.

"Aunt Christiana?" Christopher's father jumped into the conversation. He looked over at Prince Nicklaus. "You have a daughter?"

The prince looked confused and started to say something, but Christopher interrupted.

"Mom, Dad, I started to tell you a few minutes ago, but then we came to meet Prince Nicklaus." He looked at his brother and raised a brow. "The kid needs a nickname, because *that* won't get confusing quickly." Christopher turned back to his parents. She could see him take a deep breath, and the tension radiated off of him in waves. "I'll tell you the whole story later, but the pretty little girl with Julia is my daughter. Your granddaughter. Bailey."

Julia held Bailey a little tighter. What would their reaction be?

Mr. Bayfield reached out and gripped Mrs. Bayfield's shoulder. They both seemed a bit shocked, certainly, but neither said anything for an excruciatingly long moment.

Finally, Mrs. Bayfield moved, coming to stand directly in front of Julia and Bailey. "Well, hello there." She held out her hand. "I suppose that makes me your grandmother."

Bailey kept her head tucked in close to Julia's shoulder but shook Mrs. Bayfield's hand anyway.

"What would you say if you and I went to get a snack while everyone else stays here?" She leaned in closer and whispered, "Babies don't do much that's very exciting anyway."

Once again, Bailey looked to Julia for permission. "Go ahead," Julia encouraged her, but if the death grip the girl had on Julia's shirt was any indication, she wasn't comfortable with the idea. "Or would you like Alex and I to come with you?"

Bailey nodded.

"Before you go," the duke cut in. "Would you like to hold your new cousin?"

Bailey's eyes went wide as she nodded.

"Why don't you come sit in this chair then?" Duke Alexander nodded toward a seat. "I'll help you hold him."

"I will." Christopher sat in the chair and helped Bailey climb into his lap. "Hold your arms like this," he said softly, helping his daughter get situated.

Duke Alexander carefully handed his son to his niece. Christopher spoke to Bailey, but Julia couldn't make out the words. Several of the family members had phones out taking pictures.

That's when Julia noticed the cameraman in the room. Moving about as unobtrusively as he could, the man snapped pictures of all the goings-on. He'd likely been the first one invited in so he could get the intimate shots the queen and duke would cherish in the future.

After several minutes, the duke took his son back, and Mrs. Bayfield reached for Bailey's hand.

This time, the little girl took it without hesitation. Julia and Alex followed them to the same apartment they had stayed in when they were there last.

"Now, I'm hungry," Mrs. Bayfield told Bailey. "How about some scrambled eggs?"

Bailey nodded, quite excited.

"If you go to the bathroom and wash your hands super good, would you like to help?"

Rather than answering, Bailey ran off with Alex on her heels.

Mrs. Bayfield bowed her head and took a couple of deep breaths. "Quickly, before they come back, tell me what I need to know."

"I don't know many of the details of Mr. Bayfield, Christopher that is, and her mother," Julia told the woman. "He found out about Bailey as he was leaving the country for a movie shoot and couldn't take her with him. I'm the nanny for the time being. She's capable of talking, but hasn't since she moved in with him."

Mrs. Bayfield stood up straighter as the kids came back. "Thank you. Now who wants to be a helper?"

"Who's her mother?" Topher's father cut straight to the chase when they were alone a few minutes later.

"Remember Martha?"

"You dated her for a couple years, right? Then she decided she wanted to be with her ex-boyfriend instead?"

Christopher sank into one of the chairs. "One day, we were talking about getting married. We'd talked about it several times before, and I was working on a plan to propose. This day, though, she knew my work schedule was really light. We'd already talked about her staying home after we were married and starting a family. She wasn't in a career she loved anyway."

He leaned back and propped his foot up on the coffee table. "This time, she suggested we elope. It seemed like a good idea. So we did. We flew off to San Majoria then Eyjania for a couple weeks each on a month-long honeymoon. We got back. She went to her apartment to pack. I went to find her a few hours later when she wouldn't answer her phone. I found a note that she'd left me for her ex-boyfriend. A few weeks later, I got the divorce papers. All of it was handled between lawyers. I haven't seen her since she went to her apartment that day. I had no idea she had a baby."

"So how did Bailey end up here with you then?"

"Apparently, Martha died about a month ago. Her ex-boyfriend dropped Bailey off with a note. We sent off a DNA sample, but I haven't heard back yet." That puzzled him. The results should have arrived by now. He needed to contact Ida Mae and have her follow-up.

"So what's your plan?"

"I'm listed on the birth certificate as her father, but Martha never pursued any sort of financial support. She had no will. As the legal father, I'm responsible for Bailey."

"What about the boyfriend?"

Topher shrugged. "I have no idea what became of him. I did get an unsigned note from someone saying she'd need to go home eventually. I turned it over to the police, but nothing's come from it so far. Jonathan Langley-Cranston is looking into it for me, too. Or his people are. It's much more his area of expertise than mine. I don't want to ask Bailey about it, because I don't want to cause her any more trauma than she's already been through, and she wouldn't tell me anyway. She won't talk at all since she got here."

"Selective mutism?"

"I've done research. Normally, it seems like it would only apply to one kind of situation, like school. But she's in a totally new situation that doesn't change much, so apparently it applies at all times for now. And I haven't had much of a chance to get to know her yet. I'm hoping this week away will fix that."

"And Julia?"

Topher shrugged. "What about her? She's Bailey's nanny. They seem to get along well."

"And there's nothing between the two of you?" His father's raised eyebrow made Topher feel sixteen again.

"No."

"That's not what it looked like when you walked into the waiting room earlier."

"There's nothing. I was desperate, and she was the only person I could think of who might be able to help me out." Did Dad really believe he might have a thing going with the woman who had been, directly or indirectly, responsible for a rift in his brother's marriage? Even if she had been fantastic the last three weeks.

Their conversations had come easily over the phone, but they mostly consisted of information about Bailey and how her days were going, including the doctor's visits, and therapy sessions, and the visits to the speech pathologist. Those conversations contained nothing deep or meaningful, or even personal, but they formed the foundation for a very basic relationship.

"Okay." His dad's tone contained a smirk Topher didn't look over to see.

He decided not to respond, but to prove his father wrong over time. Nothing was going to develop between himself and Julia.

Famous last words. Ander's words came back to him. Words that meant nothing.

The door opened, and his mother walked in with Bailey. His daughter walked straight to him and climbed onto his lap. Topher put his arms around her as she snuggled in.

His mom nodded toward him. "I think someone's about ready for a nap."

Bailey shook her head but didn't move it from Topher's shoulder.

He chuckled. "I think you should go lie down in your room and rest for a bit, okay?"

There was no response except stifled laughter from his mom.

"She's already asleep, isn't she?" he asked.

"Just put her on our bed. One of us will stay here."

He rearranged her in his arms then stood, taking her into the nearby bedroom. Once he laid her down, Topher pulled a quilt over her. Mom had already left by the time he returned.

Dad didn't wait once Topher took his seat again. "Have you really thought this through?"

"What is there to think through?" Topher ran a hand through his hair. "I'm presuming she's my daughter. If so, there's no thinking to do. I'm her father, and that means I take care of her."

"And if the DNA comes back differently?" His dad leaned back in his seat.

Topher looked at the door to his parents' bedroom. "I don't know that it matters. I've already got a lawyer lined up. I'm on her birth certificate. As soon as we get the results, I'm going to court to get full legal custody of her. With her mother's death, legally, I'm already all she's got left. I won't let anyone take that away from me or from her. She's lost so much."

"So have you. You've lost your marriage and the first four years of your daughter's life. That's nothing to sneeze at."

"I know. But what she's lost is so much more."

"That doesn't mean you can't grieve the loss of both of those things. And she's lost four years with her father. You can't ever get those back. Neither can the rest of us. We've lost four years as grandparents. Your brother's lost four years as an uncle. It's okay to mourn that."

"Believe me, I am."

"Then make the most of the time you have from here on out. Be the best father you can be. Give her the life she needs, which may well be different from the life she thinks she wants."

His phone buzzed at him. A call from his agent. "It's Mady. But I'm glad Bailey has all of us now. Whatever else, she'll always be a Bayfield."

Chapter Eight

Julia wiped down the counter as the door to the kitchen area opened to let Christopher's mom in.

"Oh, thank you, honey!" Mrs. Bayfield set her phone on the counter. "Ander tells me all the time not to worry about cleaning up because they have people paid to do it, but it doesn't feel right to just leave the mess, does it?"

"No. I wouldn't feel right about that. Those people don't work for me." She rinsed the cloth out and hung it over the side of the sink.

"True, but you don't work here either." She whispered something to Alex, who nodded and went to the other room.

"I may as well. I'm Bailey's nanny. This was Bailey's breakfast. I'm cleaning up afterward."

"It's not quite the way it is, and you know it."

Julia just shrugged.

"It's everything coming back to you from the last time you were here, isn't it?"

"Not really. We were in the cottage last time." She should ask someone, she didn't know who, if the cottage was available. It would be nicer to have someplace slightly their own rather than feeling awkward and out of place around everyone else.

Because they still didn't belong here.

"True, but none of what happened last spring is likely a good memory."

"I can't imagine why any of you want me around," she blurted out. "I know the whole thing wasn't really my fault, but if I hadn't gone to the hospital that day there wouldn't have been anyone looking at me to help set up Duke Alexander." Tears blurred her vision. Stupid hormones.

Mrs. Bayfield laughed. "Oh, sweetheart. Nothing that happened last spring was your fault. And if you hadn't been here to stop Christiana's uncle from following her, even for a few seconds, the outcome might have been very different."

"She wouldn't have been at the cottage if we weren't there."

"Neither would he. He would have snuck into their bedroom in the middle of the night and killed or kidnapped them both. You can play the what-if game all day long, Julia, but all of that happened for a reason. What would Topher have done if Bailey had shown up but he hadn't had your number?"

"He would have called Jonathan Langley-Cranston. He got married recently and has a little girl. Kenzie would have helped him." And she would have seen Bailey and wondered about the little girl.

"Perhaps, but you're a better choice, and we both know it."

Julia gave a half-hearted shrug.

"Kenzie has her own little girl, doesn't she? And a brother-in-law who just returned from the dead? And a business to run?"

"Yes." And a baby on the way, but that wasn't public knowledge yet.

"So, just maybe, God knew what He was doing by putting you in our path last spring. So Topher would have someone to call when Bailey showed up."

There had been an awful lot of pain to put a lot of people through just to have a nanny for a little girl when another option existed.

Mrs. Bayfield's phone buzzed at her. "I have to go for now, but know that you are always welcome here, Julia. You and Alex both."

Julia nodded as Mrs. Bayfield smiled then left.

"Alex," Julia called. He came back from the other room. "It's time for us to go to our room." Hand-in-hand, they started down one of the wide corridors. Julia just hoped she remembered how to get there.

As they neared their suite, Alexander rounded one of the corners. Rather than caution like she might have expected, his face showed only friendliness.

"Hi, Julia. Alex. Are you finding everything all right?"

Alex answered while Julia nodded, though she didn't really hear her son's words.

"Duke Alexander," she started as soon as Alex was done. "Do you think..."

"I think first you can skip the duke stuff." His tone still seemed warmer than expected. "Call me Ander like my family does."

"Okay. Ander. We are incredibly grateful for the accommodations, but I wonder if it might be possible for us to stay in the cottage again?"

Now he frowned. "It wouldn't bring back bad memories? You were shot there, after all."

"No, I wasn't. The doctor decided I hit my head on something, but I fell as I tried to get away from the shot, so it all happened at the same time."

"The point remains. You were part of an attack when you stayed there."

Dare she be honest? "I know." She had to be. "But the truth is, we don't want to impose. With the new baby and Bailey, you guys just need time as family, and we're not. It would be far easier to stay out of the way in the cottage."

The frown deepened. "If we didn't want you around, you wouldn't be allowed to stay on the property at all, Julia. We would have arranged for a hotel or something. So put all of that out of your mind, and don't think another thing about it."

So, a no on the cottage. She almost asked again, but didn't want to anger him. He hadn't slept in quite a while, she was certain. Not if his wife had been in labor all night.

"The announcement was made a few minutes ago," the duke went on. "I don't think we asked you to sign any paperwork last time, and I won't now, but please do not share any photos from inside the palace or of the family without our permission."

That raised her ire. "Of course not." Did he still think she was the gold digger the media had made her out to be? "But if you'll excuse us, we're headed to our suite. It's lovely, and we thank you, but I have some work to do. Good day." She urged Alex ahead of her and didn't look back.

Knitting would occupy her time and creating patterns would occupy her mind.

Because whatever else happened, she had to remember she and Alex were not a part of this family. They were the hired help and son.

Nothing more.

Not ever.

Topher helped Bailey into her car seat for the ride to the airport before turning to give his brother a hug.

"That kid's adorable," he told Ander. "We'll be back to visit again soon. Maybe over Thanksgiving. Definitely for Christmas."

"Give Bailey some time. Once she learns to trust that you're not going anywhere, she'll open up. She already loves you. She just needs time to feel comfortable."

"I know." Topher stepped back. "Thanks for everything."

"Anytime."

This time, Topher ended up next to Bailey while Julia talked quietly with Alex in the rear facing seat. Hopefully the cameras were long gone from the airport now that the news about the new prince was out. Unfortunately, a few remained. He stifled a sigh.

The car pulled up as close to the plane as it could so the walk was short. He ignored the cameras and hoped Julia and the kids didn't see them.

It didn't take long for them to get airborne. The perks of flying in a private plane. After an hour, Julia put both of the kids to bed, just as she had on the flight to Ravenzario. Rather than settling down for the night herself, she pulled out some yarn, paper, and what he thought were knitting needles. She'd do something with the needles, then make some notes, then do some more.

It wasn't the first time he'd seen her doing this, and he had to know. "What exactly are you doing?"

She finished making a notation then looked at him. "I'm working on a pattern for a stuffed Christmas bear."

He blinked a couple of times. "I understand the words, but not what you're saying."

Was that actually a smile? He hadn't seen many of those from Julia when the kids weren't around. "I lost my job right before we went on our Ravenzario trip, but your brother hooked me up with a charity that gave me enough to get through a month or so. I'd been helping Kenzie from time to time with her yarn dyeing business. I can't dye since I'm pregnant, but I helped her do some other stuff for a while. I'd taught a knitting class or two here and there, with good reviews. My last classes ended my first week as nanny and I haven't started any more since. Back then, I expanded how many I was teaching, added crochet, and started actually writing down the patterns for stuff I made for fun. I sell them and make bags to sell, too. Those are pretty easy and don't take much time, but sell well."

"And that's what you're doing in the basement?"

"Pretty much."

"Whatever it is you're working on now isn't very

Christmassy. It's brown and orange."

Julia actually laughed. "This is a working prototype. I just use whatever I've got on hand. Once I have it all figured out, then I'll make a Christmas one as a sample. I'll sell the pattern packaged with yarn from Kenzie, or they can choose their own yarn. Between all of it, I'm making enough to stay afloat." She shrugged. "Of course, now with this job as the nanny, it's a lot easier, but I know this is temporary, and I've already committed to a big show with Kenzie before the baby comes."

Topher frowned. "When is the baby due?"

She didn't try to turn away from him. "Early December. At some point, we'll need to discuss at least a few days off. I don't expect to be paid for that time."

He hadn't even thought about that. "I can arrange to take some time off or hire someone else to take care of Bailey while I work if I can't. We'll see when we get closer." Surely he knew someone who could help him find a substitute nanny for a few weeks. Josh Wilson had a nanny who worked at the Serenity Landing Aquatic Center. She'd know someone who might want some work.

"Kenzie might be able to help. She told me she'd help me with Alex if I needed it."

Something had been bugging him. "Kenzie who?" He hadn't been able to place the name.

She tilted her head like she was thinking. "Kenzie Langley-Cranston, I guess it is now."

That came as a shock. "Jonathan's wife? The one with the little girl who went missing a few weeks ago?"

"Yes. Lorelai. She's adorable. She and Alex get along really well which is good when we do all our yarn stuff. It's a lot easier now, though. She's got the big house, and Jonathan to help rather than just the two of us making sure they stayed out of trouble."

"So all the stuff you're making in the basement, when is that for?"

Julia wrinkled her nose. "The weekend before Thanksgiving. It's a big deal, or I wouldn't ask. The show is in Serenity Landing, so no travel which is nice, but I'll be gone most of Wednesday through Sunday that week."

"What exactly do you do for all that time?"

"Kenzie and I have a booth we're sharing with another yarn business from the area, Show Me Yarn. One of each of us will be there at all times. Jonathan knows enough now that he can fill in for us in a pinch. We've also been asked to help out one of the ladies coming to teach. Lady Margaret is older and needs someone with her. I'll take her class and a few others if I have the chance."

"That's fascinating."

She smirked. "You don't have to say that."

"It really is." He never stopped to think about where hand-crafted yarn goods came from. A trade show made sense. "Maybe Bailey and I can go wander around. I bet she'd like it."

"Maybe." Julia nodded toward his daughter. "She does love her stuffed animals. A lot of it will be yarns or fiber or patterns, but there will be some finished products." She yawned. "I think I'm going to get some sleep."

"I'd love to see some pictures of your finished products sometime." Topher surprised himself with the comment, but those were the kinds of thing his mother and aunts would love.

"You can find a link on my Facebook page. We're not

friends on there, but you should be able to find it, or I can text you later." She put her yarn and stuff back in the bag and picked up another one before heading back to the lavatory.

Topher pulled out his phone and opened the Facebook app. He found Julia easily - they had several friends in common besides Jonathan - and sent a friend request before clicking on the link to her website.

The site needed an overhaul - and a dedicated domain name rather than a freebie site - but the products looked great.

Julia, it seemed, was a woman of hidden talents. Interesting.

Chapter Nine

Julia tried to keep her eyes from popping out of her head. Christopher's house was nice, very nice, but she'd never been anywhere remotely like the cottage on the beach in San Majoria. Cottage wasn't even the right word for it. Four bedrooms, four bathrooms, a gorgeous patio with a view of the western shore at an exclusive island resort. The pool in the back looked like it met the ocean, but really a few stairs led down to a stretch of the whitest sand she'd ever seen.

The sunsets would be spectacular.

She already knew that, and she'd arrived less than an hour earlier.

As soon as her things and Alex's were in their rooms, she went to make sure Bailey's were being put away . Julia would have done it herself, but a member of the resort staff was already taking care of it.

She turned back to unpack her things, but nearly ran into Christopher. With her hand on his chest, she looked up to see his smirk.

"Find everything okay?" he asked, taking a step back.

"So far. I haven't explored much yet."

"Mom!" Alex ran in from the patio. "We're right on the beach!" He ran into her with a hug.

She put her hand on his head. "I know we are."

"We're even closer than we were in Ravenzario last spring!"

They'd been on the twelfth floor of a hotel right on the beach. As fantastic as it had been, this was even better.

"Where did you stay in Ravenzario?"

Julia turned to see Christopher leaning up against the doorway, arms crossed casually over his chest. She told him the name of the hotel and its located.

"I've stayed there a couple of times. It's a nice place."

"Not as nice as this," Alex chimed in.

Julia felt her face heat, but Christopher just grinned. She ruffled her son's hair. "Why don't you go find your swim suit, and we can go outside?" She looked back to see her employer frowning. "What?"

"Does Bailey know how to swim?"

"She knows how to not drown, which isn't quite the same thing," Julia told him. "She's been swimming and had a few lessons even, but she doesn't actually swim like you think of swimming just yet. She's been recruited for the Serenity Landing Clipper Ships swim team next summer though."

"She's *four*, can't swim, and she's being recruited for a swim team?"

"Yep. Kenzie's daughter did it this year and loved it. They

teach them everything they need to know."

"We'll see."

Julia shook her head. "You've got the parental non-committal thing down pat already."

"Nice to know I've got something down." He shoved his hands in his pockets and moved away from Bailey's room. "I'm not sure I'm going to figure this dad thing out anytime soon. I have no idea. At least my brother gets to ease into it. Babies are a lot easier than little girls to start out with."

She actually snorted. "You think babies are easy?"

"No, but it's easier to start at the beginning. Baby needs are relatively easy compared to a little girl you don't know and who can't communicate with you."

"Can't communicate?" She shook her head in disbelief. "Christopher, she can communicate just fine. Just because she doesn't talk, doesn't mean she can't communicate."

"You know what I mean." He started toward the patio and Julia followed. "A baby is probably hungry or tired or needs to be changed. That's about it."

"You've never been around many babies, have you?"

"Not really."

"They can also be overtired, overstimulated, gassy, cold, hot, swaddled too tightly or too loosely, colicky, or any of a million other things. Just because they're babies doesn't mean they're easy to take care of."

"Point taken, but do you understand where I'm coming from?" He sat in one of the chairs on the deck. "I don't know what I'm doing, and if it weren't for you, she wouldn't have anyone taking care of her who had a clue."

Julia perched on the edge of the chair next to him, not

entirely comfortable with the personal conversation. "You would have figured it out somehow. You have friends with kids, and I've heard you're great at Googling things." Duke Alexander dropped that bit of information. "Give yourself a little credit."

"Maybe, but you've made it a lot easier. I don't know that I'll want to continue acting now that I have a daughter, but being blackballed before I even start wouldn't have been good." He propped a foot up on the small table in front of him. "I know they're cheesy, but I'd like to do more of these kinds of movies. They don't take very long to shoot, they're decent money, and they're clean. I won't be asked to do anything that compromises my morals."

Julia slid back in the chair. "There's nothing wrong with those movies. Lots of people love them. Even before I knew you and your brother, I thought they'd be the kind of movies you would have done if you'd kept acting."

"Do you watch them?"

"I might." She couldn't help sounding defensive.

He surprised her with his chuckle. "It's okay. My mom watches them all the time. She was ecstatic when she heard I did one."

She decided to be honest. "Okay. Then I record the new ones every week in November and December. I also record ones that I've seen before and liked. I binge watch while I wrap presents or when I just want to veg. I don't usually delete them until I need the room on the DVR."

Before he could reply, Alex and Bailey came out of the house in their swimsuits.

Christopher pushed up from his chair. "I'll go change and

get in the pool with them so you don't have to get yours on unless you want to."

He walked inside without waiting for a response. As soon as he returned, she'd put her suit on.

After all, it was her job to take care of her son - and Christopher's daughter.

Topher held Bailey's hand as they walked toward the ocean. By the end of their first full day, she'd been willing to get her toes wet, but that was about it. She'd said that today she'd go further into the water.

Rather, she'd nodded when he asked if she would.

A start, for both of them.

Bailey dipped her toes in the ocean for the first time, and Topher dipped his metaphorical toes in parenthood.

Julia and Alex had gone to the main part of the resort for the afternoon. He didn't know what they were doing, but it meant he and Bailey were alone for the first time since he left for Canada.

The waves washed up over their feet, just a little bit. Enough to get Bailey's ankles and half of his feet wet. The next wave came in a bit higher, then a little higher still.

Topher kept his eyes on Bailey as she watched the waves. "Want me to pick you up and go out a bit further?"

She looked up, fear and bravery warring in her eyes. Then she nodded and held up her arms. As Topher picked her up, he could see himself as a kid, doing the same thing with his dad. When he was older, his dad had used the situation to illustrate how God the Father is with His kids.

It had been a long time since he'd thought about that, but as he started to learn to parent, it suddenly made a lot more sense.

They were far enough in that at the next wave hit at about mid-thigh. Bailey's arms gripped his neck a little tighter as he took a few more steps.

"We'll stop right here," he told her as he shifted her weight a bit higher.

The next few waves came to his waist, small splashes getting Bailey a little wet.

"Is this okay?" He didn't know how else to communicate with her except to ask yes or no questions.

She nodded.

"Good. I've got you, Bay."

They stood out there for another five minutes or so before she pointed back to the shore. Topher turned and made his way back. Bailey wiggled to be let down a bit deeper out than she'd been before. He held onto her hand, but she wrenched it away and ran toward shore.

Julia and Alex had returned, and the kid had gone back to work on the sand castle they'd started the day before. It had been built far enough up the beach that high tide shouldn't get to it. Topher dipped under the water then followed his daughter.

Alex welcomed Bailey with a smile and a high-five. Together, they worked on the next turret.

Julia, though, struggled to sit in one of the lounge chairs.

"Here." Topher reached his hands toward her. "I'll help you lower down."

She raised a brow at him. "Will you help me up, too?"

"If you need it."

Both of her hands slid into his, surprising him with their warmth. "Lean back," he told her. "I won't let you fall."

Julia looked skeptical but did it anyway. He could feel her weight. She wasn't light as a feather, not surprising given that she was super pregnant, but she wasn't heavy either. Even in his head, he knew he'd be up a creek with those kinds of statements. He could handle her weight easily. That's all that mattered.

He took half a step forward and let her body weight control the descent. By the time she was completely seated, he had his legs on either side of the chair and leaned over her.

Her nose wrinkled as water landed on it. "You're getting me wet."

Trying to hide his grin, he shook his head, causing droplets to spray all over her.

Julia squealed and held her hands up to block it, but they didn't do much good.

Topher chuckled as he backed off and started to sit in the chair next to her. "Do you want the umbrella moved?" he asked before he did.

"Either way is fine." She pulled a towel out of her bag to dry her face. He guessed that meant she'd prefer the umbrella but didn't want to actually ask for it, so he moved it before sitting next to her.

"Thank you."

"My pleasure." The polite response had been ingrained by his parents when he was younger. "So what did you and Alex do at the resort?"

"Not much. Just wandered around. He wanted to check it out."

"And? What did you think?" This wasn't Topher's first time staying here, but he'd never stayed at the resort itself, always the resorts' cottages on the beach.

"He thought it was awesome. The pool is very cool."

Topher supposed a kid would think that. It meandered around a pool deck area, had swim up seating for food and beverages, as well as a number of water features. "Maybe we could take the kids up one day. I bet Bailey would like it."

"I'm sure she would, but doesn't that kind of defeat the purpose of a secluded hut on the beach?"

"The hut on the beach is to give us time to get to know each other away from other people," he pointed out. "But that doesn't mean we can't visit the pool at the resort."

"Your daughter's a pretty cool kid," she told him, looking toward the sand castle. "I'm praying this week goes well."

"You're not the only one." He propped one foot higher on the chair. "I think she likes me, though."

"I know she does. She so looked forward to your calls every night. They were the highlight of her day."

"Mine, too. I hated it when I couldn't call until after bedtime." He still had, though. He'd needed to check in daily with Julia to find out what was going on with his daughter.

Topher's phone buzzed with a text from his brother. "More pictures of the baby," he told her, holding his phone out so she could see.

"He's adorable."

"It's in his genes." Topher grinned as he pulled the phone back and swiped through them again.

"As is humility, I see."

That made him chuckle. He wouldn't have suspected it a month earlier, but he was glad Julia felt comfortable enough to be snarky around him. Yes, he was her employer, but they were going to be spending a lot of time together for the foreseeable future. It would be good to get along.

She pulled her knitting and notepad out of her bag, but didn't get to work until after she'd checked in with the kids. They both gave her a thumbs up sign.

Topher leaned his head back and closed his eyes. After a long few weeks, maybe he just needed a nap.

Not a long one. Just a little cat nap.

With that, he found himself slipping toward sleep and didn't even try to stop.

Chapter Ten

Julia struggled to stand, but she had no choice. Christopher had said he'd help, but he was sawing logs in the chair to her left. She could tell by the look on Bailey's face that the little girl needed to go to the bathroom. It took some maneuvering, but Julia finally managed to get upright.

She held out her hand. "Come on, Bailey. You too, Alex."

"But, Mom..." he started to whine.

Julia gave him her best mom glare, and he clamped his mouth shut. He needed to at least try and with Christopher asleep, she didn't want to leave him unsupervised.

It took less than five minutes for them to return. Christopher hadn't moved. As much as Julia hated to admit it, lowering herself back to the lounge chair was much more difficult without Christopher's help. He'd shown how strong he was with that maneuver. All of her weight had been in his hands, and he'd been surprisingly gentle as he helped her down.

As much as she wanted to doze, Julia made herself stay awake. With Christopher asleep, it fell to her to watch the kids. She did have her knitting out - for this pattern sample, it just needed to be close enough and the sand wouldn't matter too much. When she knit the actual display, she'd be much more careful.

About an hour later, Julia watched Alex and Bailey carefully as they let the waves wash over their feet and "bury" them. They wouldn't go any further in, but she wouldn't look away either.

"What exactly are they doing?"

Christopher's sleepy voice startled her, but Julia managed not to jump. "They're letting the waves bury their feet."

He looked almost as awkward as she'd felt while trying to stand up. Once on his feet, he stretched his hands out. "Want to join them?"

Her knitting lay on her lap, but she moved it to the side and reached up. Tingles covered her skin, just as they had earlier, but she knew better than to read too much into it. She'd had a crush on his character years earlier. Anything more would be incredibly inappropriate with her employer.

Christopher stood next to Bailey and talked to her about how far her feet had sunk. Julia went to the other side of Alex and just stared at her feet as the waves came in and out. When the others moved, she rested her arms on her belly and watched them splashing around, without really seeing them.

All she could think was how much she'd longed for this.

A father for Alex.

A little girl they all doted on.

Another baby on the way.

A good man to love her.

Christopher didn't, of course, but if she didn't think too deeply, the illusion would remain.

"Come on, Mom!" Alex yelled as he splashed Bailey.

The girl had a huge grin on her face, though she was only in to her mid-calf. She splashed Alex back. Christopher stood a bit deeper kicking water at both of them.

"Come on!" Alex yelled again.

"Not right now," she called back. The last thing she wanted was to get her hair full of salt water. She didn't plan to wash her hair again today, and didn't want to deal with the after effects. Dealing with it in Bailey's hair would be bad enough.

"Oh, come on!" Alex turned and said something Julia couldn't hear to Bailey. The two of them turned and ran as fast as they could through the water toward her.

Julia grinned, not worried they'd actually get her that wet. "Go ahead and try, kids."

For about five minutes, they tried to get her wet - and succeeded at getting the hem of her swim skirt wet. Nothing higher. Her hair was safe.

She even kicked some water back at them.

"That's not how you have a water war."

Julia looked up to see Christopher standing there with his hands on his hips. "I don't want wet hair right now. We can have a real water war later."

The mischievous twinkle in his eye served as her warning. He was up to something.

With her arms crossed in front of her, she narrowed her eyes into the glare that worked best on Alex. "Don't you dare."

"Don't I dare what?" His wide eyed innocent act didn't fool her, but then he held up his hands in mock surrender. "Fine." His hands came down. "No water war. But you should come farther out. The water feels nice. You don't have to go far enough for your hair to get wet."

With one eye still watching him, Julia cautiously made her way further in. When the water reached to her knees she turned back to watch the kids still splashing each other closer to the beach.

"Hey, Julia."

She glanced at Christopher. "What?"

"You know what they say, don't you?"

"What?"

"All's fair in love and water wars."

The words barely registered as she saw him take a mighty swing through the water with both arms. It seemed like a wall of water headed for her, but he was too far away and it only caught her from the waist down.

But she couldn't wait for him to try again. Unable to contain her grin, Julia started for the shore.

"You can't get off that easy!" Christopher moved quickly through the water. "You've gotta get wetter than that!"

She couldn't move as fast. "This isn't fair! I'm eight months pregnant!"

He laughed. "No, you're not."

"Close enough!"

The next splash was closer, but he'd rounded toward the front of her, and she had no choice but to move toward deeper water if she wanted to stay away from him.

Struggling to stop the laughter from spilling over, she called back. "This isn't much of a victory, you know."

"It's not a victory at all, yet. Not until you're soaked."

She turned and ran, if you could call what a pregnant woman did while nearly waist deep in water running. The splashes he made slapping his hands against the water came closer.

Julia glanced back to see a grin on his face as he closed the distance.

"If I'm going under, you're coming, too," she threatened knowing she wouldn't be able to make good on it if he didn't want her to.

"So? I'm already wet."

He'd nearly reached her.

What was he going to do when he did?

Topher felt more like a kid than he had in a long time as he chased Julia through the surf, but he hadn't thought this through. He'd almost caught her.

Now what?

Before he could make a conscious choice, he reached her. "You better take a deep breath!" With both arms wrapped around her, he held on tight and leaned them into the incoming wave, letting it take him off his feet.

He didn't let go of her as he put his feet back underneath him and helped her stand. Leaning slightly so his mouth was near her ear, Topher whispered, "Gotcha."

She twisted her head to look up at him, but no anger remained in her eyes. He would have guessed amusement, but as soon as his eyes locked with hers, the mood changed.

No longer were they two acquaintances chasing each other through the surf in a water war started by their kids.

He was a man who'd been single far too long.

She was a beautiful woman.

In his arms.

Kiss her.

The thought screamed in his head and his gaze flickered down to her slightly parted lips. What would it taste like? Salty from the sea water? Or strawberry like the lip balm she used? Maybe a little of both?

Would she let him? Or would she slap him?

Those thoughts and more flew through his mind at breakneck speed. As he decided to go for it and not worry about the consequences, something stopped him.

A voice.

"Mom!"

Her son's voice.

He felt the distance between them grow to a chasm in that second.

"Are you okay, Mom?" Alex was getting closer.

Topher let go and stepped back. "Sorry," he muttered. For so much more than the dunking.

"I'm fine." The comment was made as much to Alex as it was to Topher. "Just wet." Julia gave Topher a mock glare. "Just remember, paybacks are swell."

He smiled, though he didn't really feel like it.

"I think it's time for all of us to go inside," she announced.

"Everyone needs showers before dinner."

"Can we go swimming later?" Alex asked taking her hand as they walked back toward the beach.

"Maybe. Why don't you rinse off outside for now and change into some regular clothes? Hang your suit over the half wall to dry."

Topher followed a few steps behind, picking Bailey up when he reached her. "Why don't I help you do the same? Okay, kiddo?"

She nodded then rested her head on his shoulder.

Twenty minutes later, the two kids watched a VeggieTales movie in the living area. He could hear the water running in Julia's shower, getting the salt water out of her hair, he imagined.

Sitting in a chair that looked out over the water, he let his mind wander back to the ocean.

What had happened?

He hadn't known her before, and he'd never thought of Julia in any kind of romantic sense. It had been the absolute furthest thing from his mind since he found out she claimed to be the other woman. Sort of. Even though he knew she'd been set up, just like Ander had been, Topher had a hard time letting go of those initial hard feelings.

The objective part of his mind could rationally assess her attractiveness. She was a very pretty woman. Not glamorous like the few girls he'd dated as a teenager were now, but definitely beautiful in a wholesome, down-to-earth, stereotypically middle America, girl next door, kind of way.

Something he'd never thought to be his type.

So why now?

Proximity.

No other answer didn't leave him cringing and shaking his head.

Because the possibility of there being more to this relationship wasn't an option. She was his employee. A woman who, however inadvertently, had been part of the plot to destroy his brother, sister-in-law, and then-unborn nephew.

"Mr. Bayfield?"

He twisted in his seat to see Alex looking at him from across the room. "Yes?"

"Can we watch another one?"

Topher nodded. "Sure."

"Thank you, sir."

He winced. Did that come from ingrained politeness or the memory of the plane ride home from Ravenzario the first time? "Hey, Alex?"

"Yes, sir?"

"Call me Topher, okay? No need for the sir, stuff."

Alex hesitated, then nodded. "Will you tell my mom? She doesn't like me to call grown-ups by their first names. It's not polite."

"I'll talk to her."

The kid turned back to the TV, and Topher went back to staring out the window.

Two real relationships in his life. One lied about him getting her pregnant and used the rumors to further her own career. He'd never even slept with her.

The other married him then ran off with her ex-boyfriend and didn't tell him she was pregnant with his daughter until he'd missed nearly four years.

He heard footsteps coming from Julia's side of the house. "Christopher?" She sounded hesitant.

Topher looked up to see her standing there with her hair still up in a towel turban. She shifted her weight from one foot to the other and held an envelope in her hands. "What's up?"

She held out the mail. "This came the other day. Ida Mae asked me to give it to you as soon as you got to the house, but when we changed the travel plans, I made sure it was in my purse, so I wouldn't forget to bring it. It got buried though, and I forgot it was there."

He took it, wondering what could be such a big deal.

When he saw the logo in the return address, he knew.

DNA results.

The answer to his questions about Bailey.

All he had to do was open it, and he'd know for sure.

Was he a father? Or a sucker taking care of another man's daughter?

And, at this point, did it even matter?

Chapter Eleven

Julia couldn't stop the butterflies in her stomach as the emotions play over Christopher's face. It was important. She'd known it as soon as she saw the envelope several days earlier.

DNA results shouldn't have waited this long.

"I'm sorry," she finally whispered, not sure she wanted him to hear her. She'd rather he forget she was there.

"It's fine. It won't change the results, and I'm glad my parents got to meet her before knowing. I don't think it will matter to them anymore. They've accepted her as their granddaughter no matter what this piece of paper says." He turned it over and started to slip his finger under the flap, but stopped. "Will you open it for me?" he asked, holding it toward her. "I don't think I can look."

Julia planned to leave him to look at it without her

hovering over him, but instead she took the envelope from him. It was the least she could do after he didn't get mad about it.

Before she could open it, his phone rang.

Christopher closed his eyes, and his shoulders slumped. "That's my mom's ring tone." He pulled the phone out of his pocket. "I'll be back in a few minutes."

Julia stared as his retreating back before heading into the kitchen. Someone had left it well-stocked for them. She needed to make something to eat. After seeing what she had on hand, evaluating her own cravings, and asking the kids, Julia gathered the ingredients for pancakes. Not a traditional dinner, but both kids loved pancakes and scrambled eggs, and the baby kicked when it occurred to her.

Christopher didn't return until the eggs were nearly done and the first pancakes were coming off the griddle. "We're having brinner?"

Her heart rate sped up. "I hope that's okay." She should have asked. But if she'd waited, dinner wouldn't even be started yet. Alex, and probably Bailey, would be hangry if she waited much longer.

"I love brinner. It's so much better than the same thing for breakfast." He hopped up on the counter like a little boy. "I've always wondered why you can't have dinfast."

"Dinfast?" she asked, glancing his way as she poured more batter onto the griddle.

"Yeah. Steak and potatoes for breakfast. Or spaghetti."

Julia wrinkled her nose. "Because, ew. Who wants spaghetti for breakfast? Please don't tell me that's what you want tomorrow."

He chuckled, just a bit. "No. That's okay."

Had he forgotten the letter, or was he choosing to ignore it for now? Maybe until after Bailey was in bed so he could have some time to come to grips with whatever it said before having to face the little girl.

"I'd be open to some dinfast suggestions, but steak and potatoes are far too much work for a time of day when I'm barely coherent." She pointed the spatula at him. "I'm happy to help with breakfast preparation, but when you're home, if you want a steak before noon, you can make it yourself."

This time he gave her one of the heart-stopping smiles every teen girl had swooned over for years. "Deal."

She called the kids to the table and prepared their plates while they washed their hands. Once they were settled, she went back to the kitchen to find Christopher taking the last pancake off.

"Do we need more?" he asked.

Her stomach growled. Half of the stack of four wouldn't be enough. "Go ahead and take those. I'll make a couple more."

He went to the table while she managed to fit five on the griddle instead of the four she had been. She turned the temperature up just a bit, but kept a close eye on them to make sure they didn't burn.

By the time they were done, though, Alex and Bailey had brought their plates to the sink. Alex asked if they could go back to their VeggieTales. She told them they could after they washed their hands and faces. Her son headed for the bathroom, but Julia picked Bailey up and balanced the girl backwards on her knee.

"Let's get you clean, kiddo." She helped Bailey wash her

hands and used the washcloth to get her face. Once her bare feet were back on the floor, Bailey took off for the living room.

Julia took her plate to the table, fully expecting to eat her meal alone. It wasn't the first time, and it surely wouldn't be the last.

Instead, she found Christopher hadn't touched his food. "Is there something wrong with it?"

Christopher shook his head. "No. I just didn't think you should eat by yourself. My dad always waited for my mom when Ander and I would rush through our meals. He said it wasn't fair for when cook had to eat alone sometimes."

She didn't read anything into the comment about his parents, except that they had been good role models. Small talk dominated the conversation as they ate.

After working together to clean up the kitchen, Christopher told her to sit in the living room with her feet up and took the kids to play in the pool. Once they returned over an hour later, Christopher bathed Bailey while Alex took his own shower. After they were both in bed, Christopher came to where she was.

"It's time," he told her, still standing.

"I know." Julia took the envelope out of her knitting bag. "Are you ready to open it?"

"No. But I think I'm ready for you to."

"Are you sure you don't want to read it yourself?"

He took a deep breath and blew it out slowly. "Yeah. Go ahead." The stress in his voice tugged at her heart strings.

"Okay." She stood, not wanting to sit while he wasn't, slid a finger under the flap, and tore it open. The paper stuck a bit, but after a second it came out.

Christopher turned and walked away, his hands gripping his hips. After a few steps, he turned and came back.

The envelope fluttered to the ground as she unfolded the page. A quick scan didn't give her the information she needed, so she backed up and read it more slowly.

"What's it say?" Christopher had stopped near a window and now stared out of it.

"It says that, with 99.9% certainty, that Bailey is your little girl." A wave of relief washed over her.

Christopher's shoulders slumped as he turned around. "Thank God."

That puzzled Julia a bit. Wouldn't it have been easier for him if Bailey wasn't his daughter? Then he would have been absolved of responsibility, though it could have made for an awkward week.

"I can't imagine the trauma for Bailey if I had to tell her I wasn't her father. And then the court cases that could ensue, because by this point, I'd fight whoever came along. I'd take care of her anyway. Now, there's no one to come try to take her away from me."

What a selfless way to look at things.

Why couldn't he have been the father of one of her kids?

The thought caught Julia off-guard. Sure, Alex's father hadn't been around and barely paid child support before he died. And this baby's father wouldn't be any better unless she sued and dragged him into court. Doing so would embarrass her in front of all of her former colleagues and rip apart his family.

The one she hadn't known existed until far too late.

But wishing Christopher was the father of her baby

wouldn't fix that and could only lead to heartbreak.

Christopher started back toward her. "There's no reason to even tell her we did a paternity test unless she asks someday when she's older. A lot older."

But he didn't go to the door like she expected. Instead, he took the paper from her and read it himself. "Thank you, God," he said again.

And then he did something completely unexpected.

Christopher wrapped her in a hug.

After a shocked half-second, Julia slid her arms around his waist but the thoughts running through her head said that might be too much. In a split second, she shifted so her hands ended up on his shoulder blades. Less like a romantic hug, right?

But she still knew it would stay with her for a long time to come. Rarely had she had a hug from a guy who wasn't a potential love interest.

It was nice.

"Thank you," he whispered. His head turned slightly and, if she didn't know better, Julia would have said he kissed the side of her head.

But he couldn't have done that, could he?

That might be a question better left unanswered.

Topher let Julia go and stepped back, wondering if she was as surprised as he was by that hug. "Okay. Time to tell my parents."

Without looking back at her, he walked to the door and

went outside, pulling his phone from his pocket as he did so. The phone went straight to voice mail. A glance at his watch told him why.

Time zones were annoying.

He texted his dad to have him call in the morning, but that everything was fine. This shouldn't be shared through a text message. He texted Ander, too.

When he went back inside, Julia sat on the couch working on her knitting project. She didn't look up.

He didn't say anything to her, but went to Bailey's room. Once there, he watched her sleep.

Bailey was his daughter.

His little girl.

One thing he'd managed to do right. Sort of. It wasn't his fault he hadn't known. That she'd run off with another man. That his wife had lied in the divorce paperwork. It had taken months to finalize. She had to have known and kept it from him.

But here, now, he had a daughter. He hadn't realized a part of him had been holding back since she arrived, the part that wanted to make sure he wasn't being lied to one more time. Two hours earlier, he'd believed it wouldn't matter to him. He still believed that if she wasn't his daughter, he'd have loved and taken care of her like she was. Bailey never would have known the difference unless it became absolutely necessary.

She took a deep breath and let it out, her arm tightening around the teddy bear he'd found in some of his old things the day she arrived. He knew she had a favorite animal, but not until the flight to Ravenzario that he knew it was his old one. The beanie cap, complete with propeller, had faded over the years, but he was still soft and apparently, quite huggable.

"Do you need anything else?"

Topher turned to see Julia standing a few feet away. "No. I'm about ready to go to bed myself. Thank you for your help tonight. I appreciate it."

She gave him a small smile. "My pleasure. I'm glad the results came in the way you wanted."

"Me, too." He looked back at Bailey. "I'd love her anyway. It wouldn't have mattered."

"I know."

"Is there anything on the schedule for tomorrow?"

"No. It looks pretty much just like today and the rest of the week. There's that dinner with the show on Friday night, but that's the only thing. You weren't sure if you wanted to do that with just you and Bailey or all of us or what, so even that's not set."

"Thanks."

"Good night."

"Night." He noted the waddle in her step as she walked away. It had been less pronounced in the morning. It must get worse when she got tired, but she never complained. She disappeared around the corner, and Topher turned back to his daughter. He crossed the room, leaned over, and brushed a kiss against her hairline. "I love you, Bailey." He left her door open enough that he'd hear her if she woke up in the middle of the night.

After going through his bedtime routine, he lay down, the breeze from the ocean cooling the room.

This was the life.

The next few days were much the same, though Topher

was careful not to chase Julia through the surf again. In fact, he did his best to keep his distance.

The dinner on Friday night was fun. All four of them enjoyed it, and the kids were up a little later than normal, but woke up at the same time on Saturday. They were kind of cranky, but it gave him a chance to do more of a dad thing and not just when things were fun and easy. He tried to convince himself this was a good thing.

By the time Saturday evening rolled around, they were all ready to take it easy. Alex had the remote and flipped through the channels. Topher was texting his brother when the flipping stopped.

"Isn't that you, Topher?"

Topher looked up and grimaced. "No. That's Ander." The show cut to a commercial announcing an all weekend *2 Cool 4 School* marathon.

"Can we watch, Mom?" Alex was more excited than Topher about the prospect.

"It's up to Mr. Bayfield. If he doesn't want to, we won't."

Bailey tugged on his shirt and pointed, questions in her eyes.

"That was Uncle Ander," he told her. "We were on a TV show when we were kids." He managed to control his shudder. "You can leave it on if you want."

Julia glanced up as the show came back on. "This is a good one. There's a dance off, and Alex is the better dancer."

"He is not the better dancer," Topher scoffed. "He might say that, but he's not."

She raised an eyebrow at him. "I know you were in the episode and all, but when was the last time you watched the series as it aired? I know there were several variations of different things taped, but did you always know which one they went with if it didn't have a major effect on the plot?"

The woman had a point, but he wouldn't tell her that. "I still say the Alex character wasn't a better dancer. Chris won the contest."

"Don't spoil it!" Alex-the-kid interjected.

Julia left that eyebrow raised as she went back to her knitting. "I didn't say Alex won the contest. I said he was the better dancer."

"Let us watch, Mom!"

Sure enough, the end of the episode rolled around. Chris won the contest, even though he was in a wheelchair with a broken leg. His wheelies and spins won him the adoration of the gathered high schoolers.

"See?" Topher said. "Chris won."

"He wasn't the better dancer," Julia insisted. "Ask the kids."

"Fine. Alex, Bailey, whose dance was better?"

"Alex's," Alex answered without hesitation. "Sorry, Topher, but yours just wasn't as good."

Bailey nodded.

Topher groaned. "I know when I'm outmanned. I still say I'm a better dancer than my brother."

"I bet Mom knows the show better than you, though," Alex said. "She had the right answer."

And so, somehow the seven-year-old kid managed to maneuver both Topher and Julia into a trivia competition where the winner got one task, of their choice, from the loser.

Topher just prayed he remembered the details.

Chapter Twelve

"We don't have to go through with this," Julia pointed out while the kids both went to the bathroom.

"But we do. I'm not going to back down from the challenge."

She shrugged. "Okay then. Be right back." Julia went to her room and found the box Duke Alexander had given her. She carried it back into the living room. "Your brother said to give this to you when I felt the time was right. Something about payback for his wedding present."

Christopher groaned until it turned into a laugh. "Serves me right, I guess." He took the *2 Cool 4 School DVD Trivia* box from her. "I gave him a digital copy of the entire series for their wedding. I'm told Christiana has watched them all. Ander hasn't watched any."

"I'm guessing it's been a while since you've watched them,

too, right?"

He smirked at her. "Like I'd tell you that."

Alex opened the box. "I'll read the questions. Bay, you move the pieces for both of them, okay?"

Bailey nodded. Julia was proud of her son for finding a way to include her. She and Topher rolled to see who would go first. He won.

"What was the name of the principal?" Alex read off the card.

Christopher leaned back, a grin covering his face. "That's easy. Mr. Carlton."

"Correct."

Bailey moved Christopher's piece.

Julia's turn. "Okay, Mom. This is a two-part question. You have to get both parts right. What senior prank did Alex and Chris pull?"

Was this supposed to be hard? "They took a cow to the top floor of the school. Since cows won't go down stairs, the custodians had a hard time getting her out of the building."

"And where did they get the cow?"

Too easy. "From Mr. MacGregor's Petting Zoo."

"Correct." Bailey moved her piece for her.

Alex read Christopher's next question. "What scared Chris more than anything?"

Christopher thought long enough that Julia thought about looking up the *Jeopardy* theme song on her phone. Finally, he answered. "Losing the big game."

Alex grinned. "Wrong. Mom, you can move half the spaces he rolled if you get it right."

Julia couldn't stop her snicker. "Bunnies. Chris was deathly afraid of bunnies."

"Correct."

Christopher groaned. "That was in *one* episode and never mentioned again. I even held one in an episode after that," he pointed out. "How can that be right?"

Julia shrugged and shook the dice in her hand. "Continuity was never a strong suit for any of those shows. Where did Tori come from, or go, on *Saved by the Bell*? Or all of Shawn's step-siblings that weren't Jack on *Boy Meets World*?"

He muttered something under his breath as Julia rolled the dice.

Alex pulled the next card out and found the right category. "During high school, Alex, Chris, and the gang hung out at Mr. MacGregor's Petting Zoo and Pizza Palace. Where did they hang out in college?"

"College Station Subs and More."

"Correct."

"I knew that," Christopher muttered, as he rolled the dice.

"Who dressed up as Elvis at Alex and Bonnie's wedding?"

Julia giggled as Christopher groaned. "That would be me."

Julia wasn't quite sure how she felt when they neared the end of the game board, and it really wasn't even close. Christopher had drawn some pretty hard questions that she wasn't sure about, but he'd also missed some incredibly easy ones. Like where they went on Senior Ditch Day. Disneyland was both cliché and memorable.

"Okay, Mom," Alex held out a card. "You have to get all three of these right, then you win the game."

"What was the name of the waitress at the Pizza Palace?" Alex asked.

Easy. “Abby.”

“Correct. What was Motormouth’s real name?”

A little harder. “Maurice.”

“Correct. How did Mr. MacGregor know Chris and Alex switched shifts after he’d told them they couldn’t?”

She couldn’t stop a little bit of a gloating grin. “They wore different aftershave, and he always knew who was who because one was the same one he wore.”

“And Mom wins!” Alex and Bailey jumped up and down and hugged her while Christopher just smiled and gave a slight nod.

He leaned across the table and held out a hand. “Congratulations.”

She shook it.

“So what’s the prize?”

Julia had already decided. “I’m going to let Alex claim my prize. Maybe you two could go do something together tomorrow.” That way she didn’t have to.

Alex’s eyes lit up. “Really?”

Christopher started to clean up the game. “Sure. We can go do something.”

“Or you can dance with my mom.”

Topher froze, hand full of game pieces in mid-air.

“What?” Julia sounded surprised.

“Topher says he’s a better dancer than Duke Alexander. You’ve danced with him.” Alex shrugged. “Dance with Topher and see who’s better.”

Topher unfroze himself and continued putting the pieces in the baggie. "That's not the kind of dancing I was talking about, bud. The kind in the episode we watched."

"Okay." The kid seemed almost deliberately nonchalant. "I guess the duke is a better dancer."

He wasn't going to be goaded into something by a kid.

"Duke Alexander is a good dancer," Julia said. "But Christopher doesn't have anything to prove. I'm sure he's a fine dancer as well."

"Probably not as good as the duke." Alex picked up the game cards.

"Alex." Julia's quiet reprimand had the desired effect.

"Sorry," Alex muttered.

"No, it's okay." Topher made up his mind and pulled his phone out of his pocket. After a few taps, music started to play. He walked over to Julia and bowed slightly, holding out a hand. "May I have this dance?"

"You don't have to do this."

He looked into her eyes and tried to contain his amusement. "I know. If you'd rather live with my brother's mediocre dancing you can, or we can put this to rest here and now."

"Or you've danced with the queen. We could ask her next time we're there."

"And you really think she's unbiased."

Julia rolled her eyes and stood, slipping her hand into his. "Fine."

He led her to an area with enough room to dance and settled his other hand on her hip, but made sure to keep an appropriate distance between them. She seemed to focus her gaze somewhere near the top of his t-shirt and held herself so stiffly he didn't think she'd be able to dance at all.

"You can loosen up," he told her. "Or else this really isn't fair. If you're not relaxed, of course Ander is the better dancer."

He could see her try to relax her shoulders. "Sorry."

"Don't be sorry." He started to move, using gentle pressure to get her to move with him. Would closing the gap between them help? He was pretty far away from her, even more than her baby bump required.

By the next turn, he'd pulled her closer, but not too close.

Julia looked up at him, her eyes wide with surprise. He didn't say anything, but kept moving her around as the music played.

The music played on, and as it did, he found himself holding her closer until he could feel the warmth of her breath on skin. No longer looking into her eyes, something flooded through him, something he hadn't experienced in a very long time.

Not since Martha left him.

The rational part of his mind told him to end the dance and walk away.

But the rational part was being overwhelmed by this nearly indescribable feeling of connection with a beautiful woman.

He'd finally admitted to himself that she was beautiful, pregnancy and all. Had he ever danced with a pregnant woman? An honest response would be maybe - depending on when Bailey was conceived, but he didn't think that really counted. Neither did Christiana.

Shoving his ex out of his mind, he focused on the woman in his arms. On the electricity sparking between them. Did she feel it, too? Or was it just a result of his exceptionally long relationship dry spell?

He found his hand slipping further around her waist, until it splayed against the small of her back, anchoring her closer to him than she had been. Julia didn't protest, but slid her hand a bit further up his shoulder. Topher found his chin next to her temple, her breath teasing his collar bone.

Topher wasn't sure how long they'd danced, but his phone chirped, interrupting the music. "I guess that's our cue." His voice sounded surprisingly husky, even to his own ears.

"I guess so." Julia looked up, their gaze locking.

Unable to stop himself, he reached up with one hand and cradled her face, his thumb rubbing along her cheek. He broke the eye contact when he looked down, at her lips, just for a second.

What would it be like to kiss her? Would her lips be as soft as they looked?

Would it be as incredible as he suspected it would be?

Before he could try it out, his phone beeped again. Julia looked down and took a step back.

Topher reached for his phone on the nearby table and realized they were alone. "Where are the kids?"

"I'm sure they went to one of their rooms to watch a movie on a tablet or something. They didn't want to watch us dance."

And thank goodness they hadn't seen the last few minutes of that dance. He didn't want Alex or Bailey getting their hopes up for some sort of relationship between them. Julia getting her hopes up would be bad enough, but to break his daughter's heart so soon? Topher really didn't want to do that.

Julia moved toward his half of the house. "Who's the text

from?"

With a push of the button, he saw several new pictures from his brother. "Just more baby pictures, though I think these might be the official ones they're going to release to the public."

"I'd love to see them later." She disappeared into Bailey's room, reappearing after just a few seconds. "Come here," she whispered.

"What?"

She just motioned for him to follow. He did, and immediately understood why.

Bailey and Alex had changed into their pajamas and sat on Bailey's bed. Alex held one of her books, though it had fallen to his lap. Her head rested on his shoulder while his leaned against the top of hers.

Sound asleep.

"I don't think I can carry Alex," Julia whispered. "Can you move him?"

"Should we just leave them?"

She shook her head. "They'll wake each other up before long. If you can get Alex to his bed, I'll help Bailey lay down."

He went around to the other side, and slid his arms under the boy. Topher had picked him up before, but the dead weight of a sleeping child seemed like much more. Once on the other side of the house, Topher laid Alex on his bed, pulling a light blanket up over him.

Back out in the living area, he met Julia headed the other direction.

"She's still sound asleep. I'm going to turn in, too." She didn't look directly at him. "Good night."

She walked away. Had she been as affected by the dancing as he had been? "Good night."

Julia waited for everyone else to descend the stairs from the plane in Springfield before she tried. Had she gotten that much bigger in the last week? Stairs were much more difficult than they had been a few days earlier, especially narrow steep stairs like these.

"Here."

She looked up to see Christopher holding out a hand. Grateful, she took it and climbed down the rest. "Thank you."

"My pleasure." His hand came to rest on the small of her back as they walked toward the car.

It seemed very...coupleish. At least the kids were both already in the car, so they wouldn't see it. No one had mentioned the dancing the night before, but it had been at the forefront of Julia's mind all day.

Either Christopher hadn't been nearly as affected as she had been or he was much better at hiding it.

Once back at the house, they went their separate ways. She told him she'd take care of the unpacking and everything else the next day. He told her to take the evening off. Of course, she'd technically been on duty 24/7 for a month so an afternoon and evening off wasn't too much to ask.

Downstairs, she started a load of laundry then took Alex outside to let him run off some of the energy he hadn't expended while cooped up in the plane. Julia got out the baseball and gloves she'd bought with her first paycheck.

"Let's see what you've got." All they'd do was toss it back and forth. She didn't know how to do more than that, but Alex loved doing even that much. Now that she'd have the money and time, maybe she could get him on a baseball team in the spring.

"Can a couple of others get in this game?"

Julia turned to see Christopher standing there with his own ball glove. "Of course."

For about five minutes, the three of them tossed the ball to each other before Bailey tugged on the hem of her shirt and pointed toward the door.

"I'm going to take Bailey to the bathroom."

Christopher and Alex barely noticed as they left, so Julia asked Bailey what she wanted to do. That's how they ended up in a chair together reading *The Lion, the Witch, and the Wardrobe*. Julia had read the whole series to Alex when he was younger, and he'd been begging to read it again. They'd read a couple of chapters before leaving for the trip, so if she caught Bailey up, they could read together during the day.

She could see Alex and Christopher running around outside as one or the other would over or under throw a ball. After a couple of chapters of the book, Bailey had fallen asleep. Carefully, Julia extended the footrest on the recliner and leaned it back. With the little girl snuggled more securely against her, Julia closed her eyes. Just for a minute.

But when she bolted straight up, dusk had settled over the yard and Bailey was nowhere to be seen. Before she had too long to wonder, she heard voices upstairs and headed up to check it out.

She could see Christopher in the kitchen with her cupcake apron wrapped around him. Both kids sat on barstools with mixing bowls in front of them, stirring something she couldn't see.

She started forward as Christopher looked up.

"Hey! Did you have a nice nap?" His smile seemed genuine.

"I did. Thank you for letting me sleep." She slid onto the stool next to Alex. "What are you making?"

"I'm making a salad. Alex is mixing the insides for chicken pot pie." He leaned on the counter and looked in Bailey's bowl. "And Bay here is stirring up the brownies we're going to have for dessert."

"It looks great." Julia leaned over and took a swipe off the side of the bowl, then licked her finger. "Brownies are my favorite."

Christopher chuckled at her. "Are you supposed to do that in front of the kids?"

Julia just shrugged. "Just a little bit every once in a while won't hurt anyone."

"Can I have some, Mom?" Alex asked, with that hopeful tone in his voice.

"After they're in the oven, you can have just a little bit."

"So what are you going to do with the rest of your evening? After dinner," Christopher asked her.

"I got quite a bit of knitting stuff done while we were gone, but I have a bunch of other things I need to do as soon as possible. The show will be here before I know it. I have a ton of stuff to make."

"Alex is welcome to hang out with us for a little while this evening. I think we are going to watch some *Backyardigans*."

Topher poured the chicken mixture into a pie shell.

Alex had introduced Bailey to his favorite show. Julia had inherited a bunch of DVDs from her cousin, but Topher would stream it on the Fire TV. It would be easier to pick and choose, but she'd never been able to afford the streaming services. Julia was just glad her son hadn't moved on to more grown up television. She liked that he wasn't growing up too fast.

After dinner, Alex and Bailey climbed into one of the chairs in the living room while Topher turned on the television. Julia went downstairs to get some of her own work done. Mixed emotions filled her. She was glad her son was settling in well and that Christopher treated him almost like one of the family. But at the same time, she couldn't help feeling like she'd lost a little something - being her son's favorite person all of the time.

Hopefully, in the long run, the trade-off would be worth it.

Chapter Thirteen

"So what exactly is HEA TV proposing?" Topher leaned back in his chair and propped his feet up on the desk. After twenty minutes of conversation, he had a much better idea of what they wanted from him and what he wanted Mady to ask for in return.

Once he'd hung up the phone, he went to find Julia. He found her, and Bailey, in the basement. Bailey sat in a kid-sized bean bag chair with a picture book she was pretending to read. Julia stood hunched over a table nearby cutting fabric.

"Hey, you two."

Bailey dropped her book and ran to him, arms outstretched. Topher swooped her up and held her in front of him.

"Are you enjoying your book?"

She nodded.

"She wanted to read on her own." He looked up to see Julia

burying her fists in the small of her back and leaning into them. "She didn't want me to help her, so I thought I'd cut some fabric out. Standing here and staring at her would be kind of a waste of time."

He held up one hand. "Hey. I didn't say anything."

With her hands on her hips, she twisted one way then the other, stretching her sides. "I know, but I didn't want you to think I told her to sit there so I could do other work."

"I didn't think you would." He set Bailey on her feet. "I need to talk to Julia for a few minutes, all right?"

Bailey nodded and went back to her book.

"What do you need to talk to me about?" Julia lowered herself into a folding chair. She had to be getting more uncomfortable by the minute. He'd noticed it when she walked down the stairs of the plane and several times since then, though she never complained.

"HEA is talking to me about doing a couple of movies for them next year."

She looked up in surprise. "I thought this was a one-time thing."

"It was, but I've wanted to get back into acting for a while, and this was the first step. After everything with our names being released earlier this year, my agent got a ton of calls. I told her if HEA called, I might be interested. I want to do clean, family-friendly programming. Stuff I wouldn't be afraid to let Bailey watch. They were happy with the work I did on the movie and want me to do at least two next year."

"Two Christmas movies? I didn't think they had the same actors in two different new release Christmas movies a year."

"One Christmas, one to be determined. Possibly a fall

movie."

"Okay. What does this have to do with me? I'll take care of Bailey while you're gone."

"That's just it." He glanced over to see his daughter wasn't paying any attention to him. After taking a step, he turned and leaned back against the table. "I want her to go with me. That means you and Alex need to go, too. What time of year could we make that happen?"

"Summer would be best." She pulled out her phone and tapped a few times, showing it to him. "That's the schedule for the rest of this year. Next year's isn't up yet, but school will probably start the week of August 13, so it would be good to be back no later than that weekend. We can leave any time after the last snow make-up day on the calendar."

Topher looked at the calendar. "So basically June, July, and the first week and a half of August?"

"That's when it would be best. If you started earlier or ended later, I could always stay here with Bailey, Alex, and the baby for a week or so while you're working."

He could see something occur to her. "What?"

"But then they'll miss out on swim team and other summer stuff. Any chance you could do one mid-to-late summer, so they wouldn't miss that stuff? Do the other maybe over Spring Break, so it would only be two weeks away?"

He stared at the calendar, trying to work it out in his head. "We'll see what kind of magic my agent can work." He went back upstairs to call Mady back.

Two HEA TV movies a year wasn't much work. Only a couple of months, tops, probably less. They could film a movie in late September and early October and have it out by

Thanksgiving. He knew his movie wasn't the last one they'd filmed for the coming season.

With a new daughter, though, he probably didn't want to work near as much as he'd been thinking about two months earlier. Then he would have considered a move to LA for a TV show or, maybe, under the right circumstances, a sequel to *2C4S*. With the success of *Fuller House* and *Girl Meets World*, or even the *Gilmore Girls* reunion his mom had been so excited about, there had been discussions of it. He'd dismissed them out of hand.

The initial concepts had been for his brother's character and his wife, who married in the final episode, to be raising their own set of twins. Ander had always denied any interest in acting again at all, much less reprising their roles. Topher wondered if he could play his brother's role, but didn't think he'd want to go that route and neither would anyone else. Everyone would know it wasn't the same twin.

But even if all of that were plausible, it would mean moving, which was no longer an option. Even if he could get them to film locally, there wouldn't be enough interest for a Chris storyline - unless it was after the Alex character's death, and he had to raise his twin nieces.

Something to mention to his agent. If the network showed enough interest, surely they could make something work. Maybe they'd put it on MyBingeFlix like they had a couple of the other series. They might be easier to work with.

He called Mady, and they proceeded to have a long conversation about what he'd need from HEA TV to sign for two movies next year. They also spent quite a bit of time discussing the possibility of a spin-off show. She'd gotten a call a couple days earlier asking about his interest, but hadn't mentioned it until this conversation.

She wasn't sure they would be willing to shoot in Serenity Landing, but she'd give it a shot.

The worst they could say was no.

Julia managed to sit into the cushiest chair in Kenzie's living room. She might not be able to get up, but she'd be comfortable while she was here.

"So?" Kenzie settled into the chair across from her. "Tell me everything."

"Everything?" Julia wasn't quite sure what her friend was talking about.

"You and Christopher. Tell me about your trip!"

Julia shook her head. "There's nothing to tell." Nothing she was willing to tell, anyway, as the moments in his arms came back to her. "I'm his nanny. I helped him take are of Bailey while out of town. Now that we're home, he tries to schedule his phone calls and stuff during nap time, so he can take care of Bailey himself. I'm usually on nap duty, which is keeping a monitor near me in case she wakes up scared or something. Then I'm off in the evenings."

"So you're getting everything done you need to for the show?"

"I think so. The bags are coming along well. I have several new animal patterns to sell. I'm trying to cut all the bags out now before bending over a table gets even more difficult. Christopher and Bailey went to court today to finalize his legal custody. I got a bunch done while they were gone."

"Why don't I come over and help you with that? I've got a while before it bothers my back quite that much."

Julia breathed a sigh of relief. "That would be such a huge help."

Kenzie checked her calendar. "I think we're free every night this week. Jonathan has a bunch of meetings with people in Asia, so he's working evenings from the conference room."

"Exciting."

"So Lorelai and I will come over and help you. Christopher won't mind, will he?"

"We haven't talked about company. I suppose as long as I'm in my portion of the house, or the part I'm allowed to use anyway. It's not a big deal."

"You're not allowed to use any of it you want?"

Julia leaned her head back. "I'm the nanny, not a member of the family. Alex and I have rooms downstairs. There's an unfinished section where most of my work is set up. There's a kitchen down there I can use when it's just the two of us, and I'm not also feeding Bailey and/or Christopher. If he has to work until dinner, sometimes we eat together."

"Huh."

"What's that supposed to mean?"

"Nothing."

Julia didn't buy it but didn't push her friend. "What's the plan today?"

"We're going to work on the schedule for the show. The Show Me Yarn girls couldn't be here this evening, but one of them sent me their preferences." Kenzie pulled out her notepad. "We need to make sure someone is with Lady

Margaret at all times. That can't be a person who's taking her class."

"Why isn't the show taking care of an assistant for her? That seems like it would be their responsibility."

"They may have planned to, but she specifically requested Jonathan take care of it with people he knew personally who were connected to the yarn industry." She shrugged. "Who knows? I'm just excited we get to do it."

"She's staying here, right?"

"It's a secure location. She's actually taking over the apartment. She values her privacy and safety. I'm not exactly sure why the need for a secure location. I Googled but couldn't find any threats, just links to yarn related stuff. I think Jonathan knows more than he can say. He's kind of hinted, but he *can't* tell me. I doubt I'll see her much, if at all, except maybe on the drives to and from the venue."

"Then let's get the schedule sorted out." It took about twenty minutes, but they arranged it so most of them would be in the booth at the busiest times, but still let each of them take Lady Margaret's class and at least one other class they wanted to take.

"I'll send this to them and make sure it works. Hopefully, we're all set, but Jonathan's team wants everything scheduled before the end of the week, so we needed to get it done."

Alex chose that moment to run inside, Lorelai in his wake. "Mom! We just saw a coyote!"

"You did?" Julia struggled to stand up. "Where?"

"In the field. Mr. Jonathan said that's what it was." Alex's eyes lit up in a way she rarely saw. "I've never seen one before!"

He'd seen more wildlife in the last month than he'd seen in

his life. An advantage of living in the country, near a lake. They'd even seen a few bald eagles. That was pretty much the coolest thing ever. If they could figure out where they nested, maybe they could sneak over and look, but not too closely.

Wasn't there a nest cam somewhere? Alex would probably think that was awesome. She'd have to try to find it when she wasn't pregnant.

"That's fantastic, Alex." Kenzie held out her arms so Lorelai could climb on her lap. Julia missed Alex being able to do that. Her belly was too big for her bigger son to do so. "I haven't seen any since we moved out here, but we saw a couple at our old house."

Jonathan walked through the living room, stopping long enough to give his wife a kiss and say hello.

Julia sighed as he walked toward his office.

"It's gonna happen for you," Kenzie told her as the kids went back onto the deck where they could be seen.

"Maybe. Someday. I'm not holding my breath." The baby kicked her rib. "I've not had the best luck with men, and I'm in no rush to get my heart broken again. Or my kids' hearts."

"I doubt you'll have to worry about that. Christopher..."

"Stop!" Julia struggled to stand. "There's nothing going on with us. There's not going to be anything going on with us. Even if he found me attractive, which he doesn't, and couldn't while I look like a whale, there's too much history. He knows I had nothing to do with the rumors last spring, but I still don't think he truly trusts me." The look in his eyes as they finished the dance flashed through her mind followed by the one in the ocean. It didn't mean anything. He was probably imagining she was someone else.

Jonathan walked out of his office and opened the front door. Christopher walked in, a grim look on his face, with Bailey's hand in his. He sent Bailey straight outside while George, Jonathan's assistant, spoke quietly with his boss for a moment then followed her.

Christopher sat on the couch, his iPad in his hands. "We have to talk."

Chapter Fourteen

Before Topher could tell Julia and Kenzie what Jonathan had found, Jonathan reached a hand toward Julia.

"Let's go in the conference room. George will take care of the kids for a bit."

Julia reached up and took Jonathan's hand so he could help her stand.

Annoyance flooded through Topher. Why? It shouldn't matter if Jonathan helped her up. His fist clenched without him making a conscious choice to do it, as if it wanted to be the one to help Julia. It didn't make any sense for his hand to want something he didn't, but he was sure that was what happened.

A minute later, they were seated around the conference table with the screen on the other wall hooked up to Jonathan's computer.

"Let me pull the article up." A few clicks later, *CelebGossipNewz* was on the screen.

Complete with a picture of him and Julia in the ocean after he dunked her.

And the headline: 2C4S Alum Frolics with Brother's Ex-Mistress

When Mady called him to let him know this story had popped up, Topher hadn't wanted to believe it. His brother hadn't answered his phone, but Topher had been able to get in touch with the public relations office. They'd figure it out from their end.

Topher glanced over at Julia. Her face seemed to be set in stone, but one tear after another streaked down her cheek.

"Can you explain the picture?" Jonathan asked.

"The kids were having a water war. Julia didn't want to get her hair wet. I had to dunk her, but we went under water together then stood up. That's it."

"That look says a lot more than just goofing off with a friend."

Topher looked at it again. The look on his own face was one he'd never quite been able to pull off on screen. *Breathless anticipation* was how his director had described it a few weeks earlier. Julia's was more confusion, but definitely not the fury he'd been afraid of.

"There's nothing going on between us," he told his friend. "It was a water war. That's it." And there couldn't have been any pictures of the two of them dancing or when he kissed the side of her head after finding out Bailey really was his daughter. He still didn't know what had possessed him to do that.

"Did you read the article?"

"No."

Jonathan scrolled down to a picture of them getting off the plane in Ravenzario. "There's speculation about who Bailey is."

And a picture of him holding Julia's hand as she climbed down the airplane stairs in Springfield. Then one of his hand on her back as they walked to the car.

"Their theory is that Bailey is your love child. That Julia is her mother."

"Then where was she when everything broke loose last spring? Why would Julia have taken one child to Ravenzario and not the other?" It didn't make sense.

"These people don't care about rational thought. You know that. You know what they tried to do to Julia and your brother a few months ago. They took one picture from years ago in a school paper and a hug no one could really see and turned it into a scandalous affair. You can't expect them to have ethics."

"Why would anyone buy it?"

"Their continuing theory is that she didn't bring Bailey because she's your child not Alexander's, and she was trying to blackmail him, not you, and Bailey would get in the way of that."

"It doesn't make sense at all." Kenzie's anger seeped through her words and her body language.

"I'd never met Julia until last spring in Ravenzario. The allegations about her and Ander were all groundless. That's public knowledge. It was a set up by Christiana's uncle's loyal henchmen."

"It doesn't matter." The defeat in Julia's low voice nearly broke his heart. "They're just like any other bully. The truth is something inconvenient and to be ignored."

"And the best way to fight a bully is to ignore them, right?" Topher didn't want a confrontation.

"Maybe." Jonathan leaned back in his chair. "Bullies on the playground are one thing. This is already trending on Twitter. It'll be on Facebook before we know it. It's the antithesis of what you stood for ten years ago. You and I know it's not true, but since when does that matter in the court of public opinion?"

Topher's phone buzzed. He pulled it out of his pocket, answered, and put it on speaker. "Hey, Ander. You're on speaker with Jonathan, Kenzie, and..." Julia abruptly stood, the fastest he'd seen her stand in days, and left the room.

"How's Julia?" Ander asked. "How're you?"

"She just left," Topher told him. "I'm annoyed, mad, whatever. It's not worth my time."

Kenzie glared at him and followed in Julia's footsteps.

"If you're trying to get back into the business it is. HEA TV won't like this, and you know it."

"It's not true. If it was true, then maybe, but since when are *CelebGossipNewz* stories enough to affect contracts?"

"Since you haven't been an actor in a decade. Things have changed a lot. You're about to get a crash course. I've talked to Charlyn. We'll put out a statement that you're both above reproach, and we have no other comment."

"I appreciate that." Topher ran a hand through his hair. "It'll blow over by tomorrow. Someone else will do something stupid."

"Someone probably will, but social media has changed everything. It's not going to die, Toph."

Topher looked at Jonathan who nodded. "He's right. You

remember what happened with Kenzie over the summer. The paparazzi will likely be descending on Serenity Landing again soon. The pictures of me with Lorelai at Sam's Club lasted for days."

"Great. So what do I do?"

Ander's voice came through the phone. "You talk to Julia. Make sure she's okay. You put out a statement through Mady that none of it's true, and you'll prosecute to the fullest extent of the law should it become necessary. Your good friend Jonathan Langley-Cranston is helping beef up security on your property. After the picture of him with his shotgun, the paparazzi don't mess with him or his family. Knowing he's helping you will help deter some of the more sane ones." There was a noise in the background. "I've got to go, but we'll talk again soon. Keep me posted."

Topher turned off his phone and looked at Jonathan. "You'll help go through security measures on the property?"

"Of course, but I think your brother's right. You need to check on Julia."

"She's not my girlfriend. She's barely a friend." Was that really true? "She's an employee."

Jonathan didn't look amused. "Keep telling yourself that, why don't you?" He pointed at the picture of the two of them in the ocean. "You don't really believe it, and neither will anyone else. But even if it was true, you need to go check on her."

Topher sighed and pushed back from the table. "Fine, but only because she's a valuable employee."

Julia backed away from the conference room. She'd pulled herself together and started to go back inside, but Christopher's words drifted out to her.

Not even his friend? Just an employee?

She wished she knew where to flee. Where he couldn't find her.

Instead, she started for the front door. Kenzie would take care of Alex if Julia drove to another part of the property where she could have a break down in peace.

"What is it?" Kenzie stopped her before she could leave.

"I've got to get out of here. I can't..." Her voice caught in her throat.

"Come on." Kenzie took her hand and led her up the stairs and into the master bedroom. "Christopher won't come in here looking for you."

Mr. Benny Hercules, the little dog Jonathan had rescued over the summer, stuck his nose out from under the bed and then came toward Julia as she sank into the chair. He jumped up onto her lap, climbing up until he snuggled down on top of her belly.

"I can't do this, Kenz. I need to move."

"You're going to go back to that apartment? Or someplace worse? Really?"

"No. Move. Far. Michigan. Ohio. Belgium. I don't care, but far away. I never want to see a Bayfield brother again as long as I live."

"What brought this on? You were okay a few minutes ago."

Julia shook her head. She wasn't going to tell her friend what she'd overheard. "I can't do this. I can't put Alex or the baby through it. I can't put myself through it."

She tried to keep it under control, but the weeping took over. Mr. Benny Hercules stood on her baby bump and licked her face as the tears streamed down, then settled with his head on her shoulder.

Kenzie handed her some tissues, but Julia just held them as the sobs wracked her body.

Incoherent thoughts muddled through her mind. She wasn't good enough. She never had been. The situation with the duke earlier in the year had proved conclusively something she'd known for a long time. This only reinforced it. Alex's father. Dead end jobs. Decent jobs, sure, but never any chance for advancement. A cyber-relationship turned one-night stand with a married man. A baby on the way.

Sucked into a conspiracy to ruin the queen. Now, a tramp who slept with twin brothers, had a baby with each of them, and wanted to use those children to manipulate them.

No matter that it wasn't true. No one would remember the truth. The messages she received on Facebook every week or so were proof that the truth didn't matter. Supporters of Queen Christiana and Duke Alexander wanted to make sure she didn't interfere in their marriage. All the statements in the world hadn't made a difference and wouldn't anytime soon.

As the torrent began to slow, her thoughts unjumbled. Christopher had already paid her more than she'd ever made in her life. Most of it sat in savings. Surely it was enough to start over somewhere. She and Alex could choose together.

She finally used the tissue to clean her face and blow her nose.

"Feel better?" Kenzie asked.

Julia looked over to see her friend's eyes still closed, likely praying. "Not really, but I'll figure it out." Julia wouldn't tell her about the move until later. She'd have to be back for the show, though. It meant too much to both of them.

"If you want to splash some water on your face, you're welcome to."

Julia snuggled Mr. Benny Hercules closer. She didn't want to. She wouldn't be able to avoid looking in the mirror and seeing the splotches and horrid flush sure to cover her face at the moment.

Her phone buzzed, and she looked at it.

Where are you?

She didn't want to answer Christopher, but knew she should. Talking to Kenzie. Close enough.

I need to talk to you. Something else has come up.

She didn't reply for a minute, finally saying she'd see him in time to take care of Bailey in the morning.

No reply.

"He's left." Julia saw Kenzie staring out the window. "He took Bailey with him."

"Can we stay for a while?"

"Of course."

"I'd rather not see Jonathan or Lorelai, though. I don't want to deal with the questions."

"We can go watch a movie in the media room. Jonathan will take care of the kids." Kenzie pulled out her own phone and sent a text.

"Thanks."

By the time she and Alex arrived back at Christopher's house,the sun had set. She let them in the basement door using her key. Originally, this was how he'd told them to come and go when not working, though it hadn't quite worked out that way so far.

"Go brush your teeth." She'd warned Alex that as soon as they got home he'd have to go to bed. He didn't argue, though she knew he wanted to.

After he was in asleep, she took a quick shower and settled into her own bed. It took far longer to fall asleep than it should have. She tried to keep her wandering mind focused on where they should move. Somewhere farther north with more winter? Somewhere south with no winter at all and even worse summers?

If Alex had hated moving to Serenity Landing, he was going to loathe moving far away.

Somehow, despite little and troubled sleep, she managed to get up in time to get Alex on the bus at the end of the drive. After double checking the calendar to make sure she wasn't needed until after lunch, she went back in the basement door, planning to collapse back in her bed.

Instead, she found Christopher waiting for her.

"I thought this area was mine and Alex's," she asked, hanging her light jacket back up on the hook.

"It is."

"Then shouldn't you knock or something?"

"It's still my house."

"Whatever." She had to tell him. "This is my notice. We'll be moving as soon as I can make the arrangements."

"Why?"

She glared at him out of the corner of her eye. "You saw that article. I've had text messages from people I haven't talked to in forever. Facebook messages from people I don't know. It's best if Alex and I move on. You won't have to deal with the rumors that way either. Hire an older woman to be your nanny. There's some great ones out there."

"Bailey won't want you to leave."

"Life stinks. It's full of things you don't want to happen. She's already learned that. I hate that she's going to experience it again, but I have to protect my son and my baby, first and foremost."

"What about me?"

"What about you? You're a big boy. You can handle a few people saying you've got a girlfriend."

"There's more to it than that. It affects my career."

Julia blinked. "How does our lack of relationship outside of that as employer and employee ruin your career?"

His mouth was pulled into a thin line as he crossed his arms over his chest. "HEA TV is pulling the contract offer unless we get married."

Chapter Fifteen

Not exactly how Topher planned to tell her.

"Pardon?"

He sat on the couch and waved her toward the chair. "There's a morality clause in most contracts. HEA TV's is pretty strict. They make family-friendly programming. Scandal like this will cause them to pull contracts."

"It's three pictures. You can't read anything into the one from Ravenzario."

"There's been a bunch more come out overnight. Someone took a ton of pics while we were in San Majoria. My attorney has already contacted the resort, because I paid a lot of money for privacy."

"What other pics could they possibly have of us that are compromising in any way?"

"Helping you sit down and stand up. Us taking care of each

other's kids. It's confirmation in the minds of the tabloid press that there's more to the relationship than there is."

"And getting married is the answer. Don't think I'm gonna say yes, but thanks for asking."

"I didn't ask," he pointed out. "I told you they wanted us to."

"And you need these jobs so badly that you're entertaining the idea."

"I don't *need* the jobs, but I do want them, badly. We were also close to announcing a *2 Cool 4 School* sequel like *Girl Meets World* or *Fuller House*. It was going to film here."

She looked up at that. "I didn't know there was even interest in something like that."

"There's been interest in a reunion forever, but with the success of those shows, there's been interest in a sequel series. Ander won't do it, of course, but in the last year or so, I've been approached several times."

"How would they even do that? Your character didn't have the relationship that would lead to a sequel."

"There's part of the rub. In the last proposal we were working on earlier this week, Ander's character has twin daughters. Six or seven years old, I think. His wife has died, but he has to be overseas for an extended period of time. We hadn't quite figured out why just yet. So Chris was moving into their house to raise the girls until Alex could come back."

"It's interesting," she admitted. "I would have watched it. But you don't need the money, so it's not like having them both back out is going to leave you destitute. You'll just have to find other options."

"It's not that simple." He hadn't wanted to get into more,

but he needed some way to get out of this. "They're threatening to pull the Christmas movie and sue me for the costs. That would bankrupt me. I'd already quit working for my parents, except occasionally helping out. They sold the part of the business I was working for, so the timing was good."

"So you need to get back on HEA TV's good side."

"Pretty much." He leaned forward, resting his forearms on his knees, staring at his hands. "Would you consider a public engagement? I think that would appease them. Once things have died down, we 'break up,' and then I'll help you move wherever you want."

She didn't say anything until he glanced up. Her face was both stoic and defeated at the same time. "Sure. Whatever."

"Don't sound so excited." Even as he said it, he knew it wasn't the right thing.

"I'm a realist, Mr. Bayfield. I know my place well. I'm *just* an employee who has caused her employer embarrassment. The only way to keep it from costing you much more than your dignity is to go along with this. I could pay to move us somewhere, but I'd have about three days before I needed a new job. In the meantime, I'm exceptionally pregnant, and have to put the needs of this baby and my son first. By pretending to be engaged to you, I have stability for the foreseeable future. If you pay for our move, then I'll have money to live on until I can find child care and a job."

"Fine." He stood up. "I'll get a ring. We'll make the announcement in a couple of days. Say it was already in the works."

"Whatever you think is best, Mr. Bayfield."

She'd called him that a few minutes earlier. It bothered

Topher, but not enough to deal with a cranky, pregnant woman any more than he had to.

Back in his office, he called Mady and told her only that the announcement would be made soon, but not of the temporary nature of the arrangement.

"I don't think it'll be enough, Topher." He could hear the weariness in her voice. "They're incredibly upset that you have any kind of relationship with the woman who may or may not have been your brother's mistress."

"She wasn't!"

"I know that. But most of the viewing public isn't sure what they think."

"So what does that mean?"

"It means, I think you're going to have to marry her soon to keep HEA TV from suing. Elope in a few days, tell the world that you're planning a big wedding next summer or next Christmas, or whenever you were planning to get married in the first place."

"I'm not going to elope with Julia just to make them happy."

"I'm not sure you have much choice." She sighed. "I'll call them and let them know it's coming. While you were talking to her, more news broke."

Topher pinched the bridge of his nose. "What now?"

"The building already leased for the show."

"We haven't signed a contract. Why have they leased a building?"

"Wishful thinking? I'm not sure. The negotiations have been surprisingly easy. They want this to happen and are willing to do what they have to in order to make it happen.

It's been fast-tracked. They're already planning auditions."

"How?"

"I'm guessing a lot of this has been planned for a long time, and they're just polishing it up, tweaking it to what we've been negotiating."

"So the world knows the sequel is almost a done deal?"

"No. They know it almost was before your scandalous relationship with Julia became public."

Great. Mady had another call come in she needed to deal with, so they hung up.

Now he had to figure out if he wanted to marry Julia. And if she'd go for it.

"Wait. What?" Julia stared at Christopher. He'd only been upstairs for twenty minutes and now this?

"We get married. I'll make sure you and your kids are well taken care of. In a couple years, if you're ready to move on, you let me know. If not, we stay a couple in name only. You'll get to attend premieres occasionally if you want to. If you don't, we just say you're home with the kids because it's not your scene."

"You're really proposing a temporary marriage in name only? For real?" Julia couldn't believe her ears.

He covered his face with his hands for a moment, and then looked at her. "I don't know what else to do. Bailey's already lost so much. If the network sues, she'll lose her new home, too. I'll lose everything."

"Even your self-respect. Noted."

"Come on, Julia." He leaned back and crossed one arm over his chest. The other hand sort of pinched his eyes. "It's not my first choice either, but it'll help you and the kids, too. Not just financially, but hopefully, it'll let all of the other stuff blow over. Why would the tabloids come after you if you're my wife? There's no scandal there."

Her phone buzzed for the fourth time in as many minutes, but this was a text from Kenzie.

Who is this? And a picture of a TV screen.

She felt the blood drain from her face.

"What is it?"

Julia wrapped an arm protectively around her belly. "Just another story." She stood up and started for her room. She couldn't look at this with him right there. "I'll think about it and let you know."

Before he could say anything else, she'd shut the door to her room, locking him out. She opened the text and clicked the link in the next one.

Her heart dropped and her stomach filled with lead as she read the article. He was the father of her baby, but the story he tried to spin was preposterous. He was claiming he knew Duke Alexander was the father, as had been alleged the previous spring. Julia had supposedly tried to seduce him, so he'd think the baby was his. He deeply regretted cheating on his wife, but he was drunk when she'd propositioned him. Now she wanted him to pay child support for a kid that wasn't his.

The weight of the world pressed down on her, and she dropped her phone to the bed. Before she could try to assimilate it all, there was a light knock on the door.

"I saw the story, Jules." His voice was filled with

compassion. "Are you okay?"

"No," she managed to choke out.

He rattled the door knob, but it didn't open. A few seconds later, after more jiggling, the door opened.

She sat on the edge of her unmade bed, her fingers holding the sheets in a death grip.

Christopher sat next to her and didn't hesitate to wrap his arms around her.

Julia didn't want to, but couldn't resist leaning into him. Just for a minute, she let him take on her burdens. Make them his own. Shoulder her load so she didn't have to do it alone.

Could it hurt to let herself believe, just for a moment, that someone would take on the world with her? Take up her cause, whatever it was. Take on her worries and fears and help her bear up underneath them.

She soaked up the strength found in his arms. It would be short-lived at best, but it gave her a glimpse, a bit of hope, that someday she'd have this regularly.

"Thanks," she mumbled, trying to move away, but Christopher wouldn't let her.

"I'm sorry."

"For what?"

"If you weren't Bailey's nanny, none of this would be happening. If I hadn't chased you down to get you wet, all they'd have is some pictures of us with kids."

"And if I wasn't stupid enough to believe the lies of a player, I wouldn't be pregnant. I regret everything about that night, but I can't regret the baby, no matter how hard it is. It's not his or her fault."

"You don't know if the baby's a boy or a girl?"

She shook her head, not wanting to let him know her doctor visits had been sporadic at best, and she hadn't had time since coming to work for him. She hadn't even had an ultrasound yet.

"Then marry me. We'll figure out the end game later. I need to make this HEA TV thing work. You need at least the appearance of legitimacy or something to protect the baby from the nasty stories that could come. We can elope and release the news. Then life goes on as normal."

She struggled to get far enough away to reach for a tissue from the box on the side table. Just what every girl wanted to hear. *Marry me, then we'll pretend like it never happened.*

"Sure," she found herself saying. It would help him. It would help her. She'd figure out how God could possibly approve of this later.

"You mean it?"

"No. We should go do it before I change my mind."

"You want to get married right now?"

"Why not? Call whoever you need to call to find someone who can do it quietly. Jonathan and Kenzie were married by a judge friend of his."

"I know a retired judge who will do it."

She managed to push herself up from the bed, trying not to think of any potential implications. They wouldn't share a room, much less a bed, at any time during this farce of a thing. "Give me twenty minutes to get changed, and we can go."

"Meet me upstairs. Since Bailey's napping, I'll give Ida Mae the monitor. Hopefully, we'll be back before she wakes up."

She spent the next half hour getting dressed in the prettiest weather appropriate top she had. It was even white and fell to mid-thigh, so she could wear leggings with it along with her favorite black boots. More time was spent carefully applying her make-up and praying the headache medicine would kick in. The morning-after-bawling headache had stayed at bay until the article appeared.

Finally satisfied with her appearance, Julia grabbed her purse and headed for the stairs.

Christopher waited for her in the kitchen. He'd changed into a dark suit with a white shirt and red tie. He looked over and smiled as he started for her.

"You look lovely."

She glanced down. "Thanks."

"But I think I want to do this before we leave."

Julia didn't move as his hand cradled the side of her face and leaned toward her.

When his lips touched hers, her knees buckled, and she sunk against him and into that point of contact.

And she knew.

Marriage in name only or not, she could easily fall for the man she was going to marry. She had to protect her heart.

And that meant no more kissing.

Even if she found herself loving it.

Chapter Sixteen

Christopher slid his arm around Julia's waist, pulling her as close to him as he could. He didn't try to stop the kiss from building in intensity until something bumped him.

He stopped, his lips still on hers. "What was that?"

"The baby."

"The baby kicked me?"

"Guess so."

He kissed her again, more softly this time, before stepping back just a bit. He held out a hand. "Do you mind?"

She shook her head, so he rested his hands on either side of her stomach. It took a couple of minutes, but eventually, the baby did some sort of roll.

"That's so cool," he whispered. "I've never felt a baby moving like that before."

"It is pretty cool, but not so much when he's kicking your ribs or your bladder in the middle of the night."

"I hadn't thought about that." What did he know about pregnancy? Topher took a deep breath and stepped back, reaching into his pocket for his keys. "You ready to go?"

She looked away. "Sure. Let's do this."

He opened the door and let her precede him outside. Clicking the button for his car, he planned to open that door for her as well, but she reached it before he could and opened it herself.

Instead, he waited for her to be seated, then closed it behind her.

"Where are we going?" she asked as he turned left a few blocks down the road.

"The Pond Creek County Courthouse in Trumanville. It's closer than Springfield and less obvious if someone decides to dig for information."

"Gotcha." Her fingers twisted in the strap of her bag.

He reached over and gently extracted one hand from the other, then linked their fingers together. It came far easier than he expected. "It won't be that bad. I'm not an ogre."

She stared out the window. "I know. Just not how I pictured my wedding, even though I have two kids with two different men." Julia pulled her hand away. "Guess I still held out hope for the white dress and silver heels and a groom who actually wanted to marry me at the other end of the aisle."

Topher didn't know how to respond to that, but it couldn't have been easy for her to say.

"I know I've made more than my share of mistakes. Alex and this baby are proof of that. My faith has often been shaken and nearly shattered by my own doing. Sometimes, I let myself believe those choices don't have the consequences I know come with them. I gave up the rights to all of that years ago. Guess I let my hopes get up too far." She shrugged. "I'm fine. It is what it is. When I was honest with myself, I knew a courthouse wedding was the best I was likely to get whenever it happened."

What was he supposed to say? That she deserved more? Her heart's desire? It might be true, but he certainly wasn't helping make it happen. A "real wedding" later wasn't on his agenda. A real marriage wasn't either.

He pulled into the parking lot of the courthouse, suddenly uncertain as to the right course of action. Turning the ignition off, Topher wondered if he should discuss it with Julia. His phone buzzed, and he saw a text from Mady. With proof of the marriage, HEA TV would go forward as planned.

So he had to go through with it or lose everything.

Topher reached for his door handle. "Don't move."

Julia didn't look at him, but she didn't move either. Not until he opened her door and held out his hand to help her up. Once he closed the door, he tucked her hand into his elbow.

It didn't take long to get the forms filled out. He knew she took notice of the date his divorce was finalized.

Before he could consider it further, they were done and leaving hand in hand.

"Where are we going to do this?" she asked, holding onto the rail as she went down the steps.

"I have a friend who will marry us."

She didn't reply, but waited by the door to his car for him

to unlock it.

He let her in and sighed as he walked around to his side. Could she at least pretend to be excited? Or at least that it wasn't a death sentence?

Five minutes later, he pulled up in front of a house on the outskirts of Trumanville. A moment after that, he was pulled into a hug by Mrs. Beach.

"It's so good to see you, Christopher." She patted his back but didn't let go. "I've seen this stuff going around and don't believe any of it for a minute. I was so glad to get your call earlier."

"Thanks, Mama Beach."

She abruptly let go. "I want to meet this lovely woman."

Julia looked like a deer in the headlights as Mama Beach pulled her in for one of her famous hugs.

"It's so good to meet you," she said in that hug-strained voice women seemed to get. "Julia, right?"

"Yes, ma'am."

"None of that. Call me Mama Beach. Everyone does."

"Not when you're on the bench," Topher pointed out.

She finally let go of Julia. "Well, no. Not then. I was mean then. I had to be."

"You don't have a mean bone in your body. Stern maybe, but not mean. You've always been fair." Topher put an arm around her shoulders as they walked into the house. "That's why I called you."

Mama Beach looked over her shoulder at Julia who trailed them. "Did he tell you how we know each other?"

"No, ma'am."

Mama Beach glared at her, but didn't say anything about it.

"They grew up down the street. I think we were some of the very few people who knew what they did in California. They and my twins, a boy and girl, played together all the time. In college, he even dated my daughter a few times."

Great. He hadn't planned to mention that.

She waved a hand. "We all knew it wouldn't amount to anything, but I wouldn't have been sad to have him as a part of the family officially." Mama Beach moved away from him and turned, with her hands on her hips. "Have you told your parents about this?"

"Not yet."

"They don't want to Skype in so they can be here?"

Topher shook his head. "No. We just want it to be the two of us." He reached for Julia's hand. "It's perfect like this."

It wasn't. He'd never imagined a second wedding, but he'd always figured it would be more like the one Julia pictured.

Mama Beach stopped by the fireplace. "Then you two stand here, and let's get started."

So they were being married by a crazy, huggy, crying mama bear lady.

No waiting, no witnesses. Because Missouri didn't require either one, just someone legally allowed to perform the ceremony.

Julia didn't know what to make of that. She wasn't even sure Christopher realized Mama Beach had been crying. Clearly, the woman loved Christopher and was happy about this marriage thing.

"Dearly beloved..." she began.

Julia tried to focus, to concentrate on what exactly she was promising, despite the less than ideal circumstances. Instead, it all passed in a blur. She made the promises made by millions before her. Christopher made them back and even produced a couple of rings, something she hadn't considered.

"I just hope they fit. I didn't have a chance to make sure," he told her as he handed her the man's ring.

She took his hand and slid the band onto the fourth finger. It fit well enough. "With this ring, I thee wed. With all my worldly goods, I thee endow." That wasn't saying much.

"And now you, Christopher," Mama Beach prompted.

They switched hands, and he slipped a worn, scratched ring onto her finger. "With this ring, I thee wed. With all my worldly goods, I thee endow."

It meant something totally different coming from him. He had worldly goods, far more than she had ever dreamed of having.

Mama Beach interrupted her thoughts. "Then by the powers vested in me by the State of Missouri, I now pronounce you husband and wife. Christopher, you may kiss your bride."

Except Julia had already determined that was a very bad idea. Especially after the kiss earlier.

But how did she not kiss him...

Before she could finish the thought, her face was cradled gently in his hands and his lips brushed against hers. Once. Twice. Then back a third time for a long, searing, toe-curling kiss.

One she wouldn't soon forget.

And from the look on his face, he wouldn't either. In fact,

if they'd been home, from the look on his face, he might have invited her to move into his room.

With all that entailed.

And she didn't know that she'd be able to say no, though she knew she should.

"All right, you two. There's plenty of time for making goo-goo eyes at each other later, though I got a couple of pictures that should make the tabloids shut up." Julia looked over to see Mama Beach waggling her phone back and forth. "Now, how about a couple more?"

She posed them in front of the fire place and took a dozen pictures with her phone. "Julia, honey, what's your number? I'll send them to you both so you don't have to count on Mr. Forgetful to forward them."

Julia told her and thanked her. A few minutes later, they were back in the car, on their way home, she supposed.

"I hope you don't mind the ring," Christopher said as he turned onto the state highway heading back toward Serenity Lake.

"It's fine."

"It was my grandmother's." He held up his left hand. "This was my grandfather's. I hope it doesn't bother you that they're not new."

"Not at all." Not now that she knew where they came from.

"They were married sixty years." Heartbreak filled his voice. "Papa was driving home one night. He swerved to avoid hitting a deer and landed in a ditch. The accident wasn't that bad, but Nana hit her head and the shock, I guess, sent her into a heart attack. They got her to the hospital, where Papa refused to leave her. Once they finally looked at him, they found out he was running on pure adrenaline, and his own heart was failing. The only time he let go of her hand was when they actually shocked her."

Compassion filled her as he swiped the back of his hand across his cheek. "Even after she passed, her monitors picked up his heart beat through their hands. It wasn't long before he died of a broken heart. It hurt like hell for those of us left behind, but they wouldn't have wanted it any other way. Neither of them knew how to live without each other."

"I'm sorry." She also wanted to give back the ring. It didn't seem right to be using them in these circumstances.

"You'd have liked them, and Nana would have adopted you in a heartbeat months ago. If she'd seen what happened with Ander, she would have found you and taken care of you like any of her other grandkids."

How much different the last few months would have been if she'd had an adopted grandmother to mother her.

They turned into the driveway when something else occurred to her. "What do we tell the kids?"

His silence said he hadn't thought about it either. "Nothing for now, I guess. Neither of them have access to the Internet. We won't watch the tabloid shows with them around. We wouldn't have anyway, but make extra sure they don't see anything. It'll blow over before you know it. I'll have Mady release a statement with a couple of the pictures on my website and public Facebook page. I'm not going to sell them to some publication."

She just nodded. What did she know about how all of this worked? "And the rings? How do we explain them?"

"Just say you liked it and decided to wear it?"

What else was there to say?

When they got out of the car at the front door, Julia pulled her keys out of her purse and walked toward her car.

"Where are you going?" Christopher paused on the steps to the front door.

"It's almost time to pick Alex up from the bus stop." The bus dropped off at the end of the driveway, but the walk was far too much for her to make twice a day right now, and the drive curved with a few trees that kept her from seeing the end, or she'd let him walk up it on his own most days, weather permitting.

She half expected Christopher to offer to take her to get Alex but he didn't. Instead he said something about keeping an eye out for photographers then went inside.

Julia drove to the end of the drive and waited.

An hour after her wedding and all alone.

Alone like always.

Chapter Seventeen

Christopher leaned back in his chair as e listened to Dusty Ring, the *2C4S* creator, describe the concept for the new show. Focusing was harder than it would have been the day before. Instead, he found his mind wandering back to those kisses. Then something Dusty said caught his attention.

"Wait. What did you say about Claire?"

"Claire's agreed to be your heroine."

"Claire Cruz Cartwright has agreed to leave Los Angeles and move to the middle of backwoods nowhere - her words not a month ago - to film a television show?"

"Apparently. Her character on *2C4S* was the one that got away for Chris."

"She was in one episode." He turned it over in his head quickly. "It was a good episode." And in a quick perusal of fan fiction a week earlier while discussing this, she was the pairing most often used for the Chris character.

"You just did the movie together. What do you think about her as the love interest?"

"Works for me." They got along well. She was happily dating some non-actor guy. "What about the rest of it?"

"We're setting up auditions for twins. We'd rather use actual twins than camera tricks to make it look like twins. We're also adding a toddler boy."

"How are you going to deal with Alex being gone?"

"He's going to come home on breaks, but we'll only ever see his back or something like that. He's not gone constantly, but when the kids are out of school for the summer, we won't shoot any shows. He'll be home for three months. We'll either use you or a body double to show them hugging good-bye and waving as he drives off."

"And why isn't he home?"

"He's become a doctor, but had promised several years to Doctors Without Borders-type group before the kids were born. Or a company that paid for his business degree at a top school. They paid for his education so he owes them a whole bunch of time or has to pay back the loans with massive penalties."

"So something just plausible enough to sell but not completely buyable, even though he barely showed any interest in being a doctor ever."

"Let's face it. Continuity wasn't always our strong suit. It'll be fine."

Topher could almost see the smirk on Dusty's face. "And what's the distribution going to be? Or are you still working on that?"

"We're close to inking a deal with MyBingeFlix. We're not billing as a reboot aimed at the teens and tweens of today, but rather to the audience who grew up with you guys. The kids will be there, but it's a family comedy, not a tween show this time."

Topher shifted forward in his chair. "I like that better. Have some of the others back for guest spots. Grandparents, teachers, and such, but a different location and sets would be good, too. I don't think living in the same house would be the way to go. It's been done."

"Right. We're going nonspecific Midwest."

Topher glanced at his watch. "I've got to go, Dusty. Thanks for walking me through more of it. I'm looking forward to getting the final details hammered out. What kind of time frame are you hoping for?"

"It's insanely fast, but I'd love to start taping in January and premiere for binge watching on MyBingeFlix in the fall sometime."

"Send Mady the details, and we'll see what we can work out with my HEA TV schedule, too."

They said their good-byes and hung up. Topher headed into the kitchen where he found Ida Mae with a newly-awakened Bailey.

He picked Bailey up, and she settled into his arms, with her head on his shoulder. "Thanks for your extra help today, Ida Mae."

"My pleasure, Toph." She looked at the microwave. "But it's time for me to head out. I'll see you in the morning."

As she left, Topher realized he missed Julia and Alex. They

likely wouldn't come upstairs. They had taken to staying in the basement unless Julia was taking care of Bailey. Would that change now that they were married?

"Do you want to go see Alex?" he asked his daughter. Topher knew he was her favorite, but Alex was a close second.

She nodded and wiggled to get down, then ran toward the stairs. Topher followed more slowly and found Bailey hugging Julia before going to find Alex who was building something with his Legos.

Julia had changed out of her wedding clothes and into a pair of what looked to be baggy pajama pants and a big t-shirt. She'd pulled her hair back into a sloppy ponytail, but she still looked pretty fantastic. He'd never thought about her that way before. Was it because of the piece of paper and the rings that now said she was his wife?

Or something even more?

Julia stared out the window into the blackness of the night. As tired as she was, sleep wasn't coming easily.

Her wedding night.

She hadn't even called her parents yet. That was on her to-do list before the press release went out. It took forever to roll over, but she managed, a twinge in her back catching her attention as she did.

Odd.

Before she could go back to trying to ignore her previous train of thought, the twinge traveled around from the base of her spine to the front of her belly, growing in intensity as it did before eventually ebbing away.

Her breath caught in her throat. She lay as still as she could, praying it wasn't what she feared. Two minutes passed. Then three. Four. About the fifth minute, she began to relax, to breathe more easily. The prayers flying through her head became a bit more coherent.

But before she could drift off to sleep another pain came.

And a few minutes after that, another.

Tears had begun streaking down her face. It was far too early. Julia reached for her phone on the side table. She hadn't called Christopher since he returned from Canada, but she didn't know what else to do.

It rang until the voice mail picked up. He probably had it on "do not disturb." She called back immediately, hoping it would go through.

No such luck.

More time lapsed before the next contraction. Maybe it was a fluke. After nearly twenty minutes, the tension started to leave, until another one hit.

Time to do something. Another phone call to Christopher went unanswered, so she needed to make it upstairs.

It took far longer than normal, putting one foot in front of the other, holding onto the wall the whole time so she had to go farther. Another contraction came as she made it to the top of the stairs, but she'd have to navigate across an open space to get to the other staircase. With one hand gripping the rail and the other holding her belly, she waited it out.

As the contraction eased, she made her way to the other staircase and to the top before she had to sit down.

Tears continued down her cheeks as she wondered where

she'd get the oomph to stand again.

"Julia? Is that you?"

She breathed a sigh of relief at Christopher's voice. "I'm by the stairs."

"What's wrong?" If she hadn't been so scared, his voice would have been both sleepy and adorable.

"I'm having contractions."

"You're not far enough along for that, are you?"

"No, but I need to go to the hospital."

By this time he was crouched next to her. "Let's get you to my room while I get dressed."

She'd never been in his room, but she accepted his help standing up, and his arm went around her waist as they walked to the master bedroom.

"Do you want the chair?"

Julia shook her head. "No. If you don't mind, the bed would be better."

He didn't answer, but moved her that direction.

One portion of her mind took in the mahogany four-poster bed and mussed covers. She sank down onto it and settled onto her left side. "Thank you."

"Give me two minutes, and we'll be out of here."

They were forgetting something. "The kids!"

"Shoot." His voice drifted in from the bathroom area she'd glimpsed. "Call Kenzie?"

Julia did that, but also got no answer. She had Jonathan's number though she'd never used it before. Again, nothing.

"Call Mama Beach," he hollered.

Julia went through her contacts until she found the right one, added just a few hours earlier. Mama Beach answered, concern filling her voice as Julia explained the situation. She didn't live far and would be over as soon as she could get dressed.

Christopher emerged a minute later and helped her sit back up.

"By the time we get me to the car, she'll probably be here," Julia told him.

"And I already texted Ida Mae to come in early tomorrow so the kids don't meet Mama Beach alone." Rather than helping her stand, Christopher surprised Julia by lifting her into his arms. She rested her head on his shoulder, relaxing more than she thought possible, even as he went down the stairs.

What was it about him that made her feel safe?

He set her in a chair in the entryway while he went to get the car. She heard it pull up outside a few seconds before he walked back in. Again he carried her.

It seemed like an eternity until lights came up the driveway. Mama Beach waved them on before waggling her phone at them. Christopher took off before connecting to her via the Bluetooth in the car.

Julia leaned her head against the window, every bump the tires hit translating through the glass. It gave her something to focus on besides her worries.

Christopher walked Mama Beach through what she needed to know about the kids. He also reached over and took Julia's hand, his thumb rubbing against her knuckles. When he hung up he asked how she was doing.

"Scared," she whispered. "I haven't had a contraction since we left, but I'm so scared."

"How far along are you?"

"About 32 weeks."

"Okay. So not great, but definitely survivable." He hesitated. "Right?"

"Yeah, but not without a NICU stay. Besides all the potential health issues, I don't have that kind of money."

"Don't worry about the money." He squeezed her hand. "You're my wife now. I'll make sure it's taken care of. I need to get you and Alex on my insurance, as my family instead of as an employee. Technically, I still work for my parents so we get good insurance through them."

"Thank you."

"I'm your husband. It's my job."

Julia wasn't sure what to make of that.

The rest of the drive was silent until Christopher turned onto National near the hospital. "Where am I going?"

She told him how to get there. After putting the car in park, he went around and helped her into a wheel chair.

"I'll be back in two seconds. Just let me park."

He was gone before she could reply.

Julia started to wheel herself toward Labor & Delivery as best she could.

"Do you need some help, ma'am?" She looked up to see a nurse hurrying toward her.

"Please." Relief crashed over her in waves. The first of the people who could help.

All Julia could do now was try to relax.

And pray.

Because she hadn't stopped since before the first contraction hit.

Chapter Eighteen

Topher had never been so scared in his life, except maybe when his brother got shot protecting his royal wife. But even then they knew he'd been shot in the leg.

This was scared on a whole different level.

They took Julia back to another room and asked him to wait for a few minutes. Topher sat in the waiting room, his elbows resting on his knees and hands clasped together as he tried to put words to his prayers. It seemed an eternity before they called him back, but it probably wasn't as long as it seemed.

"Mr. Bayfield?"

He looked up to see a nurse standing there. "Yes?"

"We're moving your wife to a room. If you'd like to come with me..."

"Can you tell me what's going on?"

"When we get to the room, someone will explain everything to both of you."

That couldn't be good.

Be anxious for nothing. Be anxious for nothing. The portion of scripture repeated over and over in his head. A minute later, he was in a labor and delivery suite as they wheeled Julia in on a gurney. The nurses helped transfer her to the bed while he stood there with his hands shoved in his pockets.

One of the nurses explained everything as she did it. Started an IV. Used words like "Braxton-Hicks" and "uterine irritability" - words he knew but couldn't quite understand from the context.

After a few minutes, the two of them were alone.

"I didn't understand any of that," he admitted to Julia as he pulled a chair closer to the bed.

"They don't think I'm in labor. They think it's either bad Braxton-Hicks or uterine irritability. Basically that means my uterus is contracting, but it's not productive or moving me closer to actual labor."

"Which one means that?"

"Either one really, just different causes and treatments."

A doctor walked in, along with a nurse pushing an ultrasound machine.

"Mr. and Mrs. Bayfield, I'm Dr. McConnell. I'm the on-call doctor this evening. Mrs. Bayfield, you haven't had much prenatal care, correct?"

Julia nodded. "I couldn't afford it, but took good care of

myself. I recently got a new job with insurance, but I haven't been in to see a doctor yet. We just met a couple months ago, and got married today."

"Okay. We've got you hooked up to monitors. We're going to do an ultrasound to check on the baby and make sure everything looks good and go from there."

Another nurse came in and helped situate Julia, disconnecting the sensors attached to her belly by elastic bands.

"How far along are you?" the doctor asked, pulling a tape measure out of her pocket.

"I'm almost 33 weeks."

The doctor held the tape against Julia's belly. "You're measuring bigger than that, but let's see what we see."

Julia didn't look at Topher. "I'm certain about the date of conception. There was no other opportunity."

"Okay. Let's just take a look." The doctor sat on the rolling doctor's stool. "We'll do a more thorough ultrasound tomorrow if we can, but this it'll give us some ideas for now."

Julia's breath caught as the doctor squirted some goop onto her belly. "That's cold."

"Sorry." The doctor did seem apologetic. "It helps wake the baby up." She pressed a wand against the skin and images began to appear on the screen. For long minutes she didn't say anything, but Topher noticed tears streaming down Julia's cheeks.

"You okay?" he asked reaching for her hand.

Julia nodded. "Just seeing the baby for the first time..."

"It is pretty cool." Even if he wasn't sure what he was looking at.

"Not baby," the doctor said, turning to them with a smile. "Babies. You're having twins."

He glanced at Julia whose jaw had literally dropped open.

"What?" she whispered.

"Twins." The doctor pointed to the screen. "Two separate heartbeats. Here." She pointed to one moving spot on the screen, then another. "And here. Identical twins."

"Really?" Julia glanced at him. "Are you sure?"

"Pretty sure," the doctor admitted. "I only see one placenta which always means identical twins. They are the same gender. One of each would have definitively ruled out identical twins. But sometimes, fraternal twins will implant in such a way that their placentas overlap, and it's hard to tell if there's two. We'll check for sure after they're born. I also only see one outer sac but two inner ones which leans significantly toward identical twins. You can't *always* tell for sure, but usually." She smiled at them. "Do you want to know if you're having boys or girls?"

Julia looked at him, but Topher shrugged. "It's up to you."

She shook her head. "I'd rather wait, at least for now. Can you make a note of it though, in case I change my mind?"

"Of course. We're going to hook those monitors back up, keep those fluids going, and just watch for a while, okay?" She patted Julia on the leg. "We'll take good care of you."

"Thank you," he and Julia said at the same time.

The nurse got her resituated on her left side then left them alone with instructions to push the call button if they needed anything, and for Julia to try to get some rest.

He'd had to release her hand, but reached for it again. "Are you okay?"

"I don't know." Her eyes closed. "Twins? I don't know how

I'm going to do that."

"*You're* not. We are." He had no idea what that would look like. Sure they'd had two fantastic kisses, but they had no real relationship.

"Even if they send me home, I'll probably be on bed rest. I won't be able to take care of the kids."

"We'll figure it out." He didn't know how. Maybe his parents would come. They'd loved Julia and Alex in Ravenzario. He needed to call them anyway and let them know about the wedding. A glance at his watch said he could call in about an hour.

"Thank you for bringing me."

"Of course." It shocked him that she felt the need to say thank you. "It's my job. I'm your husband." It was their wedding night. In a labor and delivery suite.

"Yes, you are." Her eyes fluttered closed again and her breathing deepened. Maybe she was getting some much needed rest.

Topher decided he didn't care what time it was. He let go of her hand and pulled his phone out of his pocket, walking to the far side of the room to make the call. When a sleepy voice answered, he took a deep breath. "Hey, Mom. It's me. Everything's mostly okay, but we need to talk."

Julia had started to drift off, but when Christopher let go for her hand to call his parents, she paid attention to his side of the conversation. She needed to call her parents, too. They shouldn't hear about the wedding on social media.

Christopher told his parents about the wedding and a little bit of the rationale behind it, but not everything. He made it sound like it would have happened anyway. Or at least didn't imply it wouldn't have.

Then he told his mom she was in the hospital and would either be here until delivery or on bed rest if they sent her home. If she wasn't mistaken, his parents would be packed and on their way back to the States in a matter of hours. A huge weight lifted off her shoulders. Family to help would be a welcome change since her parents moved to Florida.

A few minutes later, he was back at her side, taking her hand in his.

"What did your mom say?" She needed to know she had guessed right.

"She said congratulations. She's happy for us and both excited and concerned about the babies. They've gone from no grandkids to five in a matter of a month or so." Julia detected a hint of a chuckle in his voice. "She's in grandparent heaven."

But she sensed hesitation, too. "What is it?"

"I do think she's a bit disappointed she wasn't at the wedding. She didn't get to be a part of planning the wedding for either of her sons."

"Did you tell her *we* were barely at the wedding?"

"I did. She was glad Mama Beach performed the ceremony and wants the pictures."

"I'd like to see them at some point, too."

"You didn't look at the ones Mama Beach sent you?"

Julia shook her head. She hadn't wanted to.

"How about now?"

She opened her eyes to see him pulling his phone out. He

opened the photo app and held it where they could both see.

"She got a ton of pictures of us kissing." Even in the dim room, she could see his face turn a bit red. "Sorry. I shouldn't have kissed you like that with an audience."

Julia couldn't make herself regret it. She'd enjoyed it far too much. He swiped through a few more pictures.

"Guess she used the burst thing on it." He swiped faster until he reached the end of the dozen or so pictures of the smooch that never ended. He flipped to one of them in front of the fireplace. "This one's not bad."

She had her back to him and his arms were wrapped around her, with his hands resting on her belly. She'd laid her arms over the top of his. From the shoulders down they looked great, but their faces... "We look awkward. Not exactly your best smile, Mr. ActorMan."

"I wasn't acting."

"So we're awkward. Guess it's good we don't live in an area with a lot of paparazzi." She knew it was ridiculous, but she kind of wished the pictures didn't look like they belonged on a Reddit of awkward wedding photos. Or even prom photos, because they really didn't look very wedding-y.

Christopher swiped a couple more times. "Here. This one's better."

This time they gazed at each other and not the camera. The picture hadn't been planned, and Mama Beach had caught them in an unguarded moment. Julia thought she remembered it, when their eyes had locked, just for a second.

Her breath had been taken away. And from the looks of it, Christopher's had been, too. If she'd been hoping for something out of this relationship, the look on his face would have given her that hope.

Good thing she wasn't.

Julia closed her eyes as another contraction hit. It wasn't as bad as some of the others had been.

"You okay?"

She told him.

"That's good, right?"

"I guess."

They sat in silence for a few more minutes until his phone buzzed. "Their plane leaves in a couple hours. They'll be here this afternoon. Mom said she's happy to take care of the kids indefinitely while you get the bed rest you need or if the babies come early, and you need to be up here a lot or whatever. Dad will, too."

"I'll have to thank them."

"They'll probably come here first unless you've gone home. Ida Mae will be there early to help Mama Beach with the kids. Childcare isn't really in her job description, but she'll take care of Bailey tomorrow until my folks get here. Mama Beach will come back this evening if my folks get delayed, and we need her to."

"I really like her."

"She really likes you, too." A few more minutes passed, and Julia started to drift when Christopher spoke again. "Are you okay with this whole twin thing?"

"I don't have much of a choice, do I? I'm pregnant with twins. End of story. You're the one who has a choice."

"How do you figure?"

"This - whatever it is - has barely started." She couldn't open her eyes to look at him. Whatever was written on his face, she didn't want to know. "You could leave now, or relegate us to the basement as basically completely separate living quarters. Then, once your career is more firmly established, we move out. End of story again."

"This is a marriage. That means I take care of you. You, Alex, and the babies, are a package deal."

"That wasn't what we agreed to earlier."

"That doesn't mean we weren't at least somewhat wrong. As long as we're married, I take care of the four of you."

"It's supposed to be a two-way street. I'm supposed to take care of you, too." She wanted to focus on the conversation, but despite everything, she was drifting anyway.

"I'm sure you'll have plenty of chances to take care of me. It's not..."

Darkness closed in around her as she slipped into a restless slumber.

But at least she wasn't alone.

Some wedding night this turned out to be.

Chapter Nineteen

She was finally asleep. A good thing, even if they didn't finish their conversation.

Deep inside, Topher whispered prayers he didn't quite understand - for her, for the babies, for the insane world they were about to be thrown into as parents of twins and partners in life - at least for the time being.

And what he was going to tell his parents about it. They wouldn't approve of his arguably-rash decision to marry Julia to keep HEA TV from coming after him. That's why he'd skipped over it and just said they'd eloped.

He'd deal with the rest later.

Ida Mae texted him to let him know another anonymous note had arrived. The fifth one. It said "he" would be there to get Bailey "soon." She sent it over to his lawyer, who promised to take care of it.

The rest of the morning went slowly. The doctor came back several times. The contractions slowed down then seemed to stop all together. The doctor finally agreed to send her home around noon, but she would be on bed rest for the next few weeks. Not complete bed rest, but pretty close. Topher made up his mind to hire whoever he needed to help with the house. Julia wouldn't be able to do anything, and his mom wouldn't want to do all of it.

"Do you know anyone we can hire to help with your yarn stuff? Or the bags that you sell?" he asked as they drove toward Serenity Landing.

"I think I'll be able to keep knitting and stuff. The bags won't get done, but that's okay. I can put samples out and take special orders."

He reached over and took her hand. "I know we talked about it a little bit earlier, but you don't have to do any of that if you don't want to. The whole point of me keeping the HEA TV jobs and doing the show is so I can support all of us."

"I thought it was so they wouldn't sue you into oblivion."

"Two sides of the same coin. But you don't need the income anymore."

She didn't reply, and he wondered if she dozed back off or if she just didn't want to continue the conversation. His phone rang, and he answered it on his Bluetooth, talking with Mady for a minute before promising to call her back later to finish getting the statement to the press ready.

A soft snore from the other side of the car told him Julia had fallen asleep. As they pulled into the drive, he noted the construction of pillars on either side of the entrance had begun. In a few days, it would be gated off, just to be on the safe side. His phone buzzed with a text message. His parents had landed and would be at the house soon.

He parked in front of the door. Julia was awake enough to accept his help getting out of the car, but he wasn't about to let her walk up the stairs. Instead, he scooped her into his arms again and carried her to the front door, which she opened. He kicked it closed behind him and went straight to the living room. Once she was settled on the couch, Topher went to get her a glass of water and found Bailey coming up the stairs from the basement with Ida Mae in tow.

She ran to him and gave him a quick hug before looking around.

"Julia's in the living room," he told her. She took off before he could say anything else.

"How's she doing?" Ida Mae opened the refrigerator and pulled out sandwich meat.

"Better. She's on bed rest for at least a couple weeks. My parents will be here in half an hour or so. They'll take over kid duty. Thanks for helping with Bailey yesterday and today."

"Anytime. I love her."

"Any chance she actually talked today?" He wished that one thing would change. He loved his time with his daughter, but he wanted to be able to *hear* her thoughts and ideas and opinions and not just infer them from points and nods or head shakes.

Ida Mae sighed. "No. One of these days, she's gonna open that mouth of hers and full sentences are gonna pour out. You'll wonder how to get her to shut up."

"I doubt that." He couldn't imagine that, not after she'd been silent for so long.

"Probably not, but you know what I mean."

He pulled a couple of plates out of the cabinet and began to make a couple of sandwiches for himself and one for Julia, while Ida Mae made one for herself and Bailey.

"Why don't you guys eat in the living room with us? I'm sure Julia would love to have Bailey with her a bit longer."

Ida Mae agreed and took all the plates while he followed with drinks for everyone. Julia lay on her left side on the couch while the rest of them sat around the coffee table. Bailey finished her sandwich then ran downstairs leaving the grown-ups staring after her.

"Where's she going?" Topher asked.

"She's been drawing pictures for the last couple of hours," Ida Mae explained. "She probably wants to give them to you."

A minute later, Bailey emerged with a haphazard handful of papers. She handed them all to Julia and climbed onto the couch next to her.

"These are wonderful, Bailey Bug!" Julia flipped to the second one. "Ladybugs! They're my favorite, too, you know."

Bailey nodded.

"Are ladybugs your favorite, Bay?" Topher asked. How had he not known this?

She nodded and reached for the top paper in Julia's hand. Bailey came around the table to sit on his lap and show it to him.

"What's this?" The drawing was clearly of ladybugs, but it looked to be a family of them. "Is this us?"

She nodded again and pointed to the tallest one.

"Is that the daddy ladybug?"

Another nod.

He pointed at the smallest. "And I bet this is Bailey-bug."

This time a grin crossed her face, too. She pointed to the medium bug.

"And that's Alex."

Then she pointed to the last ladybug whose belly was surprisingly large.

"And that's Julia with the babies in her belly?"

Bailey nodded again.

"Babies? Plural?" A woman's voice caught him off-guard.

Topher looked up to see his mom and dad in the doorway. How had they made it in without him hearing?

"Babies?" his mom repeated. "More than one?"

Topher moved Bailey to the side and stood up. "We're glad you're here, and yes, we found out this morning that Julia's having twins."

His mom squealed and walked right past him to hug Julia. "This is so wonderful!"

His dad clapped him on the shoulder. "Welcome to the wonderful world of being a parent of twins. You're gonna love it."

Topher just hoped his dad was right.

Julia spent the rest of the afternoon on the couch, rearranging herself enough that Alex could snuggle with her for a bit. She also had a long conversation with her parents. They talked about the babies and her new situation. They didn't quite give the marriage their blessing, something Julia didn't feel comfortable asking for anyway, but did promise to keep an open mind.

Mrs. Bayfield made dinner, and Topher brought it to her to eat while everyone else ate in the dining room. Even Christopher. Julia hadn't felt quite so alone in a while, and loneliness was a regular part of her life.

"Oh, honey. I'm sorry you're in here by yourself." Mrs. Bayfield sat in the chair across from her. "I meant to bring your food so we could eat together, but there was a bunch of stuff stuck to the bottom of the pan, and I wanted to clean it before it got worse."

"It's okay, Mrs. Bayfield."

She waved with one hand as she took a bite. "Leigh Ann, honey. You're my daughter now. Unless you'd rather call us Mom and Dad, we're Leigh Ann and James."

"Yes, ma'am." Julia wrinkled her nose. "Sorry. Leigh Ann."

"How are you feeling?"

"Okay. Tired, which is kind of ridiculous since I haven't done anything all day."

"You're making people! And trying to keep them from coming early. That's exhausting. Plus you were at the hospital all night."

"Christopher seems okay."

"Topher isn't growing humans," Leigh Ann pointed out. "Why don't you finish eating, then go take a nice, warm bath upstairs, then get some sleep?"

Julia nodded. It sounded nice. She couldn't get the bath too hot so it wouldn't be too long, but it would be enough.

Once done with dinner, Julia tried to relax against the pillows. Leigh Ann carried all the dishes to the kitchen. While she was gone, her words to Julia sunk in.

Upstairs.

She hadn't been upstairs more than twice total since Christopher had returned from Canada.

But his parents wouldn't know that she wasn't moving upstairs anytime soon.

So either he'd have to tell them, or she'd end up sleeping in his room, in his bed.

With him.

She didn't know how she felt about that.

Her insides were a bundle of conflicting emotions. On one hand, she was married to the guy, and definitely attracted to him, though it couldn't be acted on. The doctor had made that very clear. On the other hand, though, she'd never actually slept overnight with someone besides her son. If Christopher had been married to Bailey's mother, he clearly had far more experience with that than she did, even if the marriage had been short-lived.

With everything else going on, though, sharing a bed or not with her husband was really the least of her worries.

A few minutes later, the man himself walked in and squatted down next to her. "My mom suggested I take you up to our room so you can take a bath and then get some sleep. Is that okay with you?"

Julia kept her eyes closed. "I need to go downstairs first. I haven't moved any of my things yet." She lowered her voice. "And they don't know... I can stay in my room and tell them I don't want to keep you up because of my restless leg syndrome."

"That's a real thing?"

"Only when I'm pregnant, but I just might kick you."

"I'm not too worried. I'm tough." She heard him stand. "Let me help you up. We'll go downstairs, grab your suitcase and get started with moving your things upstairs."

He picked her up and headed for the stairs when his mom stopped them. "Where are you headed?"

Christopher turned around. "We haven't had a chance to move Julia's things from her room in the basement. I'm going to help her get some of it, and then I'll help Alex move his things later."

Leigh Ann waved them toward the other stairs. "I'll take care of it. Go take that bath, Julia. You'll feel better."

He looked down at her, and Julia nodded. What else was she supposed to do? He carried her up to the master suite and stopped. "Do you want that bath or would you rather just rest?"

"Just set me down here. I'll be fine. Just knock before you come in, would you?" No chance of him walking in on something he shouldn't if he knocked.

"Why don't you do any changing or anything in the bathroom, or your closet, and I promise not to just walk in there? We both can."

"My closet?" Was that a thing?

He still hadn't put her down, so he carried her into the bathroom. Once on her feet, he left his arm around her and pointed to a door. "That's your closet, unless you want the other one. On the floor plans, it's technically called 'his closet' because it's smaller. I've always used the other one because it was just me, and it's a little more convenient, and I like the layout. Plus there's this annoying little nook in it that Bailey likes to hide in sometimes."

"It's fine." The room was probably bigger than her whole apartment anyway.

"Okay. I'll have whoever brings your suitcase up close the main door so you can keep your privacy in here."

"Thanks."

With that he turned and left her alone.

Being more careful than she normally would, Julia took the bath, finally truly relaxing some after the long day and night before. And everything else.

Leigh Ann called to her that she'd left the suitcase near the door to the bathroom. The water cooled far quicker than Julia would have liked but that's what happened when you couldn't get the water too hot.

She toweled off and found her clothes, but somehow, Leigh Ann hadn't brought any of the pajamas or comfortable pants that actually fit. Biting her bottom lip, Julia headed into Christopher's closet, hoping to see something obvious she might be able to borrow.

It looked like he'd done laundry because clothes were folded neatly next to a basket on top of the dresser thing in the middle. She grabbed a pair of pajama pants and held them up. They'd be too long, but they might work. Once they were on and tied in place, she picked up a t-shirt. All of hers were too snug. It seemed kind of silly to go buy a bunch of new clothes when it had only been in the last week or so that things grew too small. She'd hoped to make it to her due date, but that clearly hadn't happened.

Of course, if she didn't get back to lying on her left side, the babies might not make it to their due date either. Julia walked back into the bedroom and sat on the side of the bed.

Before she could lay down, a knock sounded on the door.

"Hey. It's me." Christopher. "Can I come in?"

Chapter Twenty

Topher opened the door when Julia called to him. He found her sitting on the edge of his bed struggling to put her socks on.

"Let me help." In a few steps he was by her side, kneeling so he could help slide the fuzzy socks onto her feet. As he did, he noticed her pajama pants. "I have pants just like these."

"They're yours. I hope you don't mind. I need a few new clothes. I'd hoped my clothes would last, then thought about going this week, but that's not going to happen now."

He stood and realized she was also wearing his t-shirt. "It's fine. I have a bunch. Wear whatever you want." It kind of surprised him that it didn't bother him. He'd never shared clothes with anyone but his brother.

She turned and lifted her feet into the bed. "Do you have a side preference?"

Topher shook his head. "I usually sprawl on my stomach in

the middle, but I'll sleep in one of the other rooms. I don't want to disturb you."

"Your folks won't think that's weird? We just got married. Our wedding night was anything but typical and with everything else going on, don't you think they'd expect you to be here with your wife, just in case she needs you? And how is that any different than me living downstairs, which is where I spend most of my non-sleeping time anyway?"

She had a point. "If you're okay with it, then yeah it's probably better for me to stay here for a lot of reasons, including the fact that you couldn't get a hold of me last night." He sat on the bed next to her. "You shouldn't be in that position again."

"You had no reason to think I might need you." She hesitated, as though she wanted to talk about something else.

"What is it?"

"What about the kids? Alex especially. I'm moving in here with you. I'm guessing he'll be up here with us, maybe across from Bailey. We could tell him that we're moving up here because of the babies, but that doesn't explain why I'm in your room. Besides, I'm sure your parents will mention it."

"Then we tell them that we got married. Don't go into details, but just what they need to know." It hadn't hit him yet. He'd barely come to terms with being a father of one little girl, much less the son once briefly believed to be his brother's illegitimate child? As the thought flew through his mind, Topher realized he hadn't thought that way about Alex since San Majoria.

And now, Alex was his son.

Topher shook his head to clear it. This wasn't the time to

dwell on all of that. "Lay down and get comfortable. I'll get the kids, and we can talk to them together."

"Mom?" Alex's voice rang through the doorway.

"I'm in here, sweetheart," Julia called. "Can you get Bailey and come to Christopher's room?"

He didn't respond, but ran past the partially open door hollering for Bailey. A minute later, they both walked into the room.

"What're you doin' in here, Mom?" Alex asked as they crossed the room.

Julia patted the bed next to her. "We wanted to talk to you two." In a few sentences, she explained about bed rest again, but Topher sensed she was stalling for time.

"And something happened yesterday we didn't have a chance to tell you about with everything else going on." When Julia held her hand toward Topher, he took it. "Christopher and I got married. The four of us are a family now."

Alex's eyes took on a cautious look. "So that makes Mr. Bayfield my dad?"

"Step-dad," Julia quickly clarified.

"You don't have to call me Mr. Bayfield, Alex." Topher tried to be gentle, like he would if he'd married Julia for love and was trying to explain this to his new son. "I'm pretty sure we talked about it before, didn't we?" He'd noticed Alex mostly avoided calling him anything.

Alex nodded.

"Then you can call me Topher." He turned and winked at Julia. "I might be able to get your mom to call me that, too, finally."

A blush crept up Julia's cheeks. "Fine, *Topher*."

He found he quite liked the way she said it.

Then he turned to his daughter. Bailey just stood there, looking from one to the other then back again, including Alex in her stares.

Alex grabbed her in a big hug. "That means you're my sister, Bay! Just like we wanted!"

Bailey's face lit up as she hugged Alex, and they jumped up and down together.

"Just like you wanted?" Julia asked before Topher could.

Alex cringed. "Sorry, Bay."

She shrugged.

Topher looked at Julia who looked back at him.

She had far more experience with getting information out of kids. "What aren't you telling us?"

Alex put his arm around Bailey's shoulder, apparently taking his role as big brother and protector quite seriously. "Bailey and I talk sometimes. She said she wanted me to be her brother, and you to be her mom. I told her I'd share you."

Topher found himself blinking rapidly as he tried to keep up with Alex's words. He turned to Bailey, reminding himself that he didn't want to scare her. "You talk to Alex?"

Tears filled her eyes, and she seemed to shrink into Alex as she nodded.

He needed to gain her trust. "It's okay if you talk to Alex, Bailey Bug. You're not in any trouble." One of the specialists Julia had taken her to see had said it was important to let Bailey talk on her own terms and that she shouldn't get in trouble for it. "Whenever you're ready to talk to me and Julia, though, we're here to listen."

Bailey looked up at Alex who whispered something in her

ear. She nodded, but Alex didn't move his arm.

"She's afraid you'll go away, just like her mom and Gene did."

Topher stared at him. "What? Her mom and Gene? Who's Gene?" Even before Alex answered, Topher realized who it was and why it was important. The notes, the ones saying *I'll come for Bailey* were from Gene. Martha's ex-boyfriend. He'd known the man's legal name was Eugene from the private investigator he'd hired. And one of the letters had come on a scrap with "Gene" on the back like it had been torn off another piece of paper. Topher hadn't put two and two together. He needed to call his lawyer and Jonathan as soon as he could.

"She was supposed to call him dad, but Bailey never liked him so she didn't. He said she talked way too much, and if she didn't stop, he and her mom would go away and leave her behind." Bailey's tears began to flow. "And then they did."

Julia didn't think Topher was aware that he still held her hand, but his grip tightened as her son spoke.

"And that's why you didn't want to talk to us, Bay?" His gentleness with his daughter warmed her heart. "You were afraid Julia and I would leave?"

She nodded.

"And I probably didn't help when I had to leave for work right after you got here, huh?"

She nodded again.

Topher let go of Julia's hand and reached for Bailey. She let go of Alex and took the two steps into her father's arms.

Topher scooped her up and hugged her tight.

Stupid hormones meant Julia was about to cry right along with Bailey.

Oh, who was she kidding? She would have cried anyway.

After several minutes of just holding Bailey, Topher shifted her to sit on his knee. "I need you to listen super close, okay, Bug?"

She nodded.

"I don't care how much you talk, Julia and I are never leaving you, ever." He reached up and brushed her auburn hair back. "One or both of us may go away for a little bit, for work like I did, or vacation or something, but we will always, *always* come back, okay?"

Julia wondered how he could promise that when they were supposed to be married only temporarily.

"And sometimes, you might get in a little bit of trouble for talking when you shouldn't, like at church or in the library, but we'll help you learn when it's time to talk and when it's time to whisper, and when it's time to be quiet. But you can talk as much as you want most of the time, okay?"

Bailey's head nodded as she reached for him, hugging his neck. "I love you, Daddy."

Tears flowed down Julia's cheeks, and she could see fresh tracks on Topher's face as well.

"Oh, Bailey Bug, I love you so much." His voice cracked as he spoke. He let go with one arm and stretched it toward Alex. Her son hesitated for a second then let Topher hug him, too. "Thank you for listening to her, Alex. She needed a friend and an older brother to protect her until she was ready to tell us herself."

After a couple of minutes, Topher let both of them go. "Why don't we go get some ice cream to celebrate?"

Bailey and Alex screamed their assent, but Alex sobered. "What about Mom?"

Julia swiped at her cheeks. "You guys go ahead. I have to rest anyway, and I think I'm about ready to go to sleep." She gave both kids a mock glare. "You listen to Topher and be on your best behavior. Make sure you brush your teeth really good before bed."

"We will, Mom," Alex promised giving her a hug. "We'll bring you some back."

"Thank you." She thought Topher meant go to the kitchen to get some out of the freezer, but maybe he meant going out.

He leaned over and brushed a kiss against her cheek. "I'm going to take them for frozen custard at Andy's. Text me what you want? If you're asleep when we get back, I'll put it in the freezer for you."

"Thanks."

Topher swung Bailey up into his arms and rested a hand on Alex's shoulder as they walked out of the room.

Julia tugged the blankets up around her shoulders and let the contentment settle around her. Topher's bedding was far nicer than anything she'd ever owned, anything she'd ever used except at the palace and on their trip to San Majoria.

But before she could fall asleep, her phone rang. A glance at the screen told her it was Kenzie, and she did need to talk to her friend. "Hey, Kenz."

"You married Christopher!" Her friend's squeal wasn't really a question. "Why didn't you tell me?"

"It's a long story that basically revolves around all the

tabloid junk yesterday and how they were affecting Topher and HEA TV."

"So you ran off and eloped. That was quite the first kiss."

"What?" Julia blinked. "How do you know about that?"

"There were two pictures with the press release. One of your first kiss, and one of the two of you all goo-goo eyed at each other."

"I didn't know he'd sent it out yet," she murmured and wondered if she should talk to him about actually clearing that stuff with her first.

"It also mentions a reboot of *2C4S*."

"That's true. It's not a totally done deal yet, but they're going to film here in Serenity Landing. I haven't heard what titles they're tossing around yet." What would fifteen-year-old Julia think about this? Not just a reboot of her favorite show, but to have the inside scoop because she was married to the star? It was kind of insane.

They talked for several more minutes as Julia told her about the babies and the bed rest. She would have to take orders for bags at the show rather than have plenty ready to go. At least she could knit on bed rest. She'd make a bunch of the ponytail hats that had been so popular the year before. Given not much else to do, she could make several a day and take orders for more of those as well.

It seemed ridiculous, but after less than fifteen minutes of discussion, Julia had to tell Kenzie goodbye. She was simply too worn out to carry on a full conversation any longer. After drifting off to sleep, she remembered vague impressions of the children coming in to give her a kiss good night. She wondered if she remembered Leigh Ann and James poking their heads in.

She did remember, though she couldn't have really responded, the other side of the bed dipping under the weight of Topher climbing in.

The next thing she remembered with any clarity was waking up to sunshine coming in the window and an arm resting solidly around her waist.

Chapter Twenty-One

Topher had woken up with his arms around his ex-wife exactly once. The morning after their wedding, she had indignantly informed him that she was not a very snuggly sleeper and asked him not to repeat the experience.

With Julia, he was pretty sure she had woken up, but she didn't seem to be pulling away. If anything she almost seemed to snuggle further back into him, settling into his embrace.

"Good morning, beautiful." He didn't know what made him add that descriptor. She certainly was a beautiful woman, but the comment was out of character for the relationship at this point.

"Good morning." Julia shifted slightly. "Did you sleep well? I didn't kick you, did I?"

"Nope. Not even a little bit." Topher chuckled. "In fact, I barely knew you were here."

"Well, I suppose that's good. I wouldn't want to keep you up. You have a lot more to do today than I do."

With that Topher rolled away and off the other side of the bed. "Want me to help you to the bathroom?"

"I can wait for a bit if you want to get ready. I have a feeling I'm going to get really good about dozing in the next few weeks."

He chuckled again as she burrowed under the covers. He'd hurry in case she changed her mind. Twenty minutes later, he had showered and dressed in jeans and a comfortable shirt.

As he walked into the bedroom, Julia was struggling to sit up. He hurried to her side, taking her elbow with one hand and his other arm going around her back for support. "Easy now." He walked with her to the bathroom. "You have your phone, right? If you need anything, call me." He noticed again what she was wearing. "And you're welcome to borrow any of my clothes you'd like."

"Thanks."

He left her there and went to find his mother in the kitchen, making breakfast for all of them.

"I told Alex one of us would take him to school today," she said as he walked in. "He wasn't going to make the bus, but has about half an hour before he needs to leave to be there in time."

"I'll take him." Topher popped a bit of scrambled egg in his mouth before leaning over to kiss her cheek. "Thanks for breakfast, Mom."

"I also got you a wet brush for Bailey's hair." She turned a piece of bacon over in the skillet.

"What's that?"

"It's a brush designed to work well in wet hair but works great on dry, too. It'll be easier to get her hair done." She pointed the spatula at him. "And that's something you need to learn to do."

Topher cringed. "I tried, once. She didn't scream because she wasn't talking yet, but it was clearly painful."

"Yet?" His mother turned with hope shining from her eyes. "Is she talking?"

He quickly explained what had transpired the night before and how they'd planned to take both of his parents with them to Andy's, but couldn't find them.

"We went for a walk, figuring you had it all under control and needed some time with your new family." She pulled the bacon out of the pan and onto a plate covered by a paper towel.

Topher headed for the stairs to let the rest of the family know breakfast was ready, but before he could start up them, he saw the kids coming down in front of his dad helping Julia. She still wore his pajamas and t-shirt.

They all sat around the table in the breakfast nook, holding hands as his dad said the blessing. Topher had to force himself to focus more on the prayer than the feeling of Julia's hand in his.

After breakfast and a quick trip to town to drop Alex off, Topher went into his office to get some work done. He'd been asked to co-write the pilot episode of the still-untitled sequel show with Claire, under the supervision of Dusty. Some brainstorming was in order before a phone call with his agent in a couple of hours.

That call lasted far longer than he expected. Not only was he being approached by all the usual news and gossip outlets for interviews and exclusives, but DeCarter Publishing had also sent a proposal requesting his memoirs.

His memoirs? What did he have to memoir about? He wasn't even thirty yet. Maybe in another thirty years. Or forty.

He said no for now, but didn't want to close the door forever. The monetary offers for exclusive family photos irritated him. He and Mady decided to set up a photo shoot, after clearing it with Julia, and releasing the photos on his website and Facebook page. Hopefully, by releasing the pictures straight to the public, the paparazzi would back off.

Later, he found Julia in her recliner working on her second or third hat of the day. They ate dinner as an extended family, slept next to each other, and repeated the same thing for the next several days. Though she wasn't actually confined to bed, Julia stayed home on Sunday, choosing to rest and have her own Bible study.

He needed to find a study they could do together and spend some time with her doing that.

Monday rolled around, much the same as the other days, but once Alex was off to school, Topher went downstairs to where Julia already reclined with her knitting needles.

"I wanted to give you a head's up," he told her as he neared the bottom of the stairs. "I'm going to be gone most of the day. I have some meetings in town about the show and production and all of that. We're hoping to have the contracts signed in the next week or so, but we're trying to get our ducks in a row."

"Okay. Have a good day. I'll be right here." She smiled and held up another hat. "Knitting away."

Topher leaned over and kissed her forehead. "Take care of

yourself and the babies." His stomach did a weird flip at the thought of the children she carried. Children who, for all intents and purposes, would be his.

Deciding not to dwell on it, he took the stairs two at a time and headed to town.

Julia had never felt so useless in her life. Sitting in the recliner, she continued to knit another hat, but Kenzie and Leigh Ann were doing most of the work. In fact, pretty much anything she sold at the yarn festival would be a result of their help. Yes, she had started a lot of it, but none of it had been finished. Or very little anyway.

While Bailey napped, Leigh Ann stayed in the basement with Julia and Kenzie. When Bailey woke, Julia's new mother-in-law took care of her granddaughter.

"How are you doing with everything?" Kenzie asked. "I didn't want to ask with your mother-in-law here."

"Fine, I guess. Topher has been incredibly attentive and helpful. I'm still not sure it feels like were actually married, though."

Kenzie shifted in her seat. "That's not exactly what I was talking about."

Julia's eyes narrowed. "What are you talking about them?"

With a sigh, Kenzie pulled her phone out of her pocket. "This." She handed the phone over.

Julia swiped up to look at the article from *CelebGossipNewz*, complete with pictures. "Who is that?"

"That's Claire Cruz Cartwright. You don't recognize her?"

Julia expanded her fingers outward to enlarge the picture. "The girl from all the Hallmark movies?"

"One and the same. He was her co-star in the Christmas movie a few weeks ago. It comes out around Thanksgiving."

Julia pinched the pictures back in and scrolled through them. They showed her husband, with a beautiful woman, at a restaurant in Serenity Landing. It showed what appeared to be a quick hug, a kiss on the cheek, and two people eating lunch together on opposite sides of the table. "I don't know what to think."

Kenzie reached for the phone. "Look at their body language."

"What about their body language?" Julia pulled out her own tablet from the bag next to her chair. It didn't take long to find the pictures. "He's kissing her cheek. They're having lunch. He's leaning over the table to talk to her. What is it I'm supposed to be looking at?"

"Is that really what it looks like to you?" Kenzie seemed to scrutinize the picture on her own screen. "To me, it just looks like two people having lunch. The kiss on the cheek when they got there? Isn't that what all Hollywood people do? The more I look at it, the more I don't know."

Julia rubbed her stomach as a contraction hit. Should she read more into it? "I have no idea. He never kissed my cheek like that when we saw each other. He still doesn't."

"I don't think you should read too much into it, but you know the paparazzi are. You read the article, didn't you?"

"Yeah. They're certain he's having an affair already." She closed her eyes and imagined the kiss of the wedding. Surely he wasn't cheating on her, was he? Even though this had been a pretty unconventional marriage so far.

"I don't believe he's cheating on you," Kenzie stated, certainty suddenly filling her voice. "That's just not the kind of guy he, or his brother, is. Remember the accusations then? There was absolutely no truth to them last spring, and I really don't think there's any truth to them now. Do you?"

Julia turned those thoughts over in her head. She had known allegations about Duke Alexander's affair were false, because she was supposedly the other woman. This time she would be the woman scorned. But even if it hadn't been her, she never would've believed the duke would cheat on his wife. Would it make any more sense to believe his brother would? "I don't know. I don't think he would cheat on me." She didn't sound as certain as she wished she did.

Kenzie folded her arms across her chest. "Ask him. Don't beat around the bush, just come straight out and ask him if he's cheating on you. If he is, you'll be able to tell."

"He's an actor. You don't think he can lie effectively? I'm not saying I believe he's cheating on me. I'm just saying I think he could pull it off, if he wanted to lie about it."

"Being an actor and a great liar are not the same thing."

Kenzie had a point. Maybe she would ask him about it when he got home.

Footsteps on the stairs caught her attention. Bailey ran toward her, followed more slowly by Leigh Ann.

"Did you have a good nap, sweetheart?" Julia held out an arm to hug the girl.

Bailey shrugged. "I don't like naps."

"I know. I don't like them much right now either." Not when she felt like she was forced to take them.

Leigh Ann rested a hand on Bailey's shoulder. "Would you go watch TV for a few minutes, sweetie? I need to talk to Julia."

Bailey skipped to the other side of the room and turned on *Blue's Clues*.

Julia looked up at her mother-in-law. "What's up?"

Leigh Ann sighed and sat on the sofa. "I just saw some pictures, and I know what they could look like, and..."

"The ones with Claire Cruz Cartwright?" Julia logged back into her tablet. "I've seen them."

"I promise you, there is nothing going on between them." Leigh Ann's earnestness touched Julia's heart.

She zoomed in on one of the pictures again. When they were leaning toward each other over the table, they appeared to be looking at something on a tablet, not trying to be closer to each other. "I don't think there is, no matter what the websites are saying." She had to believe that. She made herself believe it. Deep down, she *did* believe it.

"Good. It's not in his nature to do that, any more than it would have been in Alexander's to have a fling with you or anyone else."

"That's exactly what Kenzie and I were talking about before you guys came downstairs. Neither one of us think anything's going on."

"And if he hasn't contacted you yet, then I'm sure he doesn't even know the story's out there." Leigh Ann seemed more relaxed.

Julia and the others turned at the sound of a door opening and voices entering the house.

"Julia?" Topher's voice drifted down the stairs. "I've got

someone I want you to meet."

Chapter Twenty-Two

We're down here, honey!" His mom's voice reached them in the kitchen.

Topher pointed toward the stairs to the basement and followed Claire. He reached the bottom about the time he heard his mom squealing.

"Claire! It's so good to see you again!" The two women hugged and did that cheek kiss thing he had never quite understood. "How are you, honey?"

"I'm good, Leigh Ann." Claire stepped back. "I'm not so sure about this whole moving to the Midwest plan, but I'm excited about the series."

"Oh, honey, you'll love it here!"

Topher didn't think his mom had used so many exclamation points in such a short period of time in a while. He went to stand next to Julia and rested his hand on Julia's shoulder. "Claire, this is my wife, Julia." That was getting easier and easier to say.

Claire held out a hand, and Julia shook it. "It's nice to meet you, Julia. I didn't think anyone would ever tie this guy down."

Julia gave a rather uncomfortable looking smile. "Well, when he asked, I just couldn't say no." She nodded toward the other woman in the room. "And this is Kenzie. She's one of my best friends."

The two women greeted each other about the time Bailey realized he was in the room. She ran toward him, yelling, "Daddy!" He didn't think he'd ever tire of hearing her voice.

"Hi, Bailey Bug." He scooped her up into his arms and gave her a big hug. "Have you had a good day today?"

She fiddled with the button on his shirt. "I missed you."

"I missed you, too, but I had a meeting this morning." He shifted her so they could see Claire. "This is my friend, Claire. She's going to be in my new TV show."

Claire held out a fist for a bump. "We were in the movie together a few weeks ago. Your dad told me so much about you, I feel like I know you already."

Bailey gave the fist bump. "Hi." She tucked in closer to Topher.

"Have a seat, Claire." He motioned toward the couch while sitting in the other recliner with Bailey. "We met to talk about the show. Claire is going to be the lead actress."

"I remember the episode where the Chris character's one great love got away." Julia tilted her head toward Claire. "Was that you?"

"It was," she confirmed.

"I loved the show growing up," Julia told her. "And I loved that episode, but didn't realize you were the actress."

"My one and only foray into that kind of teen programming. The rest was standard sitcom fare."

Voices from upstairs let Topher know his dad was back from picking Alex up at the foot of the driveway.

Kenzie stood and held a hand his direction. "Bay, why don't we go up and get a snack with Alex? Grandpa may want to come down here and talk to Ms. Claire."

Bailey wriggled down and skipped off with Kenzie.

Topher looked back and forth between his mom and Julia. "What's going on?"

"You didn't see?" Mom asked.

He raised his brows. "Does this look like the face of someone who saw something?" Before she could answer, he dug his phone out of his pocket. Eight missed calls and a dozen texts from Mady. That's what he got for putting his phone on Do Not Disturb while meeting with Claire.

A text from Mom came in. "That's the link," she told him. "Save you from looking it up."

The small preview was all he needed to see. "Claire and I are having an affair? Seriously?"

Claire pulled her phone out of her purse. "They're ridiculous. I've got messages from my agent. He must have already seen it, too."

He swiped through the article. Short on words, long on speculation. "This is ridiculous." His phone buzzed. "It's Mady." He stood and went onto the patio to take the call. She reiterated the benefits of getting a story out to *Humanity* or one of the other reputable magazines. At the very least, getting pictures up on his website and Facebook like they'd talked about before.

"Fine. I'll call a photographer today and get a rush on them." He pinched the bridge of his nose. "I think we need to get those papers signed on the show as soon as we can so the announcement can be made. That gives Claire and me valid reasons to be seen together in purely platonic settings."

"It would be good for her to be seen with your wife, too. Maybe posting a pic of the two of them together on her Facebook page or something. That's assuming they get along, of course."

"Claire came back to the house with me. We were going to have a nice evening, talking and having dinner, until all of this came up." He looked back in the house to see Claire with her phone to her ear as she paced. "I think she's talking to some of her people now. This isn't like her, either, you know. She's not going to steal some other woman's husband, no matter the circumstances. Her beliefs are one reason why I hoped she'd be back on the show years ago."

"I know this. You know this. The general public knows this. The people at *CelebGossipNewz* know this. They simply don't care." Mady sighed. "I'll see what we can do to expedite the process even more. You may need to make a trip to LA or New York to do a late night show to make the announcement."

"I can't. My wife is on bedrest. I'll do a video chat with one of them, or send Claire, but I'm not leaving Julia."

"She's been your wife less than a week." Mady's gentle tone didn't quite match the words. "Everyone knows that's not your baby."

"So?" It shocked him how much he suddenly wished it was, for many reasons. "I'm still not leaving her, even for an afternoon and evening to go do a show."

"We'll see what we can work out." Mady remained noncommittal which meant she expected him to take a few hours to go to New York, most likely. Maybe he'd at least get Claire to meet him there - or fly commercial. No way the two of them could fly a private plane together, unless maybe he took Bailey and his mom.

He agreed to talk to her again soon and set up the photoshoot as soon as he could. With another sigh, he turned and went back inside. Maybe they'd be able to put this all out of their minds and just have a nice evening.

One could hope anyway.

Julia didn't know what to do except keep knitting. Leigh Ann had told her there not to worry, and mostly Julia believed that, but she still had that little bit of doubt.

She glanced at the patio door as Topher returned. His face was a mixture of dejection and resignation until he saw her watching him. He tried to cover up his emotions, but he didn't do as good a job as he probably wished.

"It's all going to be okay," he told her as he leaned down and kissed her forehead.

"Of course it is." Claire had hung up and approached them. "How much can you be up and around, Julia?"

Julia shifted in her chair, hoping to improve blood flow to her now-numb rear end. "I can get up for a little bit. No more than about half an hour at a time a few times a day."

That seemed to please Claire. "Good. Then we're going to take you to your room, do your hair and makeup, put you in some super cute maternity clothes, and take pictures I can post on social media about how fantastic you are and how much I've enjoyed spending the day with you guys. All of that's true, but we try to get ahead of it some."

Julia lowered the footrest and pushed herself upright in the recliner. "That sounds like a good idea." But what did she know? At least Claire seemed like a nice person.

Everything she'd ever read about the woman said she was genuine.

"Let me help you." Topher scooped her into his arms. "I'll carry you upstairs and then leave you girls to do your thing."

"I *can* walk, you know." Julia liked the feeling of being in his arms, but she didn't like feeling everyone thought she was a complete invalid.

"I know, but I'm here and capable. Save your walking for when you have no choice."

Claire was on their heels when they reached the master bedroom.

A minute later, Julia was reclining on the bed she'd shared with her husband for the last few days.

Claire pointed toward the other door. "Is the closet through the bathroom? Is it okay if I find something cute for you to wear? That way you don't have to get up to find it. Or if there's something you prefer, let me know, and I'll get it for you."

"Yes, the closets are in there. Mine is the smaller one because Topher already had the big one and, honestly, he's got far more clothes than I do, anyway. Most of mine don't even fit. This is all his." The pajama bottoms and old t-shirt were not how she would have chosen to meet one of her favorite actresses, but too late now.

Claire turned and grinned at her. "Then I say we steal another one of his shirts. There's something totally adorable about a pregnant woman wearing her husband's shirt."

Julia wasn't quite sure what to think about that. She agreed, in theory, but she'd been married to Topher for such a short period of time. Everyone knew he wasn't actually the father of her babies. Was it still totally adorable in that situation?

Claire came back out of the bathroom, holding a pair of black leggings and a red and black flannel shirt. "How about this? Do you have a black tank top you could wear underneath?"

"In the dresser in my closet. Second drawer down."

Claire went back into the bathroom and emerged a minute later with the shirt from Julia's closet. "Okay. Do you need help getting changed? Do you want me to get Topher's mom? I can't imagine you'd be comfortable with me helping you, though I'd be happy to if you wanted."

Julia shook her head. "No. I've got it. If you wouldn't mind leaving the clothes over here..."

Claire laid the clothes on the bed. "I'll be right outside." She closed the door leading to the hallway behind her. It took a few minutes but Julia managed to change on her own. "You can come on in," she called.

Claire opened the door. "Now, do you mind if I do your hair and makeup? Or do you have a way you prefer to do it?"

The honest truth was Julia had never cared too much about either. "Whatever you want to do is fine with me. I have a hard time doing it these days, anyway."

After another twenty minutes, they were done. Topher insisted on carrying her back downstairs. She was back in a recliner, in the main floor living room this time instead of the basement. The chair was new, though Topher insisted he'd been planning to get one and not just because of her new restrictions. Julia didn't buy it for a minute. He'd bought it just for her.

And now Topher was kneeling down on the floor next to her while Claire stood a little further away and held her phone up in selfie mode.

"All right, guys, smile!"

Topher's arm wrapped around her shoulders, and he used a finger to tip her head toward his. She liked the feeling, the point of contact between the two of them. It made her feel like something real existed between them.

"A couple more."

Right. Claire's pictures.

"Look at each other like you like each other." The amused tone in her voice made Julia want to roll her eyes.

But Topher whispered, "Look at me."

She did, and he rested his forehead against hers. His hand came up and cupped the side of her cheek. Julia's eyes fluttered closed at his touch.

Would he kiss her?

"Perfect!" Claire's voice broke the spell being woven around them.

Julia moved away from Topher as Claire settled onto the couch. She tapped away on her phone and muttered to herself. Then she handed it to Topher. "What do you think?"

Topher took Claire's phone from her.

Check these two out! Aren't they adorable?! I was supposed to have lunch with Christopher Bayfield (Chris Slate) and his wife today in their hometown, but she was recently put on modified bed rest by her doc, so she couldn't come. After Christopher and I talked business for a while - there's some super-secret, super fun stuff coming your way soon, we hope! - we came back to their house where I get to spend the rest of the day hanging out with the brand-new Mrs. Bayfield and their two kids. Mom and Dad are DEFINITELY still in their honeymoon phase!

What do you think? Christopher and I did a movie together a few weeks ago (coming to HEA TV next month!) - what would you like to see us collaborate on next?

He passed it off to Julia. "Looks good to me, though we haven't announced publicly that she's on bed rest, but that's okay. It's probably better to do it more nonchalantly like this. What do you think, Jules?" He'd only called her that once before, hadn't he? Did she mind the nickname?

She shrugged. "Looks fine to me, but what do I know?"

"Nothing in it bothers you? Doesn't feel quite right?"

"I didn't know I was invited to lunch originally, but that's it."

"I'd planned to ask you to come, but I knew you couldn't. I also know you're a fan of Claire's movies, so I thought I'd surprise you by bringing her over for a visit. I had no idea paparazzi were in town, much less stalking me."

"I understand, but I'll feel better when the front gate is finished."

Was she more uncomfortable or scared than she'd let on?

"It'll be finished today. Jonathan's got men stationed on the property regardless."

"I know." She seemed to shake it off. "It really is nice to meet you, Ms. Cruz Cartwright. I do love your movies and never missed your show growing up."

Claire wrinkled her nose. "Call me Claire. Thank you for your support. I appreciate it, and thank you for loaning me Topher for a while today. I'm excited about the show."

Julia looked over at him. "Is it officially a go?"

"Should be in a couple days. Gotta dot the i's and cross the t's. We'll announce it next week hopefully."

"My agent's already got me scheduled on Late Night Tonight next week," Claire told him. "They've asked if you'll come, too, whether we're ready for an announcement or not."

"We'll see." He remained noncommittal. With rumors already floating about himself and Claire, he wasn't sure that was the best plan.

"You could fly out and back." Mom had stopped on her way to the kitchen and jumped into the conversation. "No need to spend the night. Maybe Bailey and I could come, too."

"She'd like that," Topher said, almost to himself. "So would Alex."

"He'd have to miss school, though, wouldn't he?" Julia interjected.

"Probably, though we might be able to leave late enough he wouldn't have to miss all day." Another thought occurred to him. "I wouldn't want to do a bunch of sightseeing though, Claire. Nothing personal, but without Julia along, even with my mom there, it would be far too easy for the tabloids to read something into it."

"Agreed." Claire curled her legs up underneath her. "You can leave here, do a little sightseeing with your mom and the kids, I'll meet you at the studio. You fly home afterward."

Something to think about.

The next afternoon, Mama Beach had helped him make arrangements with a local photographer. Anise Taylor had done family pictures for the Beach family earlier in the year, and Mama Beach had loved them.

Anise took them behind the house. After a few pictures on the dock near the lake, Topher realized he probably needed to get a boat for summer. When it was just him, it seemed pointless, but Alex and Bailey would love it.

Pictures of the four of them doing the happy family thing made up about half the photos. The rest were pictures of him and Julia. Newlyweds. His arms wrapped around her stomach with the whole hands in the shape of a heart thing. Kissing her.

Something he found himself liking more and more.

"Okay. We're going to do a fun one." Anise pulled out her phone. "Some writer friends of mine, Katie Ganshert and Becky Wade, do these Pinterest challenges. A couple years ago, they did this one." She showed them pictures from Pinterest and of both authors and their families trying to recreate it. "It's a super fun picture, but since Julia's pregnant, I'd recommend Topher hold one kid upside down and the other one make a goofy face or something." She showed the picture to the kids. "Bailey, do you want your dad to hold you upside down?"

Bailey shook her head.

"I do!" They all laughed at Alex's excitement.

Anise arranged them just right. He'd hold Alex upside

down while kissing Julia, who would do the foot pop thing commonly found in movies. Bailey would roll her eyes.

As Anise took several pictures, Topher kissed Julia over and over - and Alex laughed. He knew they'd use one of these to release.

And when Anise sent a few of them over later, Topher loved them. Bailey looked a little grumpy and rolling her eyes instead of amused, but the picture was the right one. They released it with a more detailed statement about the wedding, the babies, and Topher's plans to return full time to the world of acting.

And, a few days later, when it was official and time for the trip to Los Angeles to announce the new show, he took both kids and his mom with him. They'd decided to let Alex skip the full day of school. About the time the bus passed the end of the drive, Topher and the rest prepared to leave. Julia stood at the door, her hand rubbing her stomach.

She winced and pushed against one side.

"Everything okay? More contractions?" He wouldn't go if she needed him to stay.

"No. Baby foot trying to kick out the side of my abdomen." She winced again. "Or maybe an elbow."

"They're bouncing around?" He stared at one of his favorite t-shirts where it covered her belly. "Can I?" One hand reached tentatively toward her. The only time he'd felt a baby move in utero was right before the wedding. It might be the coolest thing ever.

Julia smiled at him. A good sign. "Sure." She reached for his hands and placed both of them on her stomach, one on either side.

After a couple of seconds, he was rewarded with a rolling movement. "That's so cool," he whispered.

"Not when you're trying to sleep."

He looked up to see only mild annoyance on her face. "I can imagine. Get some rest while we're gone. Kenzie will be here soon, right?" James had to go out of town on business so he wouldn't be there.

"Yes. Kenzie will be here until you get home. I won't be doing anything I shouldn't, though I will walk up and down the stairs on my own."

"And I didn't think I'd ever have any use for the elevator the original plans came with," he muttered. "Wish I'd left it in now."

Julia rolled her eyes. "I will be *fine.* Don't worry about us, just send me pictures."

He leaned down, his hands still on either side of her stomach, and kissed her gently. He'd been doing that more and more and finding he liked it. A lot. More than he'd ever liked kissing Bailey's mother.

"We'll be home late," he reminded her. "Even though the show tapes earlier than it airs, by the time we eat something and get to the airport and a three-and-a-half hour flight with the time change, it'll be past the kids' bedtimes. I'll try to get them to sleep on the plane, but it might be too much."

"I know. We can take Alex late in the morning if we need to."

One of the babies rolled under his hand again. Topher gave her another quick kiss then backed away. "I'll let you know when we land."

"Thanks."

He headed down the steps. "See you soon."

As he drove his mom and the kids down the drive, he glanced in the rear view mirror. She stood there with her hands folded on top of her stomach and then she waved.

An odd ache filled Topher's chest, something familiar, but something he couldn't quite identify.

All he knew is that he wanted to hurry home.

Chapter Twenty-Three

Julia had taken all of the pillows on the bed, including Topher's, and piled them behind her to make a recliner of sorts. It was comfier in here.

When they spoke before the flight took off an hour earlier, she hadn't mentioned Kenzie going home. Her friend wasn't feeling well, so Julia promised she'd take great care not to do much of anything. Dinner had been eaten and, in all honesty, Julia was about ready to go lay down anyway.

But now it was time for *Late Night Tonight*. She turned on the TV, waited through the monologue, which was amusing at best, and then Claire was up. They did the first segment on one of her upcoming movies then went to commercial. When they got back, Julia knew the time had come.

"So, something's changed since we actually booked you, right?" Terry Thompson asked her.

"That's right! Not just the ugly tabloid gossip last week, but more than that." Claire rolled her eyes at the camera and crowd.

"Now, the gossip had you and Chris Slate, whose real name is Christopher Bayfield, having an affair even though he's only been married for a couple weeks."

"Right. And it's ludicrous. He loves his wife and wouldn't cheat on her. Besides, I'd never be the other woman, either."

"You posted a picture on your Facebook account a couple hours after the rumor broke with them being all adorable and newlywedish in the background."

"And that's how they really are."

Not exactly, Julia thought, but close enough, she supposed.

"So when are you able to tell us what the super-secret project you've been working on is?"

"Right now!"

"What?" The host looked genuinely surprised.

"Christopher is here! Julia's not able to fly and be up and about too much, so he brought both of his kids and his mom out to LA today to do some sightseeing and to be here with us."

The camera cut away from the desk to Topher walking in from behind a curtain. He waved to the crowd then shook hands with Terry. He did the cheek kissy thing with Claire, then took a seat on the couch next to her. Close but not too close.

"Welcome, Chris."

"It's Christopher these days, Terry, but it's great to be here."

"Sorry, Christopher. So before we get to whatever news

you've got, I have to ask. What's it like being related to a queen?"

Julia knew Topher probably wanted to roll his eyes and ignore the question, but he put on a happy face.

"Queen Christiana is fantastic. Even better, she and my brother make each other so totally happy that it's impossible not to love her. My new nephew is adorable, and I honestly could not be happier for them."

Terry tapped his note cards on the desk. "So, don't keep us in suspense any longer! What's the big news that needs both of you here?"

Topher grinned at the camera. "The rumors have been flying pretty thick the last few weeks, but it's finally official. *2 Cool 4 School* is getting a sequel!"

Julia couldn't hide her grin as the crowd went crazy. Topher and Claire both laughed as Terry tried to quiet them down.

"That's fantastic. Can you tell us more about it yet?"

Topher shifted his attention back to Terry. "One of the things Claire doesn't love about it is that it's going to be shooting in my hometown of Serenity Landing. As much as I want to do the show, I didn't want to uproot my family to move back here. We all love where we live. We'll be able to look at the local talent for some of the roles, and some, like Claire here, will be moving to the area, at least while we're shooting."

"And that's why you were in town the other day, Claire?" Terry asked her.

"That's right. I'm looking for a place and wanted to see what the area was like, where we'll be shooting, things like that."

"I take it there's a premise for the show then. Can you tell us about it?"

"Some of it's still being hammered out, but Alexander won't be back, of course." Topher looked at the audience as they expressed their disappointment. "As much as he loved *2 Cool 4 School*, acting was always more my thing. Given his life now, his responsibilities, and his security issues, he won't be making any appearances. Just wanted to get that out there."

"But on the show, Alex is the one who married his childhood sweetheart."

"True. But unfortunately, Alex's wife has now passed on, leaving him with kids to raise on his own, including twin girls." No mention of what went down with Topher and the actress who played Alex's wife. "He's got a job that keeps him overseas most of the time, so Chris has to step in and take over the parenting duties, something he has no clue how to do."

"That's where I come in." Claire rejoined the conversation. "I was a *2 Cool 4 School* fan, too, you know. I loved doing the one episode I was on. I couldn't have done more at the time, but I always felt my character was the one that got away for Chris."

The crowds' reaction showed they agreed.

"And so, I happen to live in the same area. Chris needs help, and that romance that never was will have a chance to grow."

"That sounds fantastic." Terry tapped his note cards on the desk. "And somewhat mirrors your real life these days, doesn't it, Christopher?"

"It does," Topher confirmed. "It's a very long story I'm not going to tell now, but I'm a newlywed with two new kids, and two more on the way."

"Two? Your wife is having twins?"

"Seems appropriate, doesn't it?" Topher's grin seemed off, but Julia doubted anyone else would notice. She also noticed it took the attention off where Bailey came from.

"But everyone knows you're not the biological father of your wife's babies. The bio dad came forward a couple weeks ago and accused both of you of some pretty nasty stuff."

"All garbage. Everyone knew it, but of anyone here, Terry, I know you understand that biology isn't everything. Those kids are mine regardless of what their DNA says."

Right. Because Terry was both adopted and had adopted his wife's kids.

"Very good point. Now, does this new show have a name? Where can we watch it and when?"

"No name yet. In fact, we're going to be asking for fan participation there. The 2C4S.com website is going to run a contest for the name of the show. The winning entry will get a prize pack that includes a trip to the set and a walk-on role."

The crowd went crazy.

"As for when? We're hoping to start production early next year. Claire and I are working with Dusty Ring to write the first episode now. The release date isn't set yet, but we're looking at late summer or fall on MyBingeFlix."

Julia tuned out as the interview wrapped up. No real new information except that Claire was also working on the pilot script. The world now knew she was having twins. She clicked the button to turn the screen off and sat up further to move the pillows from behind her and situate herself to get some sleep.

Maybe when she woke up, she'd find herself a little less

alone.

Waking up alone wasn’t quite the same as it had been even a few weeks earlier. Topher hadn’t expected to miss his wife quite so much.

He hadn’t slept enough when his alarm went off, but he didn’t want her trying to get up or head downstairs without help.

His mom met him in the hallway. "You didn't sleep in your room last night?"

"No. Julia was already asleep, and I didn't want to bother her." He started down the hall. “I don't want her getting up without help, though."

Mom walked toward the stairs. "I'll get breakfast started if you want to check on her, and get the kids up. I know you told Alex he could sleep in, but he mentioned they had an assembly this morning that he wanted to go to. He could still sleep in just a little bit and not take the bus. I can take him if you need me to."

"That would be great." He opened the door to the room they shared, doing his best to be quiet. He could make out Julia's still form on the bed in the dim room. Good. She still slept.

He sent her a text telling her to let him know when she woke up, and he would come help.

Had she seen the show? Had he told her Claire was working with him on the pilot? He hated not having an idea for the name of the show yet. No one else had either. That's why they jumped at his idea of getting fan input.

The next few weeks passed quickly for him, though he knew Julia didn't feel quite the same way, but they had settled into something of a routine. He got up with the kids, his mom and dad made breakfast – when his dad was there. Once Alex was on the bus, Topher went upstairs and helped Julia get ready for the day.

He would have gladly helped more, but they didn't have the kind of relationship where she was comfortable with him doing more.

Once she was done changing clothes, or taking a shower, or whatever else she needed to do first thing in the morning, they would sit on the love seat in the room. They took turns reading a few verses from the Bible and talked about them. He usually said a prayer that included asking God to take care of the babies.

Internally, he asked God to make this into the relationship they both wanted and needed. Deep down, he found himself longing for more.

As the longing grew, he realized that's what he felt the day he left for Los Angeles. The deep desire for connection with that one special person. Given everything with his brother earlier in the year, he never would have guessed God would pick Julia for him to end up with. The more time spent with her, the more he began to understand that even though this wasn't what either one of them would've chosen, it was exactly what they needed.

Or at least exactly what he needed.

He wasn't sure how she felt, and couldn't decide if he wanted to ask.

She made more hats than she knew what to do with. When he suggested making something else to go with them, she whipped out some scarves. Then she started on baby blankets, but he didn't think she would have very many done by the time the yarn show started next week.

Each weekend, he took the kids to do something fun for part of Saturday. They went to Fantastic Caverns and a couple places in Springfield, like the Discovery Center or the Dickerson Park Zoo. Bailey enjoyed the Itty Bitty City more than Alex did.

Two weeks before the yarn show, Bailey was with his mother, and Kenzie brought Lorelai over to play while she and Julia put the finishing touches on their plan. The Show Me Yarn ladies joined them.

When he went back upstairs to go through the pilot episode again, it certainly sounded like they were having fun.

After another read through, he sent the script to Claire. They were nearly done. For now. Unless someone came up with a title they all absolutely loved, but didn't fit with the script. Many of the suggestions they received used the numbers two and four. A couple even used the number six. Julia suggested it, too, even before seeing the names that came in from the website. *Seating for Six* would require five kids or four kids and a female lead from the very beginning. Not just a potential love interest but a girlfriend, fiancé, or wife.

Topher wasn't opposed to the idea, per se. In fact, it could be interesting. Chris and his girlfriend–who–was–almost–his–fiancé, who planned to travel almost constantly, for fun, suddenly thrust into being parents. Maybe even moving up the wedding.

Before she could have had time to read it, Claire sent an email of her own. She said she hesitated to even mention it, given him and Julia, but what about a similar kind of situation? Where he and this girl he'd met once, got married in Vegas or something, but don't remember it. He moves to take care of his brother's kids, she shows up with the marriage license she found in her suitcase.

Now there's a new marriage with someone he barely knows, four new kids, and the need for *Seating for Six*.

He turned the idea over in his head. The one thing he didn't like about it was the part where they would've had to be drunk in Vegas. He hit reply and asked what kind of funny way their characters could end up accidentally married, not necessarily even in Vegas.

A few minutes later she suggested they had run into each other at a comedy club in Reno. Outside, the sign said they were looking for a real couple to get married on stage as part of the sketch. Their characters hadn't realized it was real, but as a joke, participated anyway. They didn't know the papers they were signing were legit. He goes to his brother's house taking care of four kids, who are running amok, and she shows up with the paperwork they mailed her.

Topher decided he liked it. It wouldn't take much rewriting of the pilot episode. The two characters were already surprised to be living near each other. If she showed up in the teaser at the end, with the paperwork yelling about how they were already married, that would be a great mini-cliffhanger to get people to move on to the next episode. The season finale could have his character proposing. Season two, assuming it got picked up, could be planning the wedding.

He emailed Claire back, and they put together a plan to present to Dusty. Done for the day, he went back downstairs to find Julia and her friends just wrapping things up. She had a doctor's appointment in about an hour. Though a smile stayed on her face, he noticed she rubbed her stomach a bit differently than she had before.

It concerned him some, but he didn't want to say anything unless she did.

"I hate to interrupt, ladies, but I need to borrow my wife."

"We were just getting ready to pack up anyway," Kenzie told him. "We'll be out of your hair in a few minutes. Are you ready to take your shifts next week, mister?"

He chuckled. "I'm learning. Just promise at least one of you will be there at all times, and we'll be good."

Chapter Twenty-Four

Julia did her best to keep the smile on her face, but something felt off. Not like it had a few weeks ago, but more like it had when Alex was born.

She was still officially on bed rest for a couple more hours. The week before, Dr. McConnell had told her it would likely end today, at 36 weeks, but that if she'd gone into labor in the last week, she wouldn't try to stop it. The babies were close enough to term that they *should* be okay.

After everyone else was gone, she let Topher carry her upstairs without protesting.

"You're not okay, are you?" he asked as he set her on the floor near the bathroom.

Julia shook her head. "I think I may be going into labor. The contractions aren't strong or regular or often, but they're different than before."

"Then get ready. Do we need to go straight to the hospital? Where's your bag?"

She pointed to her closet. "It's in there. I just need to get my toothbrush and stuff together and change clothes."

It took about fifteen minutes to get everything together. They let Leigh Ann know what Julia thought was going on, and then headed for town. Though they'd made the drive several times, it never failed to surprise her just how long it took. Being on the other side of the lake made all the difference.

As they neared the hospital and her doctor's office next door, Topher clarified. "You sure we don't need to go to labor and delivery?"

"I'm sure. I've had one contraction since we left. I don't even know if she'll want to keep me at this point. She may send me home or to walk the mall or something."

He didn't really seem convinced, but pulled into the other lot anyway. At least they had parking spots for pregnant women. A car left one of the spots as they pulled in. Topher hurried around to help her out of his SUV. It was far easier than trying to get in and out of her car.

His arm stayed around her waist as they went inside, up the elevator and checked in. Half an hour later, they headed over to the hospital. Her doctor wasn't convinced it was real labor, but wanted to keep an eye on her for a while just the same.

Once hooked up to all the monitors, whatever had kept the stress at bay disappeared, and emotion swept over her. Tears streaked from her eyes, across her nose, and into her left ear. It was too much. Too soon. Too much to do.

At least the nursery was done. Now she was glad Leigh Ann

had insisted. She was also glad she hadn't let Topher talk her into giving them their own rooms as newborns.

He'd also ordered both pink and blue. No matter how she'd protested that they could get it later, that they could order everything as soon as the babies were born. It was part of the point of having Amazon Prime, wasn't it? Super-fast shipping? But no. He'd decided to give whatever they didn't use to Sammy's Window - a local charity that provided clothes and other supplies to foster and adoptive parents.

At the time, she didn't know how she felt about spending money unnecessarily, but now she was glad they were already at home and waiting. Leigh Ann would put the right bedding on.

But none of that stopped the tears.

At least she hadn't progressed to sobs, and her back was to the door when it opened, and Topher slid back in.

"Mom sends her love. So do the kids. They're anxious to get up here. I told her not yet, and we'd see how it goes."

"The babies are coming," she told him with sudden conviction. "They'll be here tonight or tomorrow."

He walked around and pulled a chair up next to her. "You're sure? The doctor said..."

"I know," she snapped. "Doctors say things all the time, but sometimes you just know. This is it."

"So will they take you for a c-section then? Don't they do that with twins?"

Hadn't they discussed all of this *ad nauseum* over the last few weeks?

"Baby A was head down last week." They'd checked. "Baby B isn't, but it's not uncommon for the second baby to turn once there's a little more room. I'll have an epidural and may end up delivering both in a surgery suite. My doctor hadn't decided yet what she'd prefer." And she was on call so no dealing with a random office partner Julia didn't know. "She'll come over and check on me after she's done in the office unless I need her sooner."

"Right. I knew that."

He must be more nervous than he let on, because they'd discussed it in her office just a few minutes earlier.

"Hey." The brush of Topher's thumb across the bridge of her nose shocked her, but she managed not to jump. "Why are you crying?"

It took all her courage to be vulnerable enough to tell him. "I'm scared," she whispered, barely able to get the words out.

Even with her eyes closed, she knew he moved closer to her and then his forehead rested on her temple while an arm wrapped around her the best it could. With his other hand, he covered one of hers.

Praying with more confidence than he surely felt, Topher's words acted as a soothing balm to her frazzled nerves. He prayed for the babies, for their safe delivery, and for her. For her peace. For strength. For comfort.

And to help him be the helper she needed him to be in the next few hours, the next few weeks.

The next few years.

He'd never said anything quite like that before, and it brought Julia out of her relaxed state.

Was he thinking forever? Since when?

But as he continued, she found her rest in the sound of his voice and strength of her Savior.

"Thank you." Her voice was still a whisper, but stronger now.

"It's what I'm here for." He kept his hand on hers as he moved back, then asked a question about yarn. They'd talked a lot about yarn in the last few weeks, but the question was still insightful, and not until the nurse came in a few minutes later did she realized how skillfully he'd distracted her.

This guy just might be a keeper.

Before she could let the thought go too far, another contraction hit, this one far more intense than the others.

She gripped Topher's hand and prayed for it to go away.

Topher breathed a sigh of relief almost as big as the one Julia must have felt when the epidural finally kicked in. He'd never felt quite so helpless as when each contraction hurt her to the point of tears.

Not even when Martha left him.

Her doctor walked in as the anesthesiologist walked out. "How are you feeling, Julia?" she asked as she came to stand next to the bed.

"Better now." The tension had drained from her. "How're things looking?"

"That's what I'm here to check."

The first appointment he'd gone to with Julia had been by far the most awkward, but he still hadn't gotten used to any of this.

By the time Dr. McConnell left ten minutes later, they knew she was okay with Julia trying to delivery normally in this room, but to be aware that she could get rushed to surgery on a moment's notice if things went south with either baby.

With that, all they had to do was wait.

Well, that was all he had to do. Julia did all the work.

He tried to keep her mind off the discomfort. When they were alone, he told her about the new plan for the sitcom. She loved it and even had a few great ideas of her own for later in the season.

"Have you decided on names for the babies?" He hadn't convinced himself to ask sooner, but he'd been curious.

"No. Not yet."

"Do you have any ideas? Family members to honor, maybe?"

"I already named Alex after my grandfather and look where that got me."

"Good point, but that won't be an issue. It shouldn't have been an issue then."

She gave him a weak half-smile. "You've come a long way if you're able to say that and mean it."

"I have." The guilt sliced through him. "And something I haven't done is really apologize for all the things I said and thought last spring." He brought her hand up and kissed the back of it. "I'm sorry for the things I said, which weren't usually all that bad but a bit snarky at best, and the things I thought, which were worse."

"Thank you." Her eyes closed, and he glanced over at the machines to see a contraction spiking. "I know that wasn't easy for you."

"A lot easier than I thought it would be," he admitted. "Because the better I get to know you, the more I know none of that was true." He sighed. How to explain himself better? "I knew, on an intellectual level, that the accusations weren't true, but I didn't know, not for sure, that you wouldn't have done it if you'd had the chance. Does that make sense?"

She nodded, but didn't say anything.

He needed to make sure she understood. "Now that I know you, not only do I know intellectually that it wasn't you six months ago, but I know it's something you'd never do, even if you had the chance. It wouldn't have occurred to you to try to blackmail my brother, to claim he's Alex's father even though he's not, any of that. Even if he had been Alex's father, you wouldn't have blackmailed him, and you wouldn't have kept his son away from him all those years, either."

"I never kept Alex from his father, you know." Her eyes stayed closed. "He chose to disappear a long time ago. I didn't even know where he was when I heard he died. I haven't heard from his family in years." She hesitated. "Except for all the other weird implications, I almost wish the duke was his father, because your brother wouldn't have taken off. Or you were his father. That would be better."

Was it the drugs talking? Did epidurals make you all high like some strong pain medicines did?

Regardless, Topher knew what he wanted to give her for Christmas. Could he pull it off? He'd have to talk to Jonathan as soon as possible. If nothing else, he'd have the necessary contacts to get Topher started.

"I wish he was my son, too." The words surprised him. Not the sentiment. It had been growing for a while. But that he actually told her. "I wouldn't mind if you were Bailey's mother, either."

She didn't reply, but her grip on his hand tightened. He checked - another contraction.

"Do they still hurt?" They shouldn't, should they? Wasn't that the whole point of the epidural?

"Not really. I can still feel them. It's uncomfortable, but not really painful."

"Good."

Before they could get back to the previous conversation, the nurse came back in to check and see how Julia was doing. She'd been in and out the whole time.

"So I've got good news and bad news," she told them, and Topher felt his heart stop. "But not too bad. It's time for me to go home, so I'm going to turn you over to Laurie. She's incredible and the nurse I'd want if I was giving birth." She patted Julia on the knee. "Seriously. She's phenomenal and has kind of become our go-to gal for twins when she's here."

"Thank you for everything," Julia told her, shifting a bit on the bed.

"She'll be in to check on you again in a bit. If you need anything before then, just push the button."

"We will," Topher promised. "Thank you."

Then the two of them were alone again.

Julia shifted again, trying to get comfortable. "Tell me a story of some kind, would you? I don't care what. Maybe how you see this first season going. If you could write it however you wanted, what would that look like?"

The thoughts had been tumbling over in his head all day, so he started to tell the story. Three contractions in, she gripped his hand even tighter.

"What is it?"

"Something's not right," she whispered, the anguish evident in her voice. "I don't know what it is, but something feels really weird."

Dread filled him as he fumbled for the call button. *Please God,* was all he could manage, but it would be enough.

Chapter Twenty-Five

Everything around her had finally quieted down as Julia leaned back against the pillows. Exhausted, but happy. Scared, but thrilled.

And unsure what she would have done without Topher's support.

The births hadn't been overly difficult, at least not according to Julia's doctor, but she was worn out.

"How are they?" she asked Laurie as the nurse fixed the blanket.

"They're fine," Laurie reassured her. "They're getting cleaned up and weighed and all of those good things."

Julia had held one for several minutes before it was time to deliver the second. She'd then held both of them as long as the nurses would let her.

"Do I need to nurse them?"

"In a few minutes, as long as they're maintaining their body temperature. As little as they are, and even though they're otherwise healthy, it's possible they'll have some trouble keeping their temperatures up."

Topher took Julia's hand and cradled it in both of his. "They're fine, love."

That was new.

But she liked it.

Her eyes started to drift closed. "Can I rest then? Will you wake me?"

"Of course, honey." Laurie patted her shoulder. "It's the middle of the night. Rest is what you all need."

Julia let her mind drift. When she'd told Topher something didn't feel right, he'd called the nurse immediately. Laurie had hurried in, and then, like a NASCAR pit crew, assorted others had come to prepare the room for delivery, followed closely by her doctor.

Everything happened so fast, Julia was sure she'd never remember all of it.

She drifted and dozed for a while, though she didn't know how long. She knew Topher stayed next to her for a while, but he also spent time next to the babies.

His daughters.

He'd claimed them from the beginning, even cutting both cords.

He'd taken care of everything afterward. Calling his mom and telling her he'd let her know when the time came to bring the other kids up. Texting his brother as well as a few of her friends who would want to know. Kenzie had replied in no time.

"Hey."

She startled awake when Topher shook her shoulder. "Huh?"

"The babies are ready to eat. Laurie's going to help you down here, then they're going to take us up to the post-partum floor."

He sat nearby and snuggled Twin B while Laurie helped her nurse Twin A. Then they traded.

Both babies were beautiful. A little wrinkled and red. Smaller than Alex had been.

"How big were they?" she asked Laurie.

"This little girl here was five pounds, ten ounces. Her big sister is older by eighteen minutes and bigger by six ounces. She's six pounds even. Good sizes for twins this age."

"Good." Almost twelve pounds of baby. Julia couldn't quite wrap her head around that.

Another half hour passed before they started moving upstairs. Laurie and two orderlies went with them, one pushing her and one pushing Twin B, while Laurie took care of Twin A.

They needed names. Soon.

She had no ideas.

They went in a transport elevator, but only one floor up, the door opened and someone tried to get them to leave.

"No. Sorry!" Laurie pushed door closed button repeatedly. "Babies with temperature issues!" The doors slid shut. "There are priorities on the elevators," she explained. "Pretty much nothing is more important than babies having some issues controlling their temperature. Your little ones aren't too bad, but I'm not taking any chances with them, either. Not after how long it took the elevator to show up."

Before Julia could thank her, the door opened again, and this time they moved out.

By the time everything settled down, Julia was more than ready for sleep, but the babies needed to eat again. They were holding their own in the temperature department for the time being, but the staff still didn't want them out from under the warmers for too long.

Julia did her best to keep her modesty intact as one of her new nurses helped her with Twin A.

"Would skin-to-skin contact help with this one's temperature?" Topher asked the nurse.

She smiled at him. "It sure couldn't hurt, Mr. Bayfield."

Apparently, that was all he needed to hear. He laid the baby back in the bassinet, stripped off his shirt, then unwrapped her blankets and took her hospital t-shirt off. He gently picked her up to cradle her against his now-bare chest. With one hand, he covered her with the blankets he'd discarded then sat back down in the rocking chair.

"We're gonna snuggle, baby girl," he whispered loud enough to be heard. "She's doing that thing where she looks for food," he said louder.

"Rooting," the nurse explained. "She'll get her turn in a minute. We won't try nursing both at the same time just yet."

Julia wasn't sure she was ready for that anyway.

After trading and feeding the other baby, the nurse left the four of them alone for a few minutes.

"I think I have names," Julia blurted out. They'd been hovering just out of reach, but had finally come to the forefront.

"You have?" He only glanced up from where his gaze rested on Twin A.

"Unless you think there's a problem with it..." She nodded toward him. "...that's Anna Leigh, like your mom, but backwards and a little different. I think we should call her Annie."

"I like it." He kissed the cap on top of the baby's head. "Hi, Anna Leigh. Your grandmother is going to love that." Another glance up. "And her little sister?"

"Marissa. I don't have a middle name for her yet."

"Why Marissa?"

"Because the queen was so incredibly kind to me when she could have been mean and nasty. Marissa was her mother's name and is one of hers. If you think she'll be okay with it. That she wouldn't want to use the name herself for one of her own children." Julia was suddenly uncertain.

Topher just smiled and reached for his phone. "Why don't we find out? They should be awake by now."

Before he could dial, the phone buzzed. He swiped his thumb across and hit a button.

"Hey, brother. Good morning."

The duke chuckled over the speaker phone. "Good morning, indeed. Are you going to tell me about my new nieces or nephews?"

"Depends. Is your wife around? Can you put her on speaker?"

"Sure." He sounded puzzled, but a moment later they were both on the line. "Now spill it."

"You have two new nieces." The pride was evident in Topher's voice, as though they *were* his daughters. "Anna

Leigh, after Mom, is the oldest. Mom doesn't know yet, though," he warned. "We'll tell her later."

"She'll love it." Alexander's smile was evident through the phone.

But now the more important question. Julia tried not to hold her breath as Topher shifted, holding the baby closer.

"There's one thing we wanted to ask you about." Topher leaned closer to the phone, holding his new daughter tightly to his chest.

"What's that?"

He glanced over at Julia to see her looking at the baby in her arms. "Julia wants to name the other baby Marissa, after your mother and you, Christiana. Before it becomes official, though, we wanted to check with you."

The silence on the other end was surely because they were surprised, in a good way. He hoped.

"I would be honored, Julia, Christopher." The crack in Christiana's voice could be heard halfway around the world. "I am certain my mother would be pleased as well."

"Then Marissa it is."

"Do you have a middle name picked out?" Alexander asked.

Topher looked over at Julia, who swiped a tear off her cheek.

"Louise," she said. "After my grandmother, and it's my mom's middle name, too. Marissa Louise."

"I like it," Topher told her as she snuggled the little girl close.

"Get some rest, you four." Alexander's voice came through the phone. "It's still the middle of the night there. We'll talk to you soon."

They hung up, and he settled back in the rocker. "Anna Leigh Bayfield, Marissa Louise Bayfield, welcome to the world." He kissed the knit cap covering the little bit of hair on Annie's head.

Julia had a long conversation with her parents about the babies. They were coming for Thanksgiving. His parents and Ida Mae brought Alex and Bailey up. They were both completely taken with their new sisters.

"What are their names, Mom?" Alex sat in the rocking chair. "Who's older?"

"That is Marissa Louise," Topher told him. "She's younger."

"Then who's this?" Mom sat on the couch and held Bailey, who held the other baby.

Topher looked over at Julia. "Why don't you tell her?"

Julia took a deep breath. "That's Anna Leigh. If that's okay with you."

Mom's eyes went wide as she looked back and forth between them. "Really? Anna Leigh?"

Topher nodded. "We're going to call her Annie."

"I'm honored." She leaned over and kissed Annie's head. "Hi, Annie."

"How will we tell them apart?" Alex asked. "They're both little and look *exactly* the same."

Topher wasn't quite sure that was right, but Alex had a point. "We're not sure yet, bud. For now, we check their hospital bracelets. Maybe you and Bailey can help us come up with another way for when we get home."

The two kids promised to think of a way and left a short time later.

The next two days passed in a bit of a haze. He could only imagine what they were like for Julia. By the time they were released to go home, they hadn't come up with a solution, except to possibly dress them in different colors - or leave their hospital bracelets on as long as possible.

Topher put the SUV in park in front of the hospital. Julia sat in a wheelchair with one of the babies on her lap in the car seat. Someone else carried the other car seat. He hopped out and helped fit the car seats into their bases while Julia climbed into the front seat.

As he pulled out from under the overhang, Julia turned to look at the car seats. "I never understood moms sitting in the back seat as they drive home. The baby doesn't know. But I feel like I should be back there."

"The babies will be fine until we get home." He turned onto the freeway.

"I know they're sleeping, but what if they wake up? It's a long drive."

"It's not that far." But he did press the gas pedal a little harder. "How're you feeling?"

"Tired." She leaned her head against the side window. "I got a few hours of sleep but not that much."

Topher hadn't either, but he wasn't coming off a major physical trauma. He reached over and took her hand. "Mom and I will do whatever we can with the babies so you can get some rest."

"I don't want to bottle feed them, though. Not yet. Not if

we don't have to. I want them to be better nursers first."

"I know." That was about all he knew. He'd picked that much up from listening to her conversations with the nurses, but didn't really understand the whole thing. He just knew he needed to help however he could.

When he glanced over again, she was dozing off against the window. Not great sleep but a bit anyway.

Everyone waited on the front step for them when they pulled up. Bailey and Alex both jumped up and down as he and the newly-awakened Julia separated the car seats from their bases. Topher carried both of them inside while Julia took the steps slowly.

Once inside, Mom insisted on pictures with the whole family sitting on the couch, then some of Bailey and Alex in the big chair with each of them holding one of their sisters.

Julia tried to make his mom promise not to post the ones of the family anywhere the tabloids might get a hold of them.

"Why not?" She seemed genuinely puzzled. "You look fantastic."

"I haven't slept in three days," Julia pointed out. "I've barely brushed my hair since the babies were born much less put any makeup on."

"She's right, though," Topher told her. "I know you probably don't feel like it, but you look great. You could easily be one of those women who show other women that it's okay to be natural and normal, and that it's okay to not look like the women they all want to look like."

His mom glared at him. "I don't think you're helping, Topher." She sat down next to Julia. "I think what my son is trying to say is that there are always these celebrity moms who post pictures of themselves not long after birth, and no one feels like they can live up to those pictures. But they forget to tell the world they had a team of makeup artists and professional photographers and all sorts of tricks to make them look better than they normally do. You look like a new mom. Tired, but happy, and beautiful. It's obvious there's no filter, and that's okay."

"Isn't there a no filter hashtag?" Topher asked. "That's what I was talking about."

Julia finally nodded. "Can I at least brush my hair and change into something a little nicer?"

Topher thought his Serenity Landing High t-shirt looked just fine and told her so. His mom agreed, but told her to grab her hair brush.

A few minutes later, he sat in the big chair. Julia snuggled close to him. The love seat might have been a bit better, but he liked being this close to her. Mom directed Alex to sit on the arm of the chair next to him. Bailey sat on the other side. He and Julia each held one of the babies. She snapped a few pictures then had the older kids climb down to take a few of just the four of them.

Topher needed some time to process all of this. How he'd gone from being unable to stand this woman just a couple months earlier to holding his daughters, though they didn't have a bit of his DNA. Little Annie gripped his finger as she slept, oblivious to what was going on around her.

Right now, he wanted to be nowhere else, to think about nothing else but how his heart was suddenly wrapped up in twelve pounds of baby, their mother, her son, and a daughter he'd only just met.

Chapter Twenty-Six

Julia yawned and agreed to let Topher post the picture the next morning. The haters would find something wrong no matter what. Either she had professionals come help her, like Claire had for their first family photo shoot, and people claimed she wasn't authentic, or she'd be authentic, and people would give her a hard time for not looking perfect.

Whatever.

She kept her personal Facebook just that, personal. The only people on there should be people she could trust. Topher's Facebook was the same way, but his public page...

Well, it was public. She'd do well to avoid it and let him read her any comments he thought she should hear.

By the time pictures were done, the babies needed to be fed. Leigh Ann came upstairs with her and helped her get situated to feed both babies at the same time. The nurses had helped her get started and swore it would be a time saver.

Leigh Ann took over as the babies finished. She shooed a grateful Julia to bed before changing diapers and wrapping them back up in their swaddling blankets.

"Get some rest, sweetie." She laid first Annie then Rissa in their bassinets. "I'll keep the monitor with me. Just holler if you need something."

"Thanks, Leigh Ann."

"My pleasure," the other woman whispered as she left.

Julia drifted to sleep, wishing it would last longer than a couple hours at most.

The next week was more of the same. A seemingly never-ending cycle of feedings, diaper changes, naps, and trying to fit some time in with her son, Bailey, and even Topher before time to do it all over again. Instead of two hats or even three a day, she managed to knit two in a week's time.

The week after the girls were born, Kenzie and the Show Me Yarn ladies were over to finalize their schedules for the weekend.

"I'm going to be there as much as I can," Julia promised. She and Kenzie were the only two manning their side of the booth.

"Jonathan knows a lot more than he used to," Kenzie pointed out. "He's not taking actual shifts, but he'll be there quite a bit."

"I used to be quite the yarn buff, too."

All of them turned to see Leigh Ann walking down the stairs with Annie in her arms.

"You did?" Julia asked.

"I did. I'm happy to help out as much as I can. Perhaps

between myself and Kenzie's husband, we'll make a whole person who knows what they're talking about." Leigh Ann handed the baby off to Kenzie, who was more than happy to take Annie.

Julia grinned at the twinkle in her mother-in-law's eyes. Everyone else laughed, too. Then Kenzie took back over the meeting.

"Lady Margaret will be here tomorrow afternoon. Jonathan and I will pick her up at the airport. She's staying in the apartment at our house. We have strict instructions that she is not to be disturbed at all. Times have been prearranged or will be for us to meet her to transport her to the show. Meals are prepared and in the fridge. They just need to be warmed up."

"Isn't she like 80?" Julia asked. "She doesn't have an aide or anything to help her?"

Kenzie shrugged. "I guess not."

"So what do you need from us?" Julia yawned as she asked the question.

"When it's your turn to be her assistant, make sure she has water. Keep an eye out for unauthorized cameras in the room."

"No pictures?" Leigh Anne asked. "Is that odd?"

"A little." Julia shifted in her chair. Was it nap time yet? How would she make it through the next several days? "But some presenters don't like it. She's a little more stringent than most, though."

"She's elderly," Kenzie went on. "She may need help up or down stairs, though supposedly she's quite strong and not frail at all. She is, however, intensely personal. She doesn't like small talk. No questions about her, her family, anything like that."

Kenzie went over the rest of the rules with them. Basically, help her without being intrusive. Julia could do that. If she got some sleep.

"We'll be setting up tomorrow evening. The weather isn't supposed to get bad until Sunday evening. It's Missouri weather, though, so who knows. We should be disassembled and home by then. I don't know about you guys, but I will have started my mad dash to Thanksgiving by the time Lady Margaret leaves town Sunday evening."

Thanksgiving? Julia had managed to forget that was coming up. Bed rest and twins would do that. She glanced over at Leigh Ann who smiled as though she had it all under control. Julia needed to call her folks, too. They'd mentioned coming next week, but Julia hadn't put two and two together.

The meeting broke up and, after seeing everyone off, Julia found Leigh Ann in the kitchen. "I forgot all about Thanksgiving. I've never done a big Thanksgiving meal ever."

Leigh Ann wiped her hands on a kitchen towel. "I figured it was too much to add to your plate. It's under control. I've talked with your mom a couple times. They were going to come Tuesday or Wednesday, but with the babies here, they're coming Monday. That was the earliest they could leave."

Julia blinked. "You've talked to her more recently than I have then."

"Earlier today," Leigh Ann confirmed.

Julia wasn't sure how she felt about that, but then she shrugged it off and decided she was glad they worked it out without her. One less thing for her to have to worry about.

The rest of the evening and the next day were spent getting ready for the yarn show, taking care of the twins, and trying to get some rest in preparation for the big weekend ahead.

By five the next evening, Julia carried the first of their things in to the conference center.

"Where is our booth?" Julia asked as she followed her friend. Topher and Jonathan were emptying the SUVs. With Kenzie's pregnancy, and Julia being recently postpartum, they weren't allowed to do much of anything themselves.

Kenzie scanned the map in her hand. "I'm not sure this is right." She twisted the map this way and that, trying to figure it out. Kenzie handed Julia another piece of paper. "What booth number are we?"

Julia scanned the paper. "Booth 205. Where is that?"

Tucking a piece of hair behind her ear, Kenzie held out the map and pointed to a square. "Does this look like 205 to you?"

Squinting, Julia leaned in closer to the page. "Looks like it to me. Is that right next to the concession stand and classrooms?"

"I guess so." Kenzie looked around to orient herself. "This way."

"Did we pay for a booth so close?" Julia didn't think they had. She didn't think they could afford to, even with the Show Me Yarn ladies splitting the cost.

"I didn't think so. I took whatever she offered," Kenzie confirmed. "No one said anything about it being a prime location."

Julia shrugged. "Oh, well. I guess if she tries to come back and charge us for it, that's why we have husbands with lawyers?"

"I guess."

They found the booth, looked around, trying to figure out

the best way to set it up and be fair to both them and the Show Me Yarn people. While they talked it out, Topher and Jonathan showed up, with the other women not far behind.

With the men moving everything around, it didn't take long to get things the way they wanted them. Once the tables and shelves were set up, Topher and Jonathan, along with the other husbands, went back outside to start bringing product in.

Julia stood back and looked at the still–empty booth. It was a start.

Topher wiped his forehead with the back of his hand. The conference center was far warmer than outside. He hoisted another tub and asked Julia where she wanted it.

"What is in all of these tubs?" She put her hands on her hips and looked around. "I don't remember having this much."

He popped open the top. "These are the bags you had cut out but not sewn before you ended up on bed rest."

"Who finished them?"

Topher close the lid again. "Mom and I worked on them quite a bit. Kenzie helped some, too."

"You know how to sew?" Julia's voice sounded about like most people's did when they discovered his hidden talent.

"Mom taught both of us when we were kids. She said it was a skill that would come in handy at the most unusual times. She wasn't wrong." He cocked an eyebrow at her. "I do kind of wish you'd asked me for help though."

Julia opened the tub and pulled out one of the bags. "Did

you do this one, or did your mom?"

Topher took it from her. "Pretty sure this is one of mine."

She took it back and turned it over, her critical eye taking in all of it. "If I'd had any idea you could do this, you can bet I would have asked for your help." Julia looked up at him, tears in her eyes. "Thank you, Topher. It means a lot to me that you would do this."

He took a step closer to her and took the bag from her hands, tossing it into the tub. He framed her face with his hands, his thumbs brushing the tears from her cheeks. "Hey. What's this for?"

She sniffled. "I'm postpartum and found out you did this really sweet thing for me. Of course I'm crying."

Topher pulled her into his arms and kissed the top of her head. "It was my pleasure, honestly." He hadn't hugged her since the babies were born. It felt different, closer, without the baby bump in the way.

Julia wrapped her arms around his waist and rested her head on his chest. They stood there for several minutes until the sounds of people around them grew louder, and he let her go.

Julia turned to Jonathan. "Do you know anything about how we got such a great spot?"

"I had nothing to do with it." Jonathan held up three fingers. "Scouts honor. Just like I had nothing to do with you guys being asked to assist Lady Margaret this weekend."

Julia spun on her heel to face Kenzie. "How did it go when you guys picked her up?"

Kenzie shrugged. "You have to ask my husband. I didn't go with them after all."

Jonathan rested his hands on Kenzie's shoulders. "I told

you, sweetheart, she requested just myself and the driver meet her at the airport. You'll have plenty of time to observe her this weekend."

Kenzie's head fell forward as Jonathan rubbed her shoulders. "I know, but still. And now you're going to be working part of the weekend."

Jonathan looked around to see if anyone else was nearby, then leaned towards Topher and Julia. "Lady Margaret isn't my only client from Mevendia here this weekend. I can't say more than that though."

Topher guessed he was talking about a member of the royal family then. He knew his friend had worked with the Montevarian family many times, as well as the Ravenzarian family. In fact, when Ander's brother-in-law, Prince Nicklaus, had taken off and ended up in St. Louis, Jonathan's men who had found him. They took him back to Jonathan's house until he went home.

He also knew Jonathan wouldn't divulge the identity of his guest. Topher was surprised he had said that much. It also meant Topher would need to make sure he and Mom were here more than they had planned. Ida Mae would take care of Bailey and Alex for the next few days. Claire knew he was unavailable for the weekend unless an unavoidable emergency occurred.

The pilot episode had finally been written, and they'd started plotting out the story arcs for the whole season. They both loved how well the accidental marriage fit in with the feel of the show. The Chris character dealt not only with being a new father, but being a new husband.

The Show Me Yarn ladies and their husbands returned.

Topher needed to learn their names before the weekend ended. Under the direction of Julia and Kenzie, he and Jonathan helped arrange the product.

They didn't finish until after seven. His mom had brought the babies up to eat. An office had been set aside for Julia to use throughout the weekend. Jonathan had even arranged it so whoever had the babies would be able to park near the building and come in a back entrance. Fortunately, the girls had settled into an every-four-hour pattern. Mama Beach had offered to help as well. Topher suspected she just wanted the chance to rock the babies. Whatever her motivation, they weren't going to turn down the help this weekend. He would have to make sure she got a nice Christmas present this year.

By the time they got home, the babies were ready to eat again. Julia took care of them, while Topher spent some time with his daughter and stepson. As he listened to Alex read them a book he made a mental note to contact Daniel, his lawyer, about adoption for both kids. More and more, he wanted this marriage for the long haul, but he didn't know how Julia felt.

Annie and Marissa were legally his daughters, no matter what the biology might say. He felt as fiercely protective of them as he'd ever felt of anyone.

Maybe the time had come to start fighting for his family.

Chapter Twenty-Seven

Morning came too early. Julia sipped the only cup of coffee she'd let herself have as she tried to look coherent. Their group of five, and their assistants in the form of spouses and in-laws, had been called into a meeting before the day got started.

Topher rested his hand on her back, and she was grateful for the support. He'd been incredibly solicitous, even more than usual, since he put the older two kids to bed the night before. She wondered briefly why, but had too much else going on in her head to spend much time on it. She also knew he'd been up late working in his office many nights in the last few weeks.

"Where's the meeting?" Topher opened the door for her.

"In the room where they said I could nurse." Not technically, but close enough. The small office connected via a door off the larger room. That's where she'd be nursing.

Inside the room, everyone waited except Kenzie and Jonathan. No one else knew any more than she did, which was pretty much nothing. Since this was the group that would be helping Lady Margaret, she figured it had something to do with that.

Her suspicions were confirmed when the door opened and an elderly woman walked in, followed by Kenzie and Jonathan. The meeting was basically just a chance for all of them to meet Lady Margaret and for her to meet them, so she'd know who would be with her. Kenzie had the first shift, so Julia headed for the booth with Topher and Leigh Ann, trailing behind the ladies from Show Me Yarn.

"Topher?" She stopped before getting to the booth.

He stopped while Leigh Ann went on. "What's up?"

"We don't need the money from this show, do we?" She hurried on. "I mean, I'd thought about putting most of it back into the business, after I pay Kenzie back what I owe her, but Kenzie was telling me about a group last night, and I'd like to donate it instead. But that means I'd need money from somewhere else to replenish everything."

"That's up to you. We can either make a donation from 'family funds' or donate the money from here and replenish stock from personal money. Whatever works. I'd like to check the charity out first, though."

"Ask Jonathan about that. I know he has." She took a deep breath and glanced at the clock on the wall over the concession stands. Ten minutes before the doors opened. "It's a group called FreedomWorks. They work with trafficked women in India. They make what's called fabric yarn. They take fabric, cut it into strips, and dye it. Then they package it to sell. But these women, even if they want out of the lifestyle they've been brought up in, need a vocation to even hope to break the chains. This gives them that and gives hope." Tears filled her eyes. "I read a little bit about it, and our girls, all three of them, would have little chance to break out of that bondage if they'd been born into it. Someone else's little girl needs a chance to be free of the sex trade."

The tears overflowed, and Topher pulled her into his arms. "Hey. It's okay. I'll talk to Jonathan and, if everything's on the up and up, we'll donate. I'm sure it is, but I need to make sure. Too many scams have hit me up for money before, that's all."

She nodded against him and swallowed more sniffles. "Okay." Julia moved back and swiped at the moisture on her cheeks. "Let's go do this."

The plight of the women had been on her mind since Kenzie mentioned it the night before. As she rocked her babies, she thought about the women on the other side of the world, who had no choice in what they or their daughters would become.

In moments, the doors opened, and people began to stream in. It didn't take long for a few to stop by their booth. Being near the front doors was definitely a major change for them. At a show this size, it could take half of forever for people to start making their way toward the back of the room where Julia had expected to be.

Before she knew it, she'd sold a pattern along with some of Kenzie's yarn. Then another. Then a couple of bags and a bunch more of Kenzie's yarn. She worked almost non-stop until she felt her phone buzz, and she looked for her husband.

Her eyes narrowed as she saw a woman standing a touch

too close to him. To his credit, he leaned as far away as he could without being rude, but she was definitely in his space.

Her claws came out as she crossed the booth. "Honey?"

His deer-in-the-headlights look would have been comical if it weren't for the glare from the other woman. "Yes?"

"I just got a text from the nanny." Mama Beach kind of counted as a nanny, didn't she? "The babies are here and ready to nurse. She thought they'd like to see you, too, though."

He managed to maneuver around the woman and to her side. Slipping an arm around her waist. "Go ahead. I'm going to help this woman..."

"Bess," the woman interjected.

"...this woman with this bag then I'll be right there." His face suddenly lit up. "Mom!"

Julia turned to see Leigh Ann wave as a customer walked off.

"Mom," Topher continued. "Could you help this young lady find the smaller bag in the ladybug material? I know we made a couple of them, but the girls are here, and I'd like to go see them."

Leigh Ann smiled and moved between them and Bess. "Of course. I know right where those bags are. Go on and find your babies."

As they left the booth, he leaned down. "Sorry. She wouldn't back off."

"I know." It surprised her how secure she was in his fidelity. Not just because Duke Alexander had told the press repeatedly that men in his family did not cheat, but because of *Topher*. Even more secure than she was a few weeks earlier when the pictures with Claire came out. "Is it bad that I wish she didn't want ladybugs? Ladybugs go with Bailey, not that woman."

He chuckled and opened the door to the off-limits area. "I completely understand. Now, where are those babies?"

A sense of relief washed over Topher as they walked back into the room where they'd met Lady Margaret earlier. He hated women like Bess. Ones who thought they knew him based on a character he played years earlier. At least he'd never played a character he'd be too ashamed to be in real life.

Mama Beach was already in the room with two baby girls starting to squirm and look for their mom. Mama Beach went with Julia into the side office. Jonathan and Kenzie were both working the booth with his mom. One of the other women was in with Lady Margaret. Julia would be taking the next class. Then it would be her turn to assist.

Topher decided sit for a few minutes to give Bess time to finish and leave, and then he'd head back out to the floor.

Before he could, the door opened. Jonathan stood to the side to allow a well-dressed man about the same age as them to walk in first.

"We have about fifteen minutes before she should arrive," Jonathan was saying. "Topher, I didn't realize you two were in here. Is Julia with the babies?"

Topher nodded toward the office door. "She's in there with Mama Beach. I'm getting away from a too-forward woman."

The other two men winced.

Jonathan half-turned. "Prince William, have you met Duke Alexander's brother?"

That's why he looked familiar. Topher stood and held out a hand. "I think we may have met in passing once or twice."

The Mevendian prince shook his hand. "Good to see you again, Christopher."

"Call me Topher."

"Did I hear something about babies?"

Topher nodded. "My wife just had twins a week ago, but she really wanted to be here this weekend. She worked hard to get ready for this show. We don't live far, so friends and family are helping out."

"Congratulations."

Before the prince could say anything else, the main door opened again. The tallest of the Show Me Yarn women held the door open for Lady Margaret.

The elderly woman stopped in her tracks when she saw the prince. She inclined her head his direction. "Your Royal Highness."

He held out his hand. She let him take her gloved one. The prince leaned over and kissed the back of it.

"When I heard you were in town, I knew I needed to say hello, and thank you for your hard work preserving and passing on the Mevendian art form."

Topher wondered if the prince had any clue what she actually taught.

Lady Margaret gave a demure smile, but didn't say anything back. She walked slowly past the prince and sat in the chair reserved for her.

The door to the other room opened letting Julia and Mama Beach out, each with a baby in their arms.

"These are the beautiful babies I have heard about?" Lady

Margaret asked in her accented English.

Julia smiled and walked toward Lady Margaret. "This is Marissa Louise. She's named after the current and former queens of Ravenzario." She turned toward Mama Beach. "And this is Anna Leigh, after Topher's mother."

Topher moved a folding chair so Julia could sit next to Lady Margaret. She sat down so the other woman could see Marissa.

"May I hold her?"

The woman might be elderly, and she clearly retained her strength, bu the thought made Topher unreasonably nervous.

Julia nestled the baby into Lady Margaret's arms. The other woman cuddled Marissa close before pressing a kiss to the baby's forehead.

"She's beautiful," Lady Margaret whispered. "Simply beautiful."

"Do you have any children?" Julia asked.

For a long moment, Lady Margaret stared at Marissa. "A son. Once."

Topher didn't know how to respond, and no one else did either. What could have happened to cause such sadness when she mentioned her child?

A switch seemed to flip in Lady Margaret, and she handed Marissa back to Julia. She looked to Topher. "Would you be so kind as to get me a glass of water?"

Before Topher could do so, someone else had handed her a bottle.

A few minutes of small talk later, the "handler" for Lady Margaret had been replaced, and Julia joined the two of them heading for the classroom.

Topher said good-bye to Mama Beach and the babies.

Jonathan and Prince William were deep in conversation, so Topher left them and went back to the floor. Fortunately, Bess was long gone, and no other woman seemed to be paying special attention to him.

He joined his mother, Kenzie, and two of the Show Me Yarn women in the booth. It didn't take long for it to become clear that he didn't know nearly enough about any of this stuff, but he was learning. Several of the women, mostly grandma types, made him feel good about learning more than he ever wanted to know about something because it was important to his wife.

Nearly three hours later, when he finally saw her again, but her face glowed.

"How was the class?"

"Fantastic." She put her bag under one of the tables. "I learned a lot and taking it a second time, even though I was technically Lady Margaret's assistant, helped, too. I took lots of notes the first time then watched her closely the second time."

"That's great." Before they could talk further, a crowd of customers walked up. One after another. That's how the rest of the day went, and Topher got a crash course in all things yarn. They didn't make it home until nearly eight, and it just about time for the older kids to go to bed.

As much as he wanted to spend more time with them, he needed some quality time with his pillow just as badly. After hugs, kisses, and a short bedtime story, he headed into his room and without bothering to even change his clothes, he collapsed on the bed and fell into a deep sleep.

Chapter Twenty-Eight

Julia didn't want to admit to anyone just how taxing the day had been. Learning from Lady Margaret had been wonderful, but the timing was awful. She'd barely been able to keep her eyes open during either session she'd been in, but especially the second one when she'd already been through it once. Even paying close attention hadn't been quite enough. At one point, she'd even missed that Lady Margaret needed her water refilled until the woman sitting next to Julia nudged her and pointed it out.

Nursing the babies coincided with their arrival home. By the time she finished, Topher had put Alex and Bailey to bed, though she'd managed to get a hug from both of them.

Leigh Ann took Annie from Julia. "Why don't you get some rest, sweetie? I know you're tired."

"Where's Topher?" She tried to hide a yawn and failed

miserably. "I need to talk to him for a minute."

"I don't know. He went upstairs with the kids right after you got home, and I haven't seen him since."

"I wonder if he's in his office," she thought out loud, laying Marissa in the bassinet in the living room.

"I don't think so. I know he stayed up late working last night, but he hasn't come back downstairs."

Julia turned to look at her. "Up late?"

"You didn't notice when you got up with the babies?" Leigh Ann snuggled Annie into her shoulder. "I think he was writing the second episode of *Seating for Six* until two or three last night."

How hadn't she noticed? Had the other side of the bed really been empty that late? Had he slept with her every night since the babies were born? Her muddled mind couldn't quite keep up with everything. She'd made it through the day but not much more.

And in just a few hours she'd get to do it all over again.

"I think I'm going to take the girls and go to bed," she told her mother-in-law. "I'm beat."

"I'll bring Annie."

Julia picked up Marissa and followed Leigh Ann, who stopped at the bottom of the stairs and turned.

"I know you want to nurse the babies, and I know you haven't had a chance to pump anything yet, but if you decide to give them a little bit of formula here and there, it would be okay." Worry lines creased Leigh Ann's brow. "I'm worried about you both."

"I'll be fine. If I can get through Sunday, I'm going to collapse next week." Julia had to convince herself of that. "If you and Mom don't mind me not helping get ready for Thanksgiving, that is."

"We expect nothing from you, but you have to make it to Sunday, and it's only Thursday. Today, bringing the babies up there wasn't the easiest thing, but it worked. Why don't you let me take them tonight? At least let me take this shift. There's formula in the kitchen and bottles. I'll feed them in a few hours and you can get the one after that. Next week, when things calm down, you can go back to nursing full time."

A war waged inside of Julia. It felt like giving up. Like admitting she couldn't do it all. That she couldn't take care of her babies.

But she was exhausted.

"You won't do anyone any good if you burn out before you get to Sunday." Leigh Ann's gentle tone did far more convicting than yelling ever could. "Get some sleep."

Julia finally nodded. "Okay. But if they won't take the bottles, please come get me?"

"Of course. James is already upstairs. Let's go lay the babies on our bed, and I'll send him down for the playpen. When we get the babies settled, I'll come back for everything else. Trust us, sweetie. This is what grandparents are for."

As they started up the stairs, Julia pondered that statement. Her parents had been just a few miles away when Alex was born, but they'd adamantly stayed away and let her handle it all on her own. They'd been right to, she knew that looking back. Given the option, she would have let her parents become parents to Alex instead of being his mother like she needed to be. But things had changed.

So this was new. Letting Leigh Ann take care of the babies,

and therefore her, was nice. And different. She was more grown up. Not looking for a way out like she would have been with Alex.

James left to get the playpen as Julia kissed Marissa's forehead and laid her down on the bed. She took Annie from Leigh Ann and snuggled her for a moment then kissed her, too.

"Thank you," she whispered to Leigh Ann as she laid Annie next to her sister. "I appreciate it."

Leigh Ann rubbed a hand up and down Julia's back. "It's what I'm here for, why both of us are here. Now go get some sleep."

Julia gave her a quick hug then, after another long look at the babies, left the room. Once in the master bedroom, she realized what had happened to Topher.

His feet hung off the bed, shoes still in place, as he slept cross ways. She slipped into the bathroom to brush her teeth and change. Once back in their room, she managed to get his shoes off without much fuss then tossed a blanket over him. Maneuvering her pillow to the side, she laid across the top of the bed and let sleep claim her.

Dreams of being loved by the man in the bed with her danced through her mind. Even in the netherworld where dreams exist, she knew she had to keep her distance, but somehow, each dream ended with her in his arms.

Until the last one.

They were fighting, though she didn't know what about.

But before it could be resolved, someone shook her awake.

In the moonlight, she could see Topher's face, his eyes wide and scared.

"Where are the babies?" he demanded.

"What?" Julia couldn't make sense of his words.

"The babies are gone. Where are they?"

Her stomach dropped. What?

Topher's heart still hadn't started beating again, not when Julia wouldn't reply to his question. "Where are the babies?"

She blinked slowly, her mind clearly trying to process the information. "Your mom doesn't have them?"

"Mom?" What was she talking about?

"Your mom took the babies tonight. She's going to try to give them a bottle, so I could get some sleep. You, too. We're both exhausted."

His heart restarted and his shoulders slumped. "Thank God."

"Did you think something had happened to them?"

He shifted and sat on the bed. "I don't know. The middle of the night, who knows what goes through your mind?"

"Right."

That's when he realized something else. "Why are you sleeping sideways?"

"Because you were." Julia sat up and rearranged herself until she was in her usual spot. "But now that you're half awake, I'm moving."

Good plan. He looked at the clock to find they probably had another hour or two before time to feed the babies again. "Get some more sleep."

"I am, but tomorrow we need to talk." She was already

drifting off by the time she finished.

Great. It didn't sound bad, but saying *we need to talk* to your significant other was rarely good. Topher went to the bathroom and changed his pants, tossing his t-shirt onto the floor. Since sleeping with Julia, he'd taken to wearing one so he wouldn't make her uncomfortable, but tonight he didn't particularly care. Besides, she was already asleep.

And a few minutes later, so was he.

He didn't wake up again until sunlight streamed in the window. His wife was nowhere to be found, and neither were the babies.

After checking the clock and realizing they needed to leave in about an hour, he decided to get ready before anything else. Then he could help with his daughters.

When he made it downstairs, he found Julia asleep in the recliner, both babies snuggled into her shoulders. As carefully as he could, he took one from her, though he wasn't sure which one without unwrapping the blanket to see what color her toenails were. Painting them different colors had been Bailey's idea. He laid the baby in the bassinet then reached for the other one.

"Wha...?" Julia sat straight up as he did.

"You were sleeping," he whispered. "But you need to get ready to go. We have about half an hour. I'll get breakfast going."

She nodded and half-stumbled toward the stairs. Hopefully, she'd be bright eyed when she came back. A minute later, the older kids came down, followed closely by his mom who looked more tired than he'd seen her in a while.

"Thanks," he told her as the kids climbed on their

barstools. "I appreciate you taking the babies last night. How'd they do?"

"Fine. They actually took the bottles really well." She yawned. "I don't do the short nights quite as easily as I used to though. As soon as Alex is on the bus and either Mama Beach is here or Dad's up, I'm headed back to bed."

"That's a great plan." He kissed her cheek before pouring cereal for the older two. "You deserve it."

Julia made it back down with about five minutes to spare and looked much better than she had in a couple of days.

"Thank you again, Leigh Ann." She gave his mom a half-hug. "I appreciate it."

He pointed his glass her direction. "Just tell me next time, would you?"

Julia grinned. "He woke me up, freaking out because the babies were gone." She sat on the bar stool and hugged Alex. "Morning, kiddo. How are you?"

Alex shrugged. "Fine." He stirred his cereal. "But I can't wait for the show to be over so you guys'll be home more."

"I know, buddy. Topher and I miss you guys, too. Sunday afternoon, we'll be home, and then I'm done with yarn and shows for a while."

"Good."

Topher didn't have the heart to tell them that he'd be working a lot more on *Seating for Six* starting the first week in December. He'd probably even need to make a trip or two to LA for casting calls. Some of it he could do remotely, but the final callbacks would have to be in person. They also planned to hold some auditions locally, but he didn't have the time frame for those yet. Most of the bit parts and extras would be locals. He needed to talk to Josh Wilson, owner of the Serenity Landing Comedy Club, for his help.

The day proceeded much like the one before had. Someone brought the babies for Julia to nurse every few hours. She had one shift helping Lady Margaret mid-morning. He escaped to the office she'd been using to nurse and worked for a couple of hours. The second episode was nearly done, though it would need some edits once casting was complete.

He and Claire had a conference call with Dusty to go over some of the plans for later in the season. As he finished that up, Mama Beach showed up with the girls, and he went back out to the floor to take over for Julia.

Much of the stock had already been sold, though plenty remained to fill in the holes. He managed to sell a few of the bags he'd helped finish. Mom hadn't showed up and that concerned him a little, though they didn't really need her. Hopefully the night before hadn't been too much for her. He'd really benefited from a full night's sleep, and Julia seemed to have as well. Her overall demeanor was happier, and she seemed much more alert.

Even Kenzie noticed the change in both of them and commented on it. One of her comments struck a chord in Topher, and he couldn't wait to run it by Claire.

Whenever he could grab a few minutes, Topher went back to the office to work. An email from Ida Mae told him another letter had arrived from Gene. There wasn't enough of a threat in them for the police to do anything. He'd checked.

After a call to Claire to help brainstorm the idea he'd had for her character, he knew it was a winner. Chris, the happy-go-lucky bachelor who's taking care of his brother's kids and suddenly married to the one who got away, had been vaguely defined as a "marketing guy." That gave them enough leeway to do pretty much whatever they wanted with him.

But they hadn't really defined Claire's character yet.

Kenzie's comment about him and Jonathan learning because it mattered to their wives was inspired. Claire would have her own home business. Not yarn. That was too close to home, but maybe she wove her own fabric. Something off the wall, and Chris would have to use his marketing expertise to help her get it off the ground. It reminded him that he still needed to help Julia update her website, too.

With solid ideas for the second half of the season, he packed up his stuff when Mom showed up with the babies. By the time they finished eating this time, it would be time to go home.

For the first time in days, he felt much better about what was coming.

And Topher liked that.

Chapter Twenty-Nine

Something was different about her husband, but Julia couldn't quite put her finger on it. For the last several days, he'd been more attentive, but it went beyond that.

He almost glowed. Like Kenzie got when she found the perfect combination of dyes to create that new color she'd been dreaming about.

Julia could never do it, but Kenzie had a knack. Whatever it was, Topher was clearly on the same creative high. She didn't ask about it, though. If he wanted her to know, he'd tell her.

By the time Sunday afternoon rolled around, she was dying to know, but too exhausted to try to figure out how to ask. Leigh Ann had taken one of the overnight feedings and that helped a lot more than Julia would have thought, but she was still so tired. The sharp decrease in temperature between Friday and Sunday likely didn't help matters any. Neither did the weather front coming through.

They made it to church, though the babies stayed home with Leigh Ann and James. After being gone for so many weeks, being there was a balm to Julia's soul. They went home so Julia could feed the girls, and then to the venue to finish cleaning out their booth. Kenzie's phone rang as they packed up the last of the bags. She walked off, pinching the bridge of her nose.

She still looked stressed when she returned.

"What's going on?" Julia asked her.

"Lady Margaret's flight was canceled. She was supposed to fly through Chicago, and they're getting the major winter storm that missed us."

"Can she get on another flight?"

"Not today, and apparently she *has* to be home by tomorrow. I'm not sure what we're going to do." She tapped a finger on her arm. "Maybe Jonathan can send her in his plane, but it's not available right now. His brother and sister-in-law used it to go visit her family and pack up their things to finish moving here."

"What about Prince William?" Topher hoisted one of the tubs. "I thought Jonathan said he was leaving today, too. They're headed to the same country at least."

Kenzie's eyes lit up. "That's brilliant. I don't know why Jonathan didn't think of it." She tapped at her phone and walked back off, returning a minute later looking much calmer. "Perfect. He's going to talk to Prince William and hope it works out."

"Why wouldn't it?" Julia stacked the last few patterns into a tub. "They're going to the same place."

"They met for about twelve seconds the other day and

haven't talked to each other since." Arms full of yarn, Kenzie turned and paused. "It's weird. Almost like one of them is avoiding the other. I'm not sure Lady Margaret is a fan of the royal family. She spent all of her time in the apartment and didn't talk to any of us. Gwendolyn didn't even meet her."

"Gwendolyn?" Topher asked.

"Jonathan's cousin," Julia reminded him. "The one who's pregnant and getting married next month."

"Right."

Kenzie dropped the armful of yarn into a tub. "Gwendolyn's spent a lot of time with Jonathan's brother Philip and his wife the last few weeks. If they can get the approval, they're going to adopt her baby."

"Why wouldn't they get the approval?" Julia popped a lid on the last of her stuff.

"Because of Philip's past with drugs. They closed on the house in Spring Meadow and are getting it set up. I'm not sure when the home study will be done, but soon. If that gets a stamp of approval, they're adopting Gwendolyn's baby. If not, Jonathan and I will."

"Is that really what you want?" Julia asked her friend. "With the baby coming and all, is adopting another baby the right move?"

Kenzie rested a hand on her slight baby bump. "I don't know, but we'd already agreed to adopt the baby before we knew I was pregnant. Once Philip showed back up, and we learned they can't have children, we had a whole big discussion about it. Gwendolyn wants them to adopt, and they want to, but they have to pass this home study thing. He's been sober for a couple of years and doing very well from all the reports from his therapist and others, but we can't know for sure what the courts will decide."

She snorted. "It wouldn't surprise me if my mother-in-law tried to buy the approval though. She's over the moon that Philip's home, to the point she's stopped drinking. If the home study falls through, she's going to be almost as devastated as they will be."

"We'll be praying it goes well, then." Topher set the last of Julia's tubs on the dolly. "And that Philip can stay clean. And that your mother-in-law keeps not drinking."

Julia nodded as he spoke, because those sounded like good things.

They kept packing up. The Show Me Yarn ladies had decided to stay late the night before and clean up after the show closed, so just the three of them remained of their little group. Topher helped load everything in both SUVs.

They made it back to the house just in time for Julia to feed the twins while Topher and his dad emptied everything from the SUV into the basement. Once the girls were nestled in their swings, Julia collapsed back into the recliner with Alex and Bailey both sitting on her.

Bailey turned on an episode of *Blue's Clues*. Alex helped her draw the clues, so she could figure it out with Steve.

She'd needed this for the last few days. Time with her kids. Bailey wasn't hers, not technically, but Julia was convinced God somehow meant for the little girl to be in her life. They just fit together that well.

And she adored her little sisters. Bailey helped whenever she could. Everything from pacifier retrieval to helping with diaper duty to picking out clothes for them to wear. Alex wasn't quite as enamored, but Julia figured that probably had more to do with the fact that the babies didn't do much than not wanting to be helpful.

With her big kids snuggled next to her, and a huge weight lifted now that the show was over and packed up, Julia let her eyes drift closed.

Topher didn't like spending Sundays in his office, but he was on a roll. The second episode had been written. The third had practically written itself. He'd started the fourth. It wasn't how sitcoms usually worked, and they would probably be gone over repeatedly by others and changes would made, some of them significant changes, but it was so nice to put his creative side to work again. Even if they ended up getting scrapped all together, it had been worth it.

After a couple of hours, he emerged to find Julia sound asleep in the chair. Bailey and Alex climbed down and ran to him. He hadn't seen them nearly enough in the last couple weeks.

A glance at the clock told him showed the time had come to start dinner. Bailey and Alex joined him in the kitchen to help. Something easy. Spaghetti with tortellini. He mixed some of the red sauce with some Alfredo to make an orange sauce, his favorite.

Both kids were a big help. Julia wandered, bleary eyed, out of the living room but detoured toward the front door when the doorbell rang. She gave him a puzzled look, but he just shrugged. No one should have been able to get through the gate without being buzzed through, something he was still getting used to.

As that thought went through his head, he started for the door, too. Could it be something...

Before the thought could finish, his wife's happy squeals told him there was nothing to fear.

Bailey and Alex scrambled off their bar stools and ran past him toward the front of the house to see what the commotion was about. When he turned the corner, he found Julia hugging another woman and a man about his dad's age standing there with a suitcase.

"Gramps!" Alex shouted as he barreled into the man.

Gramps chuckled and hugged Alex. "Hey, buddy."

"Gam!" Alex turned as his grandmother let go of Julia.

Gramps knelt down and crossed his forearms over his knee. "You must be Bailey," he said. Bailey took a step closer. He held out a hand. "I'm Gramps."

She gave it one quick shake then backed up, uncertain.

Gramps didn't press her, and Topher appreciated him for that.

The older man stood up and extended a hand toward him. "I'm Kenneth. You must be my new son-in-law."

"Topher. Pleasure to meet you."

"Likewise." He turned as Alex let go of Gam. "And this is my wife, Erica."

They talked for another minute, including introducing Bailey again. Then Erica clapped her hands together. "Where's my new grandbabies?"

Julia took them, with Bailey in tow, to the living room while Topher went back to the kitchen with Alex.

"You don't have to stay in here with me, buddy," Topher told him. "You can go with the rest of them to see the girls."

Alex shrugged. "I know what the girls look like."

So that's what bothered him. "It's been a rough week, hasn't it? Learning to share your mom with two new babies?"

He gave another shrug, but didn't say anything.

"You've gone through a lot of changes lately. Moving in here, sharing your mom with Bailey, me marrying your mom, the bed rest stuff, new babies, the yarn show which took a lot of time the last few days." Topher climbed onto the barstool next to Alex and turned to face him. "I know it's been a lot for me, your mom, and Bailey to deal with, too. I can only imagine how hard it's been for you. The changes have probably been hardest on you and Bay."

"Bay's sad a lot."

"Why is she sad?" Topher suspected he knew the answer.

"She misses her mom, and you and Mom have been so busy lately..." His voice trailed off.

"That's going to change starting tonight," Topher vowed. "I still have to work and will have to go to California for a few days before Christmas, but just for a day or two. And hopefully, I'll only have to go once. My office hours here at home will be a lot more normal, and we can spend evenings together again."

He reached out and rested a hand on Alex's shoulder. "The babies will settle into a routine soon." Topher hoped. "That'll help all of us, too. Especially when they start sleeping longer at night."

"If you say so."

The timer went off before the conversation could go any further. Alex helped Topher drain the noodles and move everything to the table in the dining room.

"Will you go get everyone?" Topher asked him as he headed back to the kitchen to get two more place settings. He just hoped he'd made enough spaghetti.

Everyone gathered in the dining room with Alex clamoring to sit between his grandparents.

Dinner went well, with all of them laughing and talking. His mom and Julia's hit it off. About the time they finished, Topher's phone rang. He excused himself to take the call from Dusty about the files he'd sent earlier.

When the conversation ended, the dining room and kitchen had been cleaned up. Mom had motioned to him that she was going to take Bailey up to get her ready for bed. Alex was with his grandparents, most likely, so Topher headed upstairs.

He heard voices coming from the master bedroom. Julia was talking to someone, but he couldn't tell who.

As he reached to push the door further open and walk in, her words stopped him.

"I don't know, Mom. I don't know that I want more out of this marriage. We only got married to get the tabloids off Topher's back, so he wouldn't lose everything when the studio sued him. I knew going in he would never love me, and I'd never love him. We're just biding our time until we can separate without repercussions for him. He asked me to help him, to help Bailey. I said yes. That's it."

Topher's hand fell back to his side, pain slicing through him. Was that really how she felt? It was how they'd started, but did they really want to end up in the same place?

He took a step back and turned to walk away before he

heard anything else he really didn't want to hear.

Chapter Thirty

With all of her attention focused on folding the baby clothes in front of her, Julia didn't want to know what her mother thought about the statements she'd just made.

She'd hear it in a minute. She knew what Mom would say, and she didn't know what had caused her to confess.

"I'm disappointed to hear that," Mom finally said.

"I know." Julia tossed the sleeper onto the pile. "I know you always loved Chris Slate, and we joked about me marrying him someday, but Topher and I aren't meant to be."

"It's not that, though, you did put it down as one of your dreams, remember?"

Julia smirked. "I still have that dream board packed up somewhere."

"And it's still not what I'm talking about. You stood in

front of a judge and God and promised all kinds of things. It's even more than a promise. It's a vow, sweetheart. You *vowed* to be Topher's wife until death do you part." Mom reached out and covered Julia's hand with her own, squeezing lightly. "Unless you two had some crazy ceremony where you promised to be married until the tabloids backed off."

Julia couldn't keep the tears from overflowing her eyes. "No. It was a pretty standard wedding, except no guests attended."

"And from what you've told me about Mama Beach, she wouldn't have stood for that kind of nonsense anyway."

"Probably not," Julia whispered, swiping at her cheeks with the back of her hand.

"Do you really not want more out of this relationship?" her mom asked in that same gentle tone she'd often used when she already knew what Julia had done wrong.

"Do I *want* more and could I ever expect or end up with more are two entirely different questions." She picked at a bit of a woolly lamb on one of the sleepers. "Alex adores him and Bailey. I hate what this is going to do to them eventually."

"And Marissa and Annie, too. If you two break up in a couple of years, they'll lose the only father they've ever known, the only real father Alex has ever had."

Julia blew out a breath. "I know you're right, but I don't know what to do about it. I can't exactly seduce him at the moment, and I wouldn't want to anyway."

"Don't *seduce* him." Julia looked up in time to see her mother roll her eyes. "There's so much more to a relationship than that. Spend time together, the six of you, as a family. Spend time with Topher, learning about him and what makes him tick. Fall in love together. Chemistry will come."

Julia snorted. "Oh, there's plenty of chemistry. Didn't you see the pictures of us kissing?"

"I did, but he's an actor. I didn't know how much of was acting."

"The kisses? As far as I was concerned, none of it. From the look in his eyes, they weren't fake on his side either. But he hasn't kissed me in weeks, not really. A couple pecks on the cheek or forehead, but that's it."

"Why don't you two go out on a date in the next day or two? Between the four of us grandparents, we can handle the kids."

Julia shook her head. "I need a few days of nothing extra. I know Topher does, too. The twins aren't even two weeks old yet. My body certainly hasn't recovered. I'm planning to do a lot of sleeping and watching television with the kids the next few days. Leigh Ann said you two have Thanksgiving under control, so I'm gonna let you do that."

She nodded. "We can handle Thanksgiving. You rest and spend time with your family."

Julia took her words to heart. She slept. She spent time with her bigger kids. She watched movies with them and Topher in the evenings. He retreated to his office after the kids went to bed to work. She avoided social media, the news, pretty much everything and just focused on recovering from childbirth and a crazy week while spending as much time with her family as she could.

The day after Thanksgiving, they all piled into the media room to watch Topher's first HEA TV movie.

Kenzie, Jonathan, and Lorelai joined them. Her friend was

looking more pregnant than ever and simply glowing with happiness. She whispered to Julia that Philip and his wife had been approved to adopt Gwendolyn's baby. She also said something about Prince William and Lady Margaret making it home, though Julia wasn't sure why Kenzie went out of her way to mention that.

The movie was predictable, as most HEA TV movies were, but Julia was impressed. For having been out of the business for so long, Topher did very well. Snuggled into his side as they watched, she noticed something about the kisses between his character and Claire's.

They were convincing, but the look in his eyes was nothing like the look when he kissed her.

That left her with plenty to think about.

By Sunday, everyone had gone. They ventured to church for the first time with all four of the kids. Julia's parents had went back to Florida the day before, and Topher's parents flew out to spend the month in Ravenzario.

Julia leaned her head back against the head rest as Topher drove. "We did it."

His grin lit up the SUV. "We did. I'm pretty sure we're even going to be on time."

"Impressive for our first try."

"Definitely."

She glanced over in time to see him wince. "What?"

"I forgot to tell you about an email I got this morning."

"Okay."

"I'm going to be gone a couple of days this week. I have to go to LA for auditions."

"You're auditioning for something?" He didn't have enough

coming up already with the show and the movies over the summer?

"No. Auditions for the kids on *Seating for Six*. They want both me and Claire there to make sure the chemistry works."

"I see." And that meant she'd be home alone with all four kids for the first time.

"I know it's a lot for you to handle all by yourself." He sounded genuinely sympathetic. "Is there anyone who could come help during the day at least? Or to take one shift overnight? It's only one night, though."

"Not that I can think of off the top of my head."

"We'll figure something out. Ida Mae will be at the house. She doesn't have much to do for me right now. I'm sure she'd be happy to help."

Julia just nodded. She liked the older woman a lot, and she'd been a huge blessing. The last thing she wanted to do was impose, and Julia knew helping with her boss's offspring wasn't in Ida Mae's job description.

They pulled into the parking lot before the conversation could continue. Topher had the foresight to bring the double stroller so it was easy enough to snap the car seats in. Dropping Alex and Bailey off was simple, and then Julia followed Topher as he pushed the stroller.

After parking it on the far end of the last row, as much out of the way as he could, Topher surprised her. He entered the row first, allowing her the aisle seat next to the babies.

She could do this.

She had no choice.

Topher tapped his pen against the table as he waited for everyone else to arrive. The casting room, this time, was just a big conference room, cleared out except for a table for him, Claire, Dusty and a few others to sit. A couch sat a few feet away from the other wall to give the candidates a chance to act out the scene from the pilot.

A couple of rounds of auditions had already been held, and they were down to just a few actors and actresses for each role. Topher had seen the auditions from a distance and helped with some of the decision making, but he and Claire hadn't been there in person for the others.

They hoped to narrow it down to one, or maybe two, for each of the four children. If all went well, he and Claire would do a scene with the last of the candidates and have it all ironed out before he went home the next evening.

When they broke for lunch, he was certain who would be cast as the sons. The twin daughters were a little harder. Two sets of girls were well-suited for the parts, but they had very different looks. It might come down to which set of twins looked more related to the boys and Topher himself. They'd see how they all worked together, how they played off each other.

An uneasy feeling settled over Topher as the day went on. A stirring he didn't quite understand. He exchanged several texts with Julia, who assured him all was going well and nothing out of the ordinary had happened.

By the time he made it to his hotel, the feeling had grown but he willed it to the back of his mind. Dinner with Dusty, Claire, and a few others would be in a private room in the hotel restaurant where they'd go over everyone's notes and make decisions.

Before going downstairs, he flopped on the bed and hit the button to FaceTime Julia.

Instead, Bailey's face greeted him. "Daddy!"

"Hey, Bailey Bug. How are you?"

She shrugged. "Miss you, Daddy."

"What did you do today? Were you a big helper?" They'd talked the night before about how she could help Julia during the day.

Bailey nodded, her big eyes serious. "I helped. Gave Annie my Copter Bear when she cried."

That made Topher grin. That bear had to be over twenty years old. He loved that his daughter loved it. "You did? Did she stop crying?"

Bailey gave an exaggerated sigh, the kind only a four-year-old girl could give. "No."

During several more minutes of discussion, he learned Julia was feeding the babies, Ida Mae had baked spaghetti in the oven, and Alex was coloring in the living room.

His timer buzzed at him. "I've got to go, Bay. Take Julia the phone and tell her to call me, okay, Bug?"

"I will, Daddy! Love you!"

Before he could respond, she'd severed the connection. Topher sent a text and hoped Julia would see it soon. He had ten minutes to get downstairs, but she hadn't called back before he made it to dinner.

An hour into the meeting, his phone buzzed, and Topher excused himself to the side of the room. "Hey, Jules."

"Sorry it took so long to call you back." She sounded

distracted. "I needed to get Alex and Bailey to bed."

"Did she go to sleep okay?" Alex wouldn't give her any trouble. He was less sure about Bailey.

"I don't think she's actually asleep yet, but yeah."

"And the babies?"

"Were up a lot last night."

That explained why he'd woken up alone and noticed the bed in the nursery had been slept in. They'd put a twin bed in there for that reason, after all.

"I'll be praying they'll let you sleep tonight."

"You and me both."

But that didn't explain the uneasy feeling he'd had all day long. "And everything else is okay? Nothing unusual happened?"

"No. Everyone was kind of cranky, but that's it."

"Good. Not that they're cranky, but that nothing unusual happened." He hesitated before deciding to go on. "But something in my gut feels weird. Can you stay home tomorrow? Don't go anywhere unless maybe Jonathan or one of his guys goes with you? I don't know what the deal is, but..."

"The media again?" she asked.

"I don't think so." He glanced up to see Dusty making a "wrap it up" motion at him. "I gotta go, but please be extra careful, and let me know if anything weird happens?"

"I will."

"Thanks. I'll be home tomorrow, probably late," he promised.

"I know. We'll be here."

"I'll talk to you later. Get some rest."

"I'm going to try." She couldn't hide the sound of her yawn.

"Night."

Julia hung up before he could say goodbye.

Topher turned and went back to the table where a lively discussion was taking place about the next door neighbor and who should be cast. He had to stifle a chuckle. The neighbor woman was very loosely based on Mama Beach. He wondered if she'd pick up on it if he didn't tell her.

By the time they broke for the evening, most of the decisions had been made. The final tests would come the next day when Topher and Claire took their turns working with the other actors and actresses.

Before turning out the bedside light, Topher sent Julia a quick goodnight text. He hoped she wouldn't see it until morning. She usually had her do not disturb feature turned on, but if she was up with the girls she might see it anyway.

The next morning got off to a rocky start. The kids they'd chosen for the final round of auditions simply didn't work. No matter how hard they tried, the two boys didn't quite fit.

"So what do we do?" Topher pinched the bridge of his nose as he leaned back in his chair. "Call the other kids back in?"

"It's unlikely we could get them in today," Dusty pointed out. "Tomorrow maybe, but you're leaving tonight."

He hated to say it, but he knew what he had to do. "I'll stay another night, but we need to wrap this up tomorrow."

"We will."

Topher wished he felt as confident as Dusty sounded.

"I understand." Julia managed to press the phone more

tightly between her shoulder and cheek. "I'll let the kids know."

"I'll video chat with Bay and Alex later." Topher's voice sounded strained. "You, too, if you have time."

"It's not necessary. Save your video chat time for them. We can talk or text whenever you have time." She didn't really know that they *needed* to.

"Did the girls sleep better?"

"Somewhat." *Not really.*

"Okay. I've got to go, but please remember what I said last night."

"I do." He was being ridiculous, but she'd had no plans to leave the house anyway.

"Be careful. I'll talk to you later."

"Wait! Did you talk to Ida Mae? She said something about a letter she needed to send to your lawyer, but wanted to let you know."

Topher hesitated. "I'll talk to her. Thanks. I gotta go." Was he keeping something from her? They finished the conversation quickly and hung up.

Julia didn't know what he was being so paranoid about, but she stayed home anyway. No one had come to the front gate except for someone selling home security systems.

They clearly didn't need one. Jonathan had set them up with a state-of-the-art system already.

The rest of the day passed uneventfully. The kids all went to bed at a fairly reasonable time, and even the babies slept nearly six hours straight. *Thank you, God.*

The next morning, Julia managed to get Alex out the door on time, even though Ida Mae had called in sick. Bailey was a huge help and cooperated, rather than being trouble.

The babies had just gone back to sleep when Julia's phone rang. Alex's school nurse let her know that he had thrown up. With no one to help her, Julia was just going to have to take all of the kids.

Bailey was a big help gathering the things needed to get the babies out the door, like their car seats. Ten minutes after the call came in, they were on the road to Serenity Landing.

As much as Julia loved the house, the school wasn't close. It took almost twenty-five minutes to get there, thanks in part to a slow-moving train. She pulled up in front of the building just outside of the no parking zone. "Okay, Bailey. I'm going to have to take you and the twins in. I don't want to leave you out here, even for a couple minutes."

She pulled the double stroller out of the back of the SUV and put both car seats in it. Inside, she signed Alex out as the receptionist called the nurse's office, so he could come meet them. As both receptionists and the assistant principal oo'd and ah'd over the babies, Alex walked into the office looking miserable.

Julia gave him a big hug. "Let's get you home and in bed, buddy."

He held up a trash bag. "The nurse gave this to me in case I need it on the way home. I can't come to school tomorrow either."

"Well, hopefully you won't need it." And Topher would be home the next day. She ushered her small brood back to the car. Alex sat in the back with his head resting against the window. Bailey stayed as far away from him as she could and still be in the same seat.

The drive home didn't take quite as long, thanks to the lack of train.

She wasn't used to pressing the button to open the gate at the end of the drive. They had to sit and wait while it swung inward. As soon as it opened far enough for her to pass, she did. Rather than pulling into the garage, Julia parked in front of the front door.

"Mom?" Alex called from the back.

"Are you going to throw up, buddy?" She dreaded the sound.

"No. But someone pulled in behind us."

Julia's heart began to race. How had she not noticed? She looked in her rearview mirror. Sure enough, a car had pulled in behind them. Two men climbed out, though the driver stayed put.

"I don't like him!" The fear in Bailey's voice struck fear in Julia's heart.

"Who is that?"

“Gene!”

“Gene who?”

"My other mom’s boyfriend."

Great. Whatever was about to happen. It wouldn't be good. "Stay in the car." No. She wasn't getting out either. Instead, she waited for them to get to the window and cracked it just a bit. "Can I help you?"

"I'm here to take Bailey home."

"And you are...?"

"Her father." His voice sent chills down Julia’s spine.

"You're not her father." Julia wasn't going to let him any closer to her daughter. That's how she thought of Bailey.

"Her mother left her in my custody. I've raised her since she was born. I'm her father." The guy had to be nearing six foot, maybe even taller. He clearly knew his way around the gym.

That scared Julia. What could she do if he decided to try to take Bailey?

That's when she knew they couldn't stay. She hadn't turned the SUV off, so she slammed it into drive and pressed the gas pedal. Both men took a step back, and that's when she realized the other man was snapping pictures with his camera. She went down the drive, grateful for its circular nature. The gate had swung closed, so she pushed the button desperately hoping it would open quickly. The other car followed her. Where could she go?

Jonathan. He would be able to help.

She pushed the button on her phone and told it to call Jonathan's cell phone.

He answered on the second ring. "Hey, Julia. What can I do for you?

"I'm on my way to your house. Can you have the gate open?"

"Of course." Concern filled his voice. "What's going on?"

"I'll tell you when we get there."

"Little pitchers with big ears?"

"That's right." She hesitated, then decided she needed to tell him a little bit more. "There's a car behind me. They'll probably try to come in, too."

"Understood. We'll take care of you when you get here. Please be careful."

She knew he remembered Kenzie and the paparazzi who

had stalked her a few months earlier. Julia glanced in her rear view mirror and prayed this guy wasn't as stupid as those guys were.

Unfortunately, Jonathan and Kenzie didn't live right next door. The drive to their house took nearly fifteen minutes. The only good thing was the lack of stoplights or stop signs in between. And the speed limit was generally 55 miles an hour, except on curves.

The car behind them got too close, but not so close she felt truly afraid. Did she need to call the police? Or had Jonathan already taken care of it?

Not nearly soon enough, the drive came into view. She slowed down as little as possible and took the turn. A sigh of relief escaped when she realized Jonathan and a couple of the guys who worked for him were standing there, armed, just in case. The car behind her screeched to a halt inside the gate, but not anywhere near the house.

She pulled up to the front door, where Kenzie waited. In less than a minute, all four kids were inside with the door locked behind them. Jonathan came in from the other direction, his face grim.

"That guy says he has custody of Bailey." His tone of voice didn't help calm Julia down. "He says he's come to take her home."

Chapter Thirty-One

Topher had to stop himself from pinching the bridge of his nose. He done it far too often since he'd been in California. At least the first kid they called back had worked out. If the next one did too, they'd be all set.

"How long before the other kid gets here?" He looked at his paperwork. The kid's name wasn't easy to find, and he couldn't remember it.

"About five minutes," Dusty said. "He's not supposed to be here for another hour, but I just talked to his mom, and they're on their way."

Good. Almost over. He pulled his phone out of his pocket to see what messages he'd gotten in the last hour. A voice mail from Jonathan and another from Julia. *Weird.* He started to listen to Jonathan's, but before he could, a knock sounded on the door.

The kid arrived a little earlier than expected. Topher and Claire went around the table and got ready to do their parts of the scene. The kids had already auditioned together earlier so they knew they could work, but they had to find out for sure if this kid could work with Topher and Claire.

They spent about an hour going through different materials. The kid was uncomfortable at first, but began to find his groove after forty-five minutes.

Topher, Claire, and the others whispered together for a few minutes and decided to give him another chance. He was close. But they wanted to use something new, something they hadn't already seen a dozen times.

Topher pulled his tablet out of his bag. "I wrote a couple other episodes. I knew we might not use them, but I was having too much fun to stop." After a few taps, he'd sent the scripts to Claire, Dusty, and the others. They gave the young man about fifteen minutes to look over the script and figure out his part. If he didn't have it memorized, it would be okay. Topher spent that time talking with Dusty, and figuring out what their next steps were.

After the kid looked it over, Topher and Claire moved back around the table and went through the scene. Much better.

With that decided, Topher wanted to go back to the hotel, pack up, and head for home. Instead, Dusty had decided that since he was in town, they should have an afternoon of meetings. *Just what he wanted to do.* He came back from the bathroom to find everyone watching him.

"What?" He looked down. His fly was zipped. He didn't see any toilet paper hanging off his shoes.

"You haven't seen social media, have you?" Claire asked

him.

Topher shook his head. "No." He pulled his phone out of his pocket to see it had exploded with messages, including several from his parents. "Where do I find it?"

"Try the *CelebGossipNewz* website."

Instead of their website, he went straight to their Facebook page. After scrolling past two other stories, he found what he was looking for.

A picture of Julia looking scared, as she drove off in the SUV. The short article said she was refusing to allow Bailey to see her father. It didn't include a name or picture of "Bailey's father" in the article.

Did everyone think they were talking about him? He went to his voicemails and listened to Jonathan's first message. It just said to call him as soon as possible. Julia's first message was much the same, though not nearly as calm as Jonathan's had been. Her second message was much the same. He finally skipped to the last one. Now she sounded freaked out, and finally told him what was going on.

His ex-wife's boyfriend had shown up claiming to be Bailey's father and wanting to take her home with him.

Over his dead body.

And that seemed to be what Julia meant as well.

It made Topher extra glad he'd gone to court to get full custody officially. By the time those thoughts finished running through his head, he realized he was out the door and on his way to the hotel. He hadn't said goodbye to anyone. He sent a quick group text and said he had to get home. Julia's phone kept going to voice mail. So did Jonathan's. He walked into his room. Frantic, he got his things together, including his driver's license, which he had left there inadvertently that morning. If he'd had it with him, he would've gone straight to the airport and been on his way home already.

Instead, he tossed everything into his bag and headed down to the waiting cab. His phone finally rang as they pulled out of the hotel lot.

"Is everyone okay?" he asked, forgoing any greeting.

"Your wife is freaked out," Jonathan told him. "But that's pretty understandable."

"What happened?"

Jonathan told him in a few words about the man who'd shown up at Julia's house, and Julia's plan to go to Jonathan's rather than be alone.

Good thinking.

"Where was she? She said she wouldn't go anywhere, because I couldn't shake the feeling that something was going to happen."

"She had to pick Alex up from school. Ida Mae called in sick this morning, so Julia took all the kids with her. The car followed her through the gate, and the guys confronted her before she could get out of the car."

"I'm on my way home. I should be there in a few hours. I already called to get a plane waiting for me."

"It's really not necessary at the moment. The guy threatened me and my men, and so did the photographer with him. They've both been arrested. They won't be in jail long, but they will be there for a while."

"Still. I'm on my way. I don't like the thought of them there without me."

"I know. I just want to make sure you know that we've got

them taken care of."

"Thank you. But I'll feel better when I'm there myself. What exactly did this guy say?" He told Jonathan about the most recent letter. Jonathan said he'd let the police know.

Topher talked to Jonathan until he reached the airport. In just a few minutes, his flight was off the ground, and headed for the Midwest.

Julia held Bailey close as the little girl cried. This had all been so hard on her. Julia tried to get Bailey to tell her exactly why she didn't like this guy much, but Bailey wouldn't really say.

From what she'd gathered over the months, Julia assumed he hadn't treated her well, but there didn't seem to be any indication of true abuse. While she definitely didn't want Bailey to go anywhere, Julia did wonder if this guy had a legitimate claim to custody. Had Bailey's mother left him custody in her will? Had there been a will? Or one found that Topher didn't know about? Regardless, Topher had gone to court and been awarded custody. Surely nothing else mattered.

Kenzie walked into the room. "Alex is looking for you. He just threw up again, and he wants to go home."

Maybe she should just take the kids to the house. They would be more comfortable there, and Julia would be, too. She didn't want to impose on Kenzie and Jonathan any longer than they had to. "Do you think Jonathan would send a couple of security guards home with me? I'd rather be there, and I know the kids would, too."

Kenzie crossed her arms over her chest. "Do you really think that's the best idea?"

"That's why I asked about the security guards. I wouldn't want to be there by myself, with four kids, but if we had security, it would be okay."

"Maybe." Kenzie didn't want to let her go. Julia had known she wouldn't. "I'll talk to Jonathan and see what he thinks." Kenzie pointed a finger at Julia. "But if he says you need to stay here, you should stay here. Got it?"

"Fine." *Maybe.* Julia wanted to be at home, in her comfy chair, with her kids.

"You won't let him take me, will you?" Bailey's tiny voice broke Julia's heart.

"I won't let them take you, sweetheart." *Over my dead body.*

Jonathan walked into the room. "Kenzie says you want to go home?"

"Yes, I do very much. The kids would be more comfortable, too." Would Jonathan be okay with it?

"I've got some guards that can go with you. But do as they tell you. Stay inside. And don't go anywhere but home."

"That's all I plan to do. Unless..." Something else occurred to her.

"Unless what?"

"I need some stuff for Alex. I don't think we have any food or snacks appropriate for someone with an upset stomach."

"I'll send someone to the store for you," Jonathan told her. He shook his finger in her face much as Kenzie had. Or that's what it felt like, anyway. "But you need to go straight home. Get your kids inside and stay there. Got it?"

"Got it." She squeezed Bailey and stood up. "Come on,

Bailey Bug. We're going home."

"Not so fast. It'll take me a little bit to get everything together. Topher called a minute ago. He's on his way."

"Good. Bailey needs her dad."

As soon as Jonathan gave her the go-ahead, Julia secured the babies in the car while the kids put their seatbelts on. Security guards drove one car in front of her and another car behind. Almost like her own little motorcade.

Julia liked the feeling of safety they brought. She hated that she needed it. Three minutes into the drive home, Annie woke up, crying. Hungry. She woke up Marissa. By the time they reached the house, both girls screamed at full volume.

Julia pulled straight into the garage, rather than parking out front. She didn't get out of the car until the garage door closed. It took a bit more maneuvering, but she got both babies, car seats and all, inside while Bailey and Alex went into the living room.

A few minutes later, Julia settled into her chair with both babies nursing. Bailey had disappeared. "Where is she?" Julia asked Alex.

"I think she went upstairs."

"Can you go find her, please?"

"I feel like I'm going to throw up again."

Julia closed her eyes and prayed for strength. "Okay. Go to the bathroom. But if you see or hear Bailey, tell her to come here."

Alex ran to the bathroom, and she heard him get sick.

As much as she normally relished the time with her babies, nursing them, this time she needed to be with Bailey. Maybe she should have given them bottles, and let Bailey help. Or done half nursing, half bottles. She'd done that a few times, and it worked pretty well, mostly. Finally, both babies finished and burped. Once they were settled down into their bassinet on the playpen, Julia went to look for Alex before looking for Bailey.

"Mom," Alex's weakened voice called. "My stomach hurts."

"I know, sweetheart." Normally, when he wasn't actively throwing up, she'd snuggle with him, brush his hair back off his forehead, and just love on her baby. But right now Bailey needed her worse.

Julia checked on him and kissed his forehead, and went upstairs and did a cursory search through all the rooms. Bailey didn't show up anywhere. Julia went back and did a more thorough search, first Bailey's room, and then room by room through the upstairs.

Still no Bailey.

She went back to the first floor and looked around, but still didn't find her. Then the basement. Same thing.

Julia went back upstairs to look again, calling for Bailey the whole time.

She searched more carefully than before and still nothing. The begins of panic tried to start, but she knew the little girl hadn't gone far. She'd just gone quiet. The last place Julia thought to check was the far corner of Topher's closet. It had this weird corner/angle thing that was difficult to see into. Hadn't Topher told her once that Bailey liked to hide there?

And there, huddled on the floor in the corner, was Bailey.

Rather than scold her or make her come out of the place she clearly felt safe, Julia squeezed into the corner next to her.

She wrapped her arms around the little girl and hugged her

close. "It's okay, sweetheart. You're not going anywhere." She prayed that was true. "And your dad's on his way home. He'll be here soon. He won't let anything happen to you."

Bailey just snuggled closer, but didn't say anything. Great. She hoped they weren't back to the not talking thing.

She'd worry about that later. "I've got you, Bailey Bug. I'm not going to let you go."

With her arms wrapped around the girl she loved as much as she did her biological children, Julia prayed that everything would work out in their favor.

Chapter Thirty-Two

Topher waited impatiently for the gate to open at Jonathan's house. What was taking so long?

They were probably double checking who was at the gate, maybe even by security guards who didn't know Topher by sight. After what seemed like forever but was probably only a minute or so, the gate swung open. Topher drove through as soon as there was enough room. He left marks on the driveway as he skidded to a stop in front of the door. Where was Julia's SUV? The door opened as he reached the top step. Jonathan stood there holding the door open and then closed it behind Topher.

"Julia and the kids aren't here."

"What?" Topher couldn't believe his ears. "Where are they?"

"Alex is sick, and Bailey just wanted to be home. Julia

wanted them to be there. I sent security guards with them. They're safe. My guys told me she went straight inside the garage and didn't even get out until the garage door closed behind them."

Topher turned toward the door. "Well, I'm not staying here, then. I wish someone had told me."

"Sorry. I figured you would call when you got home and talk to either myself or Julia before you made it this far. I've been dealing with a few other things. I knew your wife and kids were safe."

"Got it." Topher knew Jonathan had other things going on in his life and his work besides taking care of Julia and the kids, especially if they were already home. It didn't mean Topher wasn't annoyed that Jonathan wasn't with them, and that no one had called him.

“I'll call you later."

He sped back out of Jonathan's drive and onto the road. He pushed the speed limit as much as he dared, but it still took far too long to get to his house. The gate seemed to take forever to open after he pushed the button. He didn't wait for the garage, though. Pulling up in front of the house, he put the car in park, pulled the keys out, and ran up the stairs.

"Hello?" He didn't see anyone. "Where is everyone?"

He didn't hear anything. He walked into the living room to find the twins sound asleep. *Good.*

"Hello?"

"In here," came a weak voice.

Topher looked around. The bathroom? Sure enough, he found Alex sitting on the floor with his back to the wall. Topher squatted down near him. "You feeling any better, buddy?" He reached out and brushed Alex's hair off his forehead. The kid felt warm. "Stomach still bothering you?" *Please don't throw up*. He couldn't handle it.

Alex nodded. "I feel blech."

"That's no fun." Topher ruffled Alex's hair. "Do you know where your mom and Bailey are?"

Alex shook his head. "I think they might be upstairs, but I'm not sure."

Topher whispered a prayer Alex would feel better then started for the stairs. "Hello? Bailey? Julia?" His first stop was Bailey's room, but they weren't there.

"In your closet," he heard Julia call.

His closet? Before he could think it through, he was through his room and into the closet. Where were they?

Julia stood up from that weird little corner. She reached down and scooped Bailey into her arms. Before she could make it across the small room, Topher had reached her side. He took Bailey, who was already reaching for him. She gripped his neck and buried her head in her arms.

"I don't want to go with him, Daddy."

"You won't have to. He's not your dad. Remember? We went and saw the judge, and the judge said you get to live with me forever."

"I 'member."

"That means you can never be taken away." Topher sat down in the chair in the sitting area of his bedroom. The statement wasn't entirely accurate, he knew that, but it would be quite the battle for anyone to take his daughter away from him.

Any of his kids.

As he snuggled Bailey close, that thought stayed with him.

He considered the twins his own in many ways, but Alex? The thought had crossed his mind more than once. Did he really think of Alex as his son?

Yes. He did.

The boy had wormed his way into Topher's heart, much like Julia had. He'd decided he wanted to make this family work, but he hadn't had much of a chance to discuss it with Julia or figure out whether she wanted the same thing. He never had talked to his lawyer about adoption either. Daniel would know what to do.

He'd make that his top priority as soon they ran Gene off.

Julia walked out the door, but stopped and came back when he called for her.

"Where are you going?"

A carefully neutral look crossed her face. "I'm going to check on my son. He's been throwing up most of the day."

"He's in the bathroom downstairs."

"I know." She disappeared down the hall.

Did she not want the same thing he did? Or did it have more to do with everything going crazy today and feeling overwhelmed?

Here, alone, with four kids, all of whom needed her after being chased by a crazy guy and photographers. That could be overwhelming.

And she was still only a few weeks postpartum.

He'd hired her as a nanny, but maybe the time had come to make sure she had the help she needed, too.

Julia headed down the stairs to find her son. He was still sitting in the bathroom, huddled against the wall.

"Why don't I take you upstairs and help you get ready to take a nap?"

Alex nodded and stretched up a hand.

Julia took it and helped him up. With her arm wrapped around his shoulder, they walked up the stairs and then to his room. She helped him get out pajamas then sent him into his bathroom to change. A minute later he came out and climbed into the bed she'd turn down. She pulled the covers up over him and leaned down to kiss his forehead. "You do feel warm, sweetheart." Fortunately, not quite warm enough for to her go find the thermometer. "Why don't you get some rest?"

"Will you stay with me?"

Julia smiled at how little he sounded. He was getting so big, so old, but when he was sick, he still just wanted his mom. She laid down on top of the covers and let her mind drift while he fell asleep.

Topher had been most solicitous once the yarn show ended, until he had to leave for LA. Nothing too over the top, but helping with the babies and the older kids and just kind of taking an interest in her and what was going on.

Did he want something more out of this relationship? Did she? She did. She knew she did, but was she willing to take the risk without knowing what he wanted?

As she lay there, she daydreamed about what it would be like to be in a real relationship with Topher. To have him kiss her again. Like he meant it. What it would be like to actually sit next to each other, to be in that new phase of a relationship were you can't get enough of being together. Is that what it would be like? Or would they go straight to the... She couldn't quite think of the right word. Apathetic, wasn't it, but she couldn't think of anything else. The part of a relationship where they didn't necessarily take the other person for granted, but kind of took the relationship for granted, kind of. The part of the relationship where they became so comfortable with each other and there just wasn't much trying too hard and uncomfortable and awkwardness anymore.

In some ways, it would be nice to be that comfortable with him so quickly, and not to wonder if he really liked her or what he was thinking.

After a little while, Alex's even breathing told Julia he'd finally fallen asleep. She carefully eased herself out of the bed and headed for the kitchen. She needed to make something for dinner. It was part of her job.

She met Topher in the hallway outside Bailey's room.

"She fell asleep," he whispered.

"Even though it will mess with bedtime, I kinda hope she stays that way for little while."

"Me, too. It's been a long day for her, and she needs the rest." She headed down the stairs with Topher on her heels. "How did the auditions go?"

"They went fine, I guess. All the roles have been cast. Sets are being designed, and we're still hoping to start shooting in February or so."

"So you're hoping to premiere next fall?"

"Yes. It would be good timing."

"Do you think that guy will be back?" Julia asked without looking him directly in the face. "I don't know what he hopes to gain. But clearly there's something that he wants."

"He probably wants money." Topher slid onto one of the barstools. "He thinks if he threatens to try to take Bailey, I might just throw money at him to get him to go away. The letters just said he was coming to get her."

"What letters?"

He sighed. "I didn't want you to worry, so I didn't tell you about them. I've gotten a few anonymous letters saying, 'I'm going to come for Bailey,' but nothing more. I turned them over to my lawyer, the police, and the FBI. Money would be new, but not unimaginable."

"Would you give it to him?" Julia open the cabinet and pulled out a 9 x 13 dish.

"Probably not. He doesn't deserve it. She's my daughter, I have full legal custody of her, and I see no reason why I should be extorted. He has no legal claim to custody of Bailey."

"So there's nothing to be worried about?"

"Other than him being a nuisance, I don't think so."

Surely Topher would do something, something legal anyway, to make the guy go away. Julia mixed together the ingredients for chicken pot pie while Topher worked on his tablet. About the time she put it in the oven, his phone rang.

"Hello?" She couldn't hear who was on the other end of the phone. Topher's expression went from calm to furious in a matter of seconds, and she knew. "You're not taking our daughter."

Julia didn't know what to do to try to help, so she prayed. That was probably the best thing she could do anyway. After listening for a few minutes, and reiterating over and over again that Bailey wasn't going anywhere, Topher hung up the phone.

"What does he want?"

"He wants our daughter." Topher's sardonic laughter filled her with dread. "He said he'll take $1.5 million instead, though. That his pain-and-suffering over losing his daughter is worth at least that much."

"Are you going to pay it?"

"I couldn't even if I wanted to." Topher's hands balled into fists. "But I don't want to. And I won't. I need to call my lawyer." He got up and headed for his office.

Julia prayed his lawyer would be able to do what was necessary to protect their little family. Even if things fell apart between her and Topher, he needed Bailey, and Bailey needed him. And that was the most important thing.

Topher breathed a sigh of relief. Daniel assured him the other man could do nothing, short of kidnapping, and Topher wasn't going to let that happen.

Daniel reassured him that he'd call Gene as well as the police and make sure they were aware of what was going on. He'd take care of all of it and let Topher know if the guy didn't back off.

While he waited to hear back, Topher tried to work on some other stuff, but his mind wandered.

Christmas was coming up. He'd heard enough from Bailey to know his little girl hadn't really had a real one, ever. If he had to guess, Alex hadn't either - and Julia probably hadn't had one in a very long time.

He needed to make Christmas plans. They were supposed

to go to Ravenzario at some point over break, though the timing hadn't been confirmed. Maybe they'd stay home for Christmas itself then leave the day after. Let the kids have a real Christmas morning at home.

Topher made a note to check with Julia about passports for the babies. They could rush order them if they needed to. A glance at his watch told Topher it had been nearly an hour. He wanted to pick up the phone and call Daniel, but he needed to trust the man.

Opening a new document on his computer, Topher started a Christmas list. Bailey and Alex could get bedroom makeovers, just the way they wanted them. He could probably go ahead and order ladybugs for Bailey. Alex was more difficult, but Topher could give him a card with a note on it explaining the present. Or he could ask Julia what kind of room Alex would like.

What else? Maybe a drone with a camera for Alex. Bikes for both of them. He was typing up his thoughts when his phone rang.

"Yes?"

"He won't bother you anymore," Daniel promised.

"How can you be so sure?"

"Because when I was doing that research a few months ago, I discovered some things the DEA was very interested in knowing. I might have implied to him that if he went away, I wouldn't pass the information along." Topher could hear the chuckle in the other man's voice. "A more appropriate promise would be that I wouldn't pass the information along *again*. I called my buddy at the DEA, and all he would say was that they were on it. They also have copies of all of the letters you gave me. So do the FBI."

"Good." And doubly good that Bailey wasn't going to be anywhere near that man. After a couple more minutes of conversation, Topher hung up and went to find his daughter.

Julia was pulling the casserole dish out of the oven. "Bailey's not up yet, and I doubt Alex will want to eat. I didn't think tonight's dinner through."

Topher waited just long enough for her to set it down then grabbed her around the waist and twirled her around. Julia's squeals filled his ears as her arms wrapped around his neck. "Doesn't matter. It's over. That man will never come near us again!"

She squeezed him tighter. "Topher! Really? That's wonderful!"

He set her down but didn't let her go and told her what Daniel had said. "He thinks we'll find out he never really wanted Bailey. He handed her over to me, made a few vague threats, let us get attached, then came back to get money. That's all he ever wanted." Julia beamed up at him the whole time.

A thought struck him. "Why don't you run upstairs and check on the older kids? Put on a nice dress, and we'll have dinner in the dining room."

Her expression changed to perplexed. "Um, sure." He hated to let her go, but he did. "The biscuits are in the oven. There's a timer," she called back over her shoulder.

Biscuits?

Topher shoved that thought out of his head, gathered two place settings, and hurried into the dining room, glad he hadn't changed out of the suit he'd been wearing to the auditions. Candles were already in place on the table, but spread out. He moved a couple of them closer, so they could pretend the rest of the table didn't exist. Napkins out of the china hutch finished the place settings.

Glasses. They needed glasses.

No wine. Julia was nursing. Apple juice would look right, but wouldn't go well with whatever she'd made. The timer went off, and Topher pulled the biscuits out of the oven, praying they were done.

He'd no sooner taken the food into the other room and lit the candles than she walked in.

"What's all this?"

Some of his nerves dissipated, but others took their place. Suave and flirtatious he could do, but far more rested on this than any other first real date. "A candlelight dinner with my wife." He pulled out her chair. "Your seat, milady."

She gave him a puzzled look as she sat down. "Thanks."

Once seated, but before reaching to dish up the food, Topher took her hand. "Do you mind if I pray?"

Julia shook her head and squeezed his hand as he prayed a heartfelt prayer thanking God for His provision.

With his napkin in his lap, Topher turned his attention to the food. "I have to admit, I'm not quite sure what this is."

"Chicken pot pie without the pie crust," she explained reaching for a biscuit. "This is how my mom always made it anyway. The gooey pot pie insides are kind of like gravy." She split a biscuit open on her plate then spooned the mixture from the casserole dish over it. "It's super easy to make, too. Two cans of veggies, diced up cooked chicken, two cans of cream of mushroom or chicken, and a can or two of milk so it's not quite so thick. Mix with some shredded cheese, top with some more, and into the oven it goes. Mom would bake it with biscuits on top, but I could never get them to cook right, so I make them on the side."

While she finished talking, Topher filled his own plate and started eating. Not what he was used to, but good. The meal was filled with small talk until they were both finished. That's when he reached over and took her hand.

"May I have this dance?"

Chapter Thirty-Three

Julia wasn't quite sure what he was up to, but she wasn't about to turn down the chance to dance with Chris Slate either.

No.

Not Chris Slate, though her teenage self would never believe what had transpired in the last months.

Topher Bayfield.

Her husband.

She nodded and let him help move her chair. He took her hand and led her a few steps toward the door to the kitchen. Stopping, Topher pulled his phone out of his pocket and tapped a few times before setting it back on the table.

Jazz music spilled out of the speaker.

Billie Holiday. Our Love is Here to Stay.

Topher pulled her close, his arm wrapping solidly around

her waist as he chuckled. "I didn't pick this song on purpose, just a jazz station."

Julia wrapped her hand around the back of his neck. "Is it an appropriate song?" It took everything in her to ask the question.

He hesitated as his thumb rubbed up and down her spine through the material of her dress. "I don't know. Is it?"

With her eyes closed, Julia took a deep breath then answered. "I kind of wish it was."

His chin rested against her temple. "Me, too."

The ache filled her chest. "Do you really mean that? After everything..."

"Sh." She felt his chin turn as he pressed a kiss against her hair. "I was wrong last spring." They were words she never thought she'd hear him say. "You weren't to blame for any of it, but I blamed you anyway, and I shouldn't have. I dreaded calling you to ask if you'd come live here and help take care of Bailey."

"Why?" Did she really want to know?

"Because I wasn't sure you could really be trusted. But you dropped everything to take care of my little girl and made sure I got to know her even when I was so far away. Then you helped me get to know her in person. And you didn't hesitate, not really, when it came to marrying me to protect her new stability. Thank you."

"I can honestly say it's been my pleasure. I don't know what I would have done if I'd ended up on bed rest back at my little apartment."

"I have no doubt you would have figured something out. You are incredibly resourceful."

She felt color climb into her cheeks. "Thanks."

"I don't know when or how it happened, not really, but I'm falling for you, Jules." Topher tucked her hand in close to his chest as she tightened her grip on the back of his neck. "I think of your kids as my kids. I want to adopt Alex, and for you to adopt Bailey, if that's okay with you and her. I'm not sure how she'd feel about it, because she does love her mom, you know?"

"I understand."

"And I wouldn't want to adopt Alex without approval from both of you. And his biological father, I suppose."

"I'm kind of surprised we haven't heard from his family, trying to get their fifteen minutes of fame."

"What would Alex think?"

"I think he'd be all for it." And a huge weight off Julia's shoulders for many reasons. If anything ever happened to her, her ex's family wouldn't be given custody.

"And you?"

"Definitely."

"I didn't see who you put down as the girls' father."

"No one, at first. I wasn't sure what to do. I don't want their biological father anywhere near them, but you're not their bio dad either. I should have asked, but I didn't." She hesitated. "But since we were married before their birth, you're legally considered their father, so I finally put you down. I just hope it was okay since you're not their biological father."

"I'll find out. I don't want their biological father anywhere near them."

The song had changed more than once while they did little more than sway to the music.

"I'm falling for you, too," Julia blurted out. "I had a crush on both of you years ago, like half of America's teenage girls, but I always preferred Chris, even though most girls liked Alex. I even have a dream board where I said I wanted to marry you."

He was kind of flattered, and wanted to see the dream board someday, but for now... "I'm not Chris Slate, though."

"I know that. I knew that then. I didn't know who you were, of course, but I knew you were more than your public persona. The dream board was a silly fourteen-year-old girl thing. I've known I was falling for the real you since the first video chat with Bailey while you were in Canada. I could see how much you already loved her, even though you weren't one hundred percent certain you were her father. I resisted it, even to myself, for months, but the last few days especially, I've known I want more."

"I heard you talking to your mom last week." The confession surprised her as she tried to remember the conversation.

"Which part?"

"Where you didn't think we'd ever love each other."

"Then you missed the part where we talked about how I wondered how to make this real."

His grip on her waist tightened more. "I guess I did." Topher let go of her hand and tipped her chin upward. "I want more. I want this to be real. Like my parents, my grandparents, or my brother. I want a real marriage."

Julia couldn't look him straight in the eye. "You know what I wished for earlier today?"

"What's that?"

"I wished we were already at that place where we're so comfortable together that we don't even feel we need to try anymore. You know, when you don't try to stifle the burp, or where I don't feel the need to have my hair perfect and make up on just to eat breakfast."

"I understand what you're saying, but I kind of hope we're never at the point where we don't try."

"I know. I just want it to be okay to show up for Saturday morning breakfast in pajamas with bed head."

He chuckled. "I'm not sure I've ever seen you with bed head."

"I've seen you." The color crept into her cheeks again. "You have pretty adorable bed head. My hair just looks like a rat's nest."

Topher didn't contradict her statement, but before she could say anything else, he surprised her as his lips claimed hers.

Topher wasn't sure what possessed him to kiss Julia, but now that he was he didn't want to stop.

He tightened his hold on her so he could kiss her more fully.

Before he could make a conscious decision to take the kiss deeper or further, Julia pulled away.

"Did you hear that?" she whispered.

"Hear what?" He didn't hear anything but the rapid beating of his own heart.

"That's Alex." She gave him a hard, swift kiss. "I need to check on him."

One more quick kiss, and she was gone, but he heard

another voice upstairs, this one calling for him.

Topher followed the same path Julia had taken up the stairs, but stopped when he reached Bailey's room. "Yes, sweetheart?"

Bailey sat in the middle of her bed, covers pulled up to her waist. "You weren't here when I woke up, Daddy." The accusation in her voice nearly broke his heart. Had she expected him to stay while she slept? If he had known that he would have, but the honest truth was that his time had probably been better spent with Julia.

"I'm right here, Bailey Bug." He crossed the room and sat on the bed next to her. "Come here." He opened his arms and she climbed willingly onto his lap. “Everything's okay, sweetheart."

"Will you let him come take me?"

"I already talked to my lawyer, and he already talked to that man. It's over. He won't ever bother us again."

"Are you sure, Daddy?"

He pulled her closer. "I am. But if he ever does come back, I'll do the same thing all over again, and make sure he goes away." He better not ever come back.

“Good."

They sat there for a short time until Bailey said she was hungry.

"Julia made dinner."

"Do you think Julia could be my mommy?" Bailey's tiny voice and the uncertainty in it made Topher want to reassure her that nothing would please Julia more. But before he could, Bailey spoke again. "Do you think my first mommy would mind?"

She'd asked a loaded question Topher had no idea how to answer. Not truthfully. "I think your first mommy would want you to be happy and safe and taken care of. Do you think asking Julia to be your mommy is the way to do that?" Seemed like a safe way to put it.

Bailey nodded, but didn't say anything else.

"Well, then why don't you ask her?"

"Would Alex share his mommy with me?"

Topher kissed her head. "I bet he would." He and Julia hadn't discussed when to talk to the kids, but it seemed like the right time. "Would you be okay sharing your daddy with him?"

Bailey nodded vigorously. "Then he could really be my brother."

"You're right. Why don't we talk to them about it in a little while? Maybe when Alex feels better."

Bailey seemed to not hear the last part, because she climbed down and took off toward the door, hollering for Alex. Topher quickly followed.

Julia and Alex were coming out of his room. Alex looked better than he had earlier in the afternoon.

Bailey stopped in front of them with her hands on her hips. "Alex, I'll share my daddy if you share your mommy. Isn't that a good deal?"

Alex looked up at his mom. Julia looked like she wasn't sure what to make of Bailey's statement.

Sorry, Topher mouthed at her. She shrugged.

"Well?" Bailey asked. Topher was kind of surprised she didn't stomp her foot.

"I'll share my mom with you, even if your dad doesn't want

to adopt me." Alex didn't look at Topher as he spoke. "If your dad and my mom want my mom to adopt you, then you could be my sister for real."

Bailey spun on one foot. "Tell him, Daddy."

"I would be honored to be your father, Alex." Topher bowed slightly at the waist. "If you want me to. I want to be your father, and Annie and Marissa's. For real."

The shouts that filled the hallway nearly deafened Topher. He couldn't help but laugh as the kids jumped around in circles.

Julia looked about the same, and then grimaced as another noise was heard. "I think we woke the twins up."

While Julia took care of the babies, Topher made Alex some toast, and heated up some chicken pot pie for Bailey. By the time Julia was done feeding the girls, the older kids were done eating too. They ran into the living room where she snuggled Annie. Topher picked up Marissa from the bassinet then sat down next to his wife. He cradled the baby in one arm and wrapped the other around his wife, pulling her closer to him. He kissed her forehead.

"This is perfect," she whispered.

"It was all Bailey's idea, you know." He kept his voice down. "She brought up adoption."

"Seems like God knew the right timing for all of it." Julia leaned her head against his shoulder.

Topher grinned. "I guess He did. I guess all those glimpses of a future we both had over the last few months were just waiting for the right time to come true."

Bailey and Alex climbed onto the couch with them. Bailey turned on an episode of *Blue's Clues* while she snuggled next to Julia. Julia turned her head and leaned up just enough to kiss Topher on the side of his mouth. "Yep. I think this is just about perfect."

Topher couldn't have said it better himself.

Epilogue

Excited squeals woke Topher before the bouncing on the bed did.

"It's morning!" cried one voice.

"Christmas morning!" yelled the other.

"We're awake." His wife's sleepy murmur echoed his own thoughts. "I'm pretty sure you woke the babies up, too."

"I think they woke the entire county." Topher reached his hands over his head and stretched before opening his eyes to see his son and oldest daughter perched on the end of the bed. "Merry Christmas."

"Merry Christmas, Daddy!" Bailey scrambled toward him with Alex not far behind.

Topher pulled both of them into a hug then let them go. "Did you already go to the bathroom?"

"Yes," they cried in unison.

"Well, Mom and I haven't." He pushed himself further into a seated position. "Why don't you go sit on the top step, and we'll get up? In a few minutes, we'll go downstairs together."

Or he and Julia would go down first. They'd discussed it in the wee hours of the morning with her head on his chest and his arm wrapped around her back holding her close. She'd get situated feeding the babies if they were hungry. He'd have a camera out and then let the kids come down.

A perfect plan.

One that would have been better in a couple more hours, but such was life with kids.

"You know," Julia started, sitting up next to him. "It's your first Christmas, too."

Topher snorted. "Not hardly."

"It's your first Christmas as a parent. That's a whole different thing than as a kid."

She had a point, and he leaned over to kiss her, trying not to let his mind wander back to the night before after she'd gotten the all clear from her doctor.

They took turns in the bathroom and admonished the kids to stay put while they each carried a baby downstairs. Once the cinnamon rolls were in the oven and Julia was nursing the twins in her chair, he went to set up a camera.

"Are you glad we didn't go to Mevendia for the wedding yesterday?" she asked.

Topher looked over at her and grinned. "Miss my first Christmas morning with my kids in our own house? Nah. I'm glad we stayed." While getting everything ready for the kids, he thought back over the last few weeks. They had been fantastic. After the younger kids were in bed, they'd talked about everything under the sun, including their past relationships. She told him about the biological fathers of her children and how glad she was to finally be able to trust her judgment in men. He told her about Martha - and Margie McCoy, his former co-star who had dragged his name through the mud as *2C4S* ended. Their marriage was starting to feel like a real relationship.

He went to the bottom of the stairs. "Okay, this is how it's gonna work. You can open your stockings now. We'll all open presents after breakfast, okay?"

They shouted their agreement. Topher went back to the living room and turned on the camera on his phone before telling them they could come down.

Julia was right. It was different to see the looks on his kids' faces. They both absolutely lit up. They'd decorated the tree a few weeks before, but the presents had appeared after bedtime on Christmas Eve.

They found their stockings, but before either one dumped them out, Alex picked up the other two, the ones Topher hadn't known were there. "Here's yours, Dad," he said as he handed one to Topher. The other went to Julia.

Topher propped his phone up on the end table where it could still see Bailey and Alex. "I didn't know we got stockings, too," he whispered to his wife.

She shrugged. "It's not much, but yes. It's got stuffing in it, too, to make it look fuller than it is. Otherwise, it would look pretty empty."

He dumped it on the floor in front of him. Mostly assorted candy, but a small box caught his eye. "What's this?" he asked, picking it up.

"Something I thought you might like."

He shook the box a little bit until the bottom fell out. He picked up the key. It was oddly shaped, unlike anything he'd seen before. "What is it?"

She didn't answer, so he picked up the small slip of paper and unfolded it.

I know it's corny, but I didn't pick out the ring you wear. I didn't even help decide which ones to use. I love your grandparents' rings, and it's the one I put on your finger the day we said, "I do," so I don't want to replace it either. I thought through a bunch of options and searched online, but everything was pretty hokey.

One idea kept standing out, though I didn't like any of the executions I found, so I made my own.

This is the key to my heart. It can fit on your keyring without anyone thinking it looks girly or weird or out of place, but it's different enough that you'll never mistake it for a house key either.

When you look through your keys for the right one for your office or the set or whatever, you'll see this key and know that my heart belongs to you. It has since the first glimpse of hope snuck through months ago (or when I saw the first episode of 2 Cool 4 School, whichever).

I love you, Christopher Bayfield. I think I have for pretty much forever, and I don't plan to ever stop.

Topher's vision blurred as he read the note and he leaned over to kiss her square on the mouth. "I love it, Jules. It's perfect." Another kiss. "And I love you." He asked Bailey to bring him one of the presents under the tree. "I was going to save this for later, but..." He took the twins one at a time and laid them in their bassinet while Bailey handed it to her.

She ripped open the paper and shook the lid off the box. Shooting him a puzzled glance, she pulled out the pile of papers. "What's this?"

"The adoption paperwork for the kids. Daniel is still getting it all set up, but we should be able to get it finalized by the end of January."

Julia leaned over and kissed him, tears glistening in her eyes. "Thank you."

"My pleasure. I wish I'd been able to get it done before Christmas, but there just wasn't enough time."

"This is perfect."

The kids interrupted their conversation. He'd explain it to them later. Everything else under the tree was fun or useful, but nothing overly deep and meaningful. "I do wish I had something more." He'd made a large donation to FreedomWorks on her behalf, but that was it.

"I don't want anything else," she told him. "I have you. I have the kids. Before you know it, you're going to legally be the father of four. It's all I need."

She handed him one of the babies, though he didn't look to see which one as Alex and Bailey distracted them with their exclamations of joy over mundane things like chocolate mini-candy and mechanical pencils and boxes of crayons.

No longer did he have to settle for glimpses of the life he longed for. He didn't have to watch his brother and sister-in-law or his parents or even Jonathan and Kenzie. Instead, he just had to look at his family. So much bigger than it had been even six months earlier.

It wouldn't always be easy, but looking around at the ones

he loved most, he knew it would all be worth it..

Dear Reader,

Thank you for joining Christopher, Julia, Alex, and Bailey in *Glimpsing Hope*! I appreciate you and hope you enjoyed it! This is the second book in the Serenity Landing Second Chances series! Next up is Crown Prince Richard of Mevendia! YAY! That story is out now! More YAY!

FreedomWorks has been mentioned a couple of times in this series. It's an organization run by a couple who work through the Assemblies of God. They work hard to get women in the sex trade in India out of that life - and to give them hope. You can find out more on their www.ThatTheyRemainFree.com website, but to protect their ladies from further exploitation, details of what they do and their actual identities are not shared. If you feel led, you can find out more on their website, including ways to donate. You can also find their yarn at your local Hobby Lobby.

The Show Me Yarn ladies are real, too! In fact, they're dear friends of mine! If you've followed my Facebook page, you may have seen me writing in a friend's rec room. That's the room where they do all of their dyeing (for now - they're working on getting their own space). I've even helped a little bit - including brainstorming names for some of their colors. HUGE thank you to Ginger, Christa, and Ester! If you like all things yarn, check out their Facebook page, Show Me Yarn, and Etsy site – www.etsy.com/shop/showmeyarn!

Bailey... Bailey is named for the sweet daughter of one of my oldest friends (longest friends? Because we can't be getting OLD!). I've known Amy since I was five and started first grade in a new school in a new town in a new state. I met Jeremy when he started attending our school much later. I remember (vaguely) their first date. They got married. Had a son - Liam, who is the very picture of God's love personified. Then Bailey was born on 9/12. Her time on this earth was far, far too short, but she impacted so many. Fiona came along not too long after that. I've loved getting to watch her - and Liam - grow through the wonder of Facebook.

Someday, I hope to bring you the story of the real Bailey, via Amy's own words. Both Liam and Bailey have/had the same genetic disorder, that has given Amy and Jeremy and their families some of the biggest trials...and the biggest blessings. The strength and courage of Amy, Jeremy, and the millions of other parents like them never ceases to amaze me. I'm so grateful for Amy's continued friendship - and the glimpses of hope she and others give the rest of us of Christ-like love here on earth.

In a few pages, you'll find the first chapter of *Reclaiming Hearts* – Prince William's story! YAY!

In just a few more pages, you'll find chapter 1 of *Grace to Save*, the first book in the Serenity Landing Tuesdays of Grace series! It's the story of Travis Harders and his daughter, Cassie. Travis is the theater teacher at Serenity Landing High School and both have shown up from time to time in other books. It's a story that's very near and dear to my heart, to the core of who I am.

It's a story of prodigals, and redemption, and mercy, and oh-so-much grace.

You can find it available now on Amazon.

Just a reminder, *Good Enough for a Princess*, book 1 in the Montevaro Monarchy series is FREE on all retailers! Though it was two series ago, that book is the beginning of the events that lead to *Glimpsing Hope.* Many of you have likely already read *Finding Mr. Write*, but if not, it too is FREE on all retailers!

I see a meme floating around Facebook from time to time that tells readers what they can do to help their favorite authors. Buying their next book or giving a copy away is kind of a no-brainer, but the biggest thing you can do is write a review. If you enjoyed *Glimpsing Hope* would you consider doing just that?

I would LOVE to hear from you! My email address is books@candidpublications.com. To stay up-to-date on releases, you can sign up for my newsletter (there's fun stuff - like a super special novella that will be coming FREE before the beginning of my next royalty series next year!! You'll also get notices of sales, including special preorder pricing! And I won't spam!) or there's always "What's in the Works" or "What I'm Working On Now" on my website :). You can find my website and blog at www.carolmoncado.com. I blog about once a month at www.InspyRomance.com. And, of course, there's Facebook and my Facebook profile, Author Carol Moncado. If you recently liked my Facebook *page* (Carol Moncado Books)...I hope you'll "follow" the profile as well. Facebook recently changed the rules again which means very few people (often 1-5% of "likes") will see anything I post there. Following the profile will show you my book updates, updates about books from authors I love, funny cat (or dog or dinosaur!) memes, inspirational quotes, and all sorts of fun stuff!! I hope to see you there soon!

Thanks again!

Acknowledgments

They say writing is a solitary endeavor, and it absolutely can be. Sitting in front of the computer for hours on end, talking to imaginary people.

And having them talk back ;).

But the reality is no one walks alone. Since I began this writing journey nearly six years ago, I can't begin to name all of those who've helped me along the way. My husband, Matt, who has always, *always* believed in me. All of the rest of my family and in-loves who never once looked at me like I was nuts for wanting to be a writer. Jan Christiansen (my "other mother") has always believed in me and Stacy Christiansen Spangler who has been my dearest friend for longer than I can remember.

Ginger Solomon, author of *One Choice* and a bunch of other fantastic books (but *One Choice* is still my favorite!), has been invaluable with her proofreading services.

Then there's my writer friends. My NovelSista, Jessica Keller Koschnitzky, sister of my heart. She is part of my BritCrit gals. Joanna Politano (who has talked me down off more virtual ledges than anyone), Jen Cvelbar (the best case of misidentification *ever*, not to mention best conference roomie), Kristy Cambron (who is more beautiful inside and out than any one person should be allowed to be), and Stacey Zink (who never, ever fails to have a fabulous encouraging word) are BritCritters, too. We do a lot more living than we do critting, and I wouldn't have it any other way. All five of them are beyond gifted as writers, and I thank God they're in my life. There's my MozArks ACFW peeps who laugh with me, critique, and encourage to no end. Then there's the InspyRomance crew, the CIA, my Spicy peeps (you know who you are!), and all of the others who've helped me along on this journey.

And Tamela Hancock Murray - my agent extraordinaire, who despite the lack of "anything in it for her" has supported me in this crazy indie journey.

I said I could go on for days, and I could keep going. On and on. I know I've forgotten many people and I hate that. But you, dear reader, would quickly get bored.

So THANK YOU to all of those who have helped me along the way. I couldn't have done this without you and you have my eternal gratitude. To the HUNDREDS of you (I'm gobsmacked!) who pre-ordered and encouraged me without knowing it as that little number continued to climb, you have my eternal gratitude. I hope you stick around for the next one!

And, of course, last but never, *ever*, least, to Jesus Christ, without whom none of this would be possible - or worth it.

Available Now

Prince William Richard Stephen Jedidiah, first in line for the throne of Mevendia, hurt in every place he could possibly hurt.

But why?

Groaning reached his ears, and he realized it came from him. Blinking his eyes open, he found the plane shrouded in darkness. He was on board his family's plane, right? He tried to think back.

Yes. He was flying home from Serenity Landing. There had been turbulence after the pilots said they'd be landing in Eyjania due to weather. Then... nothing.

"Lou? Frankie? Lane?" The pilots and steward were nearby. They had to be.

But something else niggled at his memory.

Some*one* else.

"Lady Margaret?" His voice turned more frantic. He was responsible for getting the elderly woman home safely. "Lady Margaret, are you all right?"

No reply.

William pulled his phone out of his pocket and turned on the flashlight. Lane was in his jump seat near the back of the plane. Blood oozed from a gash on his forehead. With a flip of the release, William took his seatbelt off and went to Lane's side. He was breathing and his pulse was strong. Hopefully, Lane was just unconscious for a few minutes longer than William himself had been.

Ignoring the throbbing pain in his ankle, William worked his way forward.

He found Lady Margaret slumped over in her seat, breathing but with no signs of bleeding. Closer inspection showed her hair askew. So the woman wore a wig. Interesting. But not interesting enough. He needed to find Lou and Frankie.

"Sir?" Frankie's voice came from the cockpit. "Is everyone okay back there?"

"I think so," William called, heading that way. "They're both unconscious, but they're breathing." Lane was their paramedic, though both pilots had some training.

"We'll be back in a minute," Lou called.

Without waiting for them, William unbuckled Lady Margaret's seatbelt and carried her to the couch where he laid her down. By the time he did, Lane was stirring.

"Careful, Lane. You've got a gash on your head." William probably did, too, but this wasn't the time.

"Are you all right, sir?" Lane's eyes were barely open, and he already asked about William. His family had worked for William's for generations.

"Fine." Not accurate, but close enough. When the adrenaline rush ended, there would be a price to pay. He already knew that. It almost made him glad his security team had traveled ahead and not with them. Lane was a member of the security office, though he didn't actively work on a security team except as needed. His presence had been enough to convince William's normal team to go ahead.

Lou and Frankie, also trained with security just in case, emerged from the cockpit. "We're fine," Frankie assured him.

"Good." William stood with his hands on his hips. "Now what?"

"Now we try to get help. We're not too far from town, but our radio went out before we could send a mayday." Frankie crossed his arms across his chest in thought. "We need to find shelter, and then a couple of us can go for help."

"I don't think I can," Lane told them. "I'm pretty sure my arm's broken."

William looked at the debris around the cabin. Some of the stowed luggage had come loose from its bins. He didn't know who the rest of the luggage belonged to, but a piece of it must have hit Lane.

Lou and Frankie exchanged a look. "We're going to go scout around for a few minutes and see if we can find anything. There's supposed to be cabins in this area. I think your family's property is close, sir."

"I'm not familiar enough with the area around the property to tell."

After another minute of discussion, Lou and Frankie took powerful flashlights and opened the emergency exit. They'd be back in a few minutes before going further.

A groan from the couch caught William's attention.

"Take care of her, sir." Lane leaned his head back against the bulkhead. "I'm gonna stay right here."

William knelt next to the couch. "Lady Margaret? Can you hear me?"

Several more groans came out before a word did. "*Liam?*"

Liam? No one had called him that in years. And even then...

Rather than let the memories overwhelm him, he pushed them to the side and told himself she just didn't pronounce his name right after such a traumatic experience.

"It's Prince William, Lady Margaret. We were in a plane crash."

"We were?" She sounded more alert and struggled to sit up.

"Please be still, Lady Margaret. Don't try to sit up yet."

"Where are we?"

"As best I can tell from what the pilots said earlier, a fairly large meadow in the mountains of Eyjania."

She pushed herself up with one arm until she reached a seated position. "How far from town?"

"I'm not sure. The pilots are outside, scouting around to see if there's a cabin nearby."

Before she could respond, Lou came through the door.

"We found a cabin on the edge of the clearing. If you have a small overnight bag you can grab, that might not be a bad idea. We're farther from town than we thought."

It took nearly half an hour to get Lane's arm into a sling,

check William and Lady Margaret out a bit more thoroughly, and find the overnight bags.

The cold settled in. November in these mountains could be harsh. Frankie had gone ahead to the cabin, hoping to get a fire started or find a telephone.

Lou helped Lane out of the plane, leaving Lady Margaret for William.

"Let me help you," he insisted. "I know you didn't need my help getting into the plane, but this is non-negotiable."

She didn't even try to turn him down.

The feel of her hand wrapped in his larger one unsettled him. Something seemed familiar about it, though he had no idea what. He'd never even heard of the woman until a few months earlier when dancing with a friend's wife.

Jonathan Langley-Cranston had taken Kenzie to a Mevendian wool festival earlier in the day, and she had gushed about the whole thing, including Lady Margaret. He'd never met the elderly woman until a few days ago.

Once on the ground, Lou led them around the tail section of the plane. In the distance, they could see lights. That's where they headed, snow and cold seeping deep into their bones. None of them had dressed for knee-deep snow.

Long minutes later, they reached the cabin. The rush started to abate and William knew the adrenaline crash would soon follow. The aches and pains he'd been able to push past would then come rushing to the forefront. He kept a grip on Lady Margaret's left hand with his, while his right arm went around her back to help her up the slick stairs to the porch.

But when they reached the top step, William's ankle gave away, and he crumbled where he'd stood.

Lady Margaret stumbled backward, falling into the snow drift. He looked helplessly up at Lou and Frankie.

Now what?

Lady Margaretha of Delatreaux wanted to cry, but didn't dare. Not with her disguise still in place. Tears would ruin her make up.

One of the pilots hurried carefully down the stairs while the other helped Prince William to his feet.

William looped an arm around the pilot's shoulders and didn't put much weight on one leg.

"Give me your hand, ma'am."

Maggie looked up to see the other pilot standing over her.

"We need to get you inside."

She nodded and took his offered hand. He helped her up and to the porch, this time without the tumble.

"Forgive me for noticing, ma'am, but your wig has slipped."

Maggie's hand flew to her head. It was still there, but definitely out of place.

"No worries, ma'am. My grandmother often wore a wig when her hair thinned. It's unlikely anyone knows, and I promise you, we can be trusted."

She gave a curt nod, but it was so much more than that. A wig was one thing, but what if William found out who she was?

Her first moments awake flooded back to her. Had she called him *Liam*? No one ever called him that, except her, in their most personal, private moments together.

Once inside the cabin, she took a quick survey then picked up her bag and headed for the bedroom on the other side of the living area. Surely none of the men would object to an elderly woman using the only bedroom.

At least one of them, but not William, called after her. She ignored him. Using the flashlight on her blessedly-undamaged phone, she found a mirror and straightened her wig. At least the wig cap kept anyone from seeing her natural hair color.

A minute later, one of them knocked on the door. “Ma’am, that room’s not heated. You need to be out here by the fire.”

“I will be fine,” she called. “I’m changing into dry clothes.” But even as she said it, she reconsidered. Her fingers were numb. Straightening the wig had taken all of her effort.

She had two outfits in her overnight bag, one for Maggie and one for Lady Margaret - just in case. Teeth chattering and fingers fumbling, she managed to take off the outfit she wore over her bodysuit.

Her wet bodysuit.

But it wasn’t wet all the way through. She’d be fine. It took some effort, but she managed to pull on pants and a tunic before emerging from the bedroom.

“I will be sleeping in here,” she announced. “Now that I have dry clothes on, I will be quite warm.”

The three men looked to Prince William who simply nodded.

Good. He wasn’t going to pull rank on her. She turned her back and shut the door behind her. As soon as her things were shoved back in the bag, Maggie scrambled under the covers and prayed they would warm her up.

But the process was slow. Too slow.

She drifted back to Serenity Landing as darkness overcame her.

Maggie refused to curtsy to Prince William.

Not this time. Even if he was giving her a lift home from Serenity Landing on the royal plane.

She *had* curtsied several days earlier when he'd shocked her with his arrival at the festival in the town of Serenity Landing, Missouri, but she wouldn't do it again.

Her car pulled to a stop near the Mevendian royal plane. A gentleman waited to open her door. She just had to remember not to act her age.

Prince William was being kind enough to offer her a lift home. A snowstorm in Chicago meant her flights were canceled. Being stuck in the States was not on her agenda. Not even close. She had to be home by morning or all kinds of crazy would break out.

"Ma'am?"

Maggie reached out a hand and let the man assist her out of the car. "Thank you," she murmured. *Don't say much. Don't answer questions. Don't get too close.*

That was her motto when in her alter ego's clothing as she was at the moment.

No one knew Lady Margaretha of Delatreaux was Lady Margaret of Aquitaine Toulouse, world-renowned teacher of the lost Mevendian technique of spinning yarn.

She neared the plane and ignored Prince William's offer of assistance up the staircase. Despite his kindness, he didn't deserve the time of day from her.

He'd know that if he knew her true identity.

When was the last time they'd actually spoken to each other?

Somehow he'd ignored her in the receiving line at his brother's wedding. That took skill.

Maggie surveyed the inside of the plane quickly and chose a comfortable chair that seemed to be far enough away from the others that he might not bother her.

"Are you sure you wouldn't prefer to sit back here, ma'am?" The steward stood next to a couch.

"No." One word answers. Keep it simple.

William gave her an odd look, one she recognized from the days when they were much closer. Closer than anyone knew.

He thought she was being rude.

Too bad.

The prince settled into a chair on the other side of the plane and back several feet. A few moments later, the pilot instructed them to buckle in and prepare for take-off.

She had to make it to the other side of the Atlantic without anyone finding out who she really was.

Not even the one man who should know her better than anyone else.

All of the next generation of royals from the Commonwealth of Belles Montagnes have found love.

Except one.

Crown Prince William of Mevendia has done an

exceptional job of keeping his private life out of the public eye. It's been half a decade since he was last romantically linked with anyone, and even then, no one actually knew who she was.

Margaretha Delatreaux had once fancied herself in love with a prince. Maybe she still did. Promises broken still cause her heart to ache, and she longs to repair the damage the last words they'd flung at each other had done.

After a chance encounter, a life or death situation, a foreign country, and unflattering press, just maybe they'll have a second chance at reclaiming hearts.

Previews may not be in their final form and are subject to change.

Available Now!

September 11, 2001

A ringing jolted Travis Harders from a deep sleep. He cursed as the phone knocked to the floor with a clatter. "This better be good," he snapped when he got the handset in place.

A glance at the clock nearly made him groan.

4:07.

"You'll be hearing from the police soon."

He rubbed the sleep out of his eyes with the heel of one hand and tried to process the statement. The words didn't really register as the guy, whoever he was, kept talking until Travis interrupted. "What? Who is this?"

"Mark's dad." Right. Travis's best friend. "You remember us? The ones who treated you like family? Let you live with us?"

Travis's stomach sank. Mark's family had practically adopted him when he moved from southwest Missouri to the Big Apple. They had filled the gap in his life left by parents who disapproved of Travis's choice to move to New York. Mark's parents let him spend holidays and birthdays with them, with Travis making only the obligatory phone calls back home.

But none of that explained why Mark's dad would be calling the police.

"Who is it?" a sleepy Jennifer asked.

Travis covered the mouthpiece and whispered to his girlfriend, "No one." His feet hit the cool floor, and he headed for the other room. At least he had a place to escape to. Being an out-of-work-actor-turned-barista didn't pay much, but he'd lucked into a fabulous apartment. Closing the French door behind him, he tried to focus on the voice yelling from the other end of the line.

But he only caught "my daughter" and "spring break" and "drugged."

If possible, Travis's stomach clenched further as that night flooded back to him. Memories of bringing her back to this very apartment when she was in no condition to go home without risking the wrath of her parents. But after what happened between them…it was only right for him to be on the receiving end of her dad's anger. "I don't know what she told you sir, but…"

"I know all I need to know," he bellowed.

Even though he was in the other room, Travis lowered the volume on the handset. "I take full responsibility for…"

"You're right, you do!" He let loose a string of obscenities. "You'll spend years in prison! Drugging a girl! Sleeping with her!"

"What?" His whole world spun. Travis regretted every

minute of that night after they got back to the apartment, but he hadn't drugged her. He didn't even know where to get those kinds of drugs. They weren't in love, never had been, but to place the blame solely on him? The next morning, they'd talked about it enough to know she hadn't blamed him.

What changed? Feeling sucker punched, Travis hung up on the man. What he said didn't matter. Travis would find out when he was on trial for something he didn't do. On autopilot, he dressed for his five a.m. shift. Coffees of the World wasn't the best job, but it had flexible hours and had led to finding this sublet. There was no shortage of interesting characters to populate his imagination. Like the skinny brunette with the shoulder length bob who worked for Morgan Stanley and always ordered a short nonfat mocha, decaf, no foam, no sugar, no whip. She could be the heroine in one of his screenplays even if he never knew her name.

He kissed Jennifer's hair and told her he'd call after work. Five flights of stairs later, the sounds of the city waking up greeted him as he walked toward the train that would take him to the Trade Center. Standing at the top of the subway steps, he changed his mind. Travis headed for his car parked a couple streets over and called in.

Two hours later, he stopped in McLean for gas about seven thirty, filling up the tank of his Toyota Corolla hatchback. Three hours after that, he could still drive for a while longer before he'd need to stop again. He contemplated leaving the state, but decided not to, instead turning northward before leaving Allegany County.

He'd gone through more emotions than he knew he had, none of them good. Anger. Fear. Frustration. Blame. Worry.

Intimidation. In western New York, things were more peaceful than they ever were in downtown Manhattan, but his insides were in utter turmoil at the thought of an arrest and trial.

His favorite heavy metal CD blared from the speakers. During the lull between songs, Travis could hear his cell phone vibrating on the passenger seat where he'd tossed it. After an hour and a half of the stupid thing ringing nearly nonstop, he finally snatched it up.

"What?" Travis growled.

"Are you okay?" Though he only talked to her twice a year, there was no mistaking his mother's voice.

Or the panic in it.

The tremor set him on edge. "Yeah. Why?"

"Thank you, Jesus," she whispered, though Travis couldn't figure out what she was thanking Him for. "Where are you? You got out okay? Were you working? There was no answer at your apartment."

Why was Mom calling just to ask if he was okay? Why was she frantic? "I'm in western New York State. Out for a drive. Get out of where?" Could Mark's dad have called already?

"You don't know?" Frenzy changed to disbelief.

"Know what?" Travis held the phone against his shoulder as he downshifted into a turn.

He could hear the tears over the static-filled line. "Two planes, Trav. They hit the Towers. Both of the buildings are on fire."

His heart thudded to a stop. "What?" Hadn't a bomber hit the Empire State Building in WWII? But two planes? On a brilliantly clear day? No weather in sight. "How bad is it?" he croaked.

"They're saying it's a terror attack. The Pentagon is on fire. There's another plane out there somewhere. Big jets, Travis. I saw the second one hit. The explosion. Papers flying everywhere. The people..." Her voice broke. "You really weren't there?" she confirmed.

"No, Mom. I'm not anywhere near there." But he needed to find a place to stop. A television. He had to see for himself. Tens of thousands of people would be dead and dying. Did he know any of them?

"There are people jumping, falling, out of the upper stories. I can't imagine." He could almost see her pacing around the kitchen alternately running her hands through her hair and wringing them together. "They're jumping from a hundred stories up. What could be so bad to make that the better option?" Her voice caught. "I don't know how I can watch this, Trav, but I can't turn away. All I can do is pray."

Pray. Right. A face flashed before Travis. The uptight former-football-player-turned-businessman from the 102nd floor of the North Tower with his caramel macchiato and corny joke of the day. Was he one of those jumping?

She gasped then whispered. "Dear God, no. No!" Her scream made him move the phone even as his stomach sank.

He pulled into a café parking lot near Danville. "What?"

"The tower. It's gone. Just gone. The south one, I think." Her voice trailed off in prayer.

The shock he'd felt after the phone call from Mark's dad paled compared to what he felt now. "Mom, I gotta go." Jen. His friends. His coworkers. He needed to make calls of his own. Find out if they were okay. And Mark. His best friend had been a firefighter for a year. He'd be down there. Inside one of the Towers. Travis hadn't talked to him since that night, the March before, but part of him, the part that still believed there was a God in heaven, whispered a prayer that Mark was somewhere safe as faces of customers and friends flashed through Travis's mind.

The blonde. The cute, petite one who ordered a crunchy, cinnamon pastry and half caf, double tall, easy hazelnut, non-fat, no foam with whip extra hot latte on Tuesdays. She flirted shamelessly, though he knew she was recently and happily engaged to some guy in Tower Seven. Her family lived near his in Serenity Landing, Missouri, and she worked at the Marriot World Trade Center in the shadow of the Towers. Could it have survived the collapse? Was Joanna now buried underneath the rubble?

"Be safe, Travis. Do you have somewhere you can go? They're evacuating Manhattan."

"I'll be okay." He hesitated. "I love you, Mom. You, Dad, Jay. I love all of you. I'll call when I can, but I have to try to find out about my friends, about my girlfriend. I'll talk to you soon."

His mom's "I love you," came through the line as he clicked his phone off.

He started his first call as he walked into the café. Call after call failed as he stood with others, watching the screen in horror as the second tower crashed down. His problems. Mark's dad. Mark's sister. All of it fled as the enormity of what was happening sunk in.

The whole world had changed.

December 18, 2001

"It's a girl."

Abi Connealy collapsed back onto the bed, tears streaming down her cheeks as a newborn squawk filled the delivery room.

A girl.

A million thoughts flew through her mind, few of them happy, as a nurse laid the baby on her chest. So small. So scrunched up and red. Dark hair. Abi couldn't see her eyes as she wrapped her arms around the tiny bundle. "Hi, baby," she whispered. "I'm so glad you're here."

"How are you?"

Abi looked up at Brenda Wardman. Her brother's girlfriend had been a rock the last few months. She didn't need to clarify, because Abi knew what she meant. "I don't know." The voice mail she'd left her parents on the way to the hospital remained unanswered unless Brenda knew something she didn't.

Her fingers brushed over the cheek of the tiny girl. "She's perfect, Bren." Another tear fell, this one landing on her new daughter's face as Abi closed her eyes.

The nurse took the baby to the warmer and did whatever it was nurses did, but Abi didn't see any of it. Her eyes remained closed, and she clasped Brenda's hand as more hot tears streaked into her ears. Just under twenty-four hours of labor meant she didn't have the energy to wipe them away. She knew she didn't have the will to do so even if she could have.

"Do you know what you're going to do?"

Abi wanted to yell at her friend for bringing up the most difficult decision of her life just moments after the birth of her daughter. But since Abi hadn't made up her mind beforehand,

Brenda needed to know to help make the arrangements.

Except Abi didn't know.

Not for sure. She knew what the smart decision was, though her head and her heart didn't agree. But she had to put her baby first. "I'll have them call."

"It's going to be fine," Brenda tried to reassure her, but Abi heard the doubt in her friend's voice.

Right.

Fine.

Once the social worker arrived, she'd never be fine again.

Somehow, Abi managed to doze for several hours during the afternoon, but after listening to the message from her parents, the one that told her all she needed to know without really saying anything, her eyes refused to close. Instead, she stared at the bracelet encircling her wrist, rotating it around time and time again.

A knock sounded half a second before the door pushed open. "Hi, there, Abi. Someone's looking for her mama." The nurse compared the baby's bracelet to Abi's before lifting the blanketed bundle out of the clear bassinet. "The card says you're giving her formula?"

There was no judgment in the woman's voice, but Abi felt her own condemnation eating away at her. All she could do was nod.

After a few minutes of helping them get situated, the nurse started to leave, but stopped before walking out the door. "The emotions are normal, honey. They get everyone at one point or another."

Abi nodded but didn't take her eyes off the little cheeks sucking in and out. She memorized the sounds, the smells, the essence of the tiny bundle in her arms. Or tried to. Even as she did, she knew it would never work. In the morning, a social worker would come and Abi would sign the papers put in front of her.

And she'd never see her daughter again.

But when the social worker sat in the chair by the window, asking the questions, one tripped Abi up.

"Do you know who her father is?"

The night was burned in Abi's memory banks. Part of it anyway. When she hesitated too long, the worker prompted her again. Abi nodded. "Yes. I know who the father is."

"Then we'll need his signature, too."

"He doesn't know," she whispered. "I haven't talked to him since. I was going to, but then 9/11..." Her voice trailed off.

"Was he in the Towers?" the social worker asked as gently as she could.

Abi shook her head. "I don't he was. I mean, I know he wasn't one of the three thousand, but I don't know if he was there or not." She'd called his apartment from a pay phone a few weeks later. When he answered, she hung up.

"If you know who he is, we have to have him sign away his parental rights, sweetie."

Something she hadn't considered when she made this plan.

The nurse walked in, once again pushing the bassinet. Her face fell when she saw the social worker. "I'm sorry. I didn't realize you were..."

With a swipe of the overused Kleenex, Abi wiped her face. "I wasn't sure, but now I can't anyway."

The social worker left a couple of fliers and walked out with a sympathetic smile. The nurse awkwardly helped Abi get situated to feed her daughter one more time.

"Do you have a name you like?" The woman sat on the edge of the bed holding Abi's empty water bottle.

"Cassandra."

"That's beautiful."

"It was my grandmother's name. She died this past summer." The grandmother who would have adored meeting her great-granddaughter, who would have taken Abi and the baby in when she needed somewhere to turn. Had given Abi hope she'd do just that before succumbing to a sudden, massive stroke.

Abi didn't have anyone else like that in her life. Brenda would if she could, but there was no way. Abi had no other family. No one else in her life who would support her no matter what.

Darkness descended, but Abi refused to send little Cassie back to the nursery. She didn't know what she planned to do about adoption, but she wouldn't give up another minute with her baby.

Yet another round of tears leaked down her face as Abi cuddled the tiny bundle against her chest. With all but one light turned out, the desperate whisper ripped from her throat. "God? Are you there?" She'd never prayed before, but this seemed like the time to start if there ever was one. "I don't know what to do."

Baby Cassandra yawned and blinked her eyes open, staring up at her mother. The light caught them just right and struck Abi with the bright blue.

Then it hit her.

The one place she could take her daughter where she'd be

safe. And loved.

December 23, 2001

Two days before Christmas, Abi sat in a coffee shop on Long Island and waited. Calling him had taken every ounce of courage she had. Leaving the voicemail took more.

Sitting there, Abi didn't know if she could go through with it. The stroller with her little girl sat to her right. On the other side of it, Brenda sat with her back to the door. Diners nearby sipped on gourmet coffee, but Abi focused on the stationary in front of her. She arrived early so she could write the note, but the paper remained nearly blank.

When she'd arrived at her parents' Long Island home after leaving the hospital, a note reiterated her father's threat. Since then, Abi had planned what to say, but realized she'd never make it through even the shortest speech. She'd planned the words to write, but now the time had come to put pen to paper, and she only managed his name. A glance at her watch told her she didn't have much time. If she didn't write it now, she'd have to make the speech. No way could she do that.

She picked up the Mont Blanc knock-off she'd received for graduation from her grandmother and scribbled a few lines. Her heart squeezed as she reread the note. She couldn't be a student and a mom. But this? Abi had her suitcase packed. She wouldn't return to her parents' home but would crash at Brenda's for a few days while her friend went out of town. Brenda knew most of what happened, but not everything. Abi's fingers furrowed through her hair, and she turned to stare out the window. There he stood. His six-foot frame seemed shorter with his shoulders slumped and hands shoved deep in the pockets of his coat. He looked at his watch and trudged across the street.

The bell over the door jangled. Abi crossed through the unfinished sentence, scribbled a last sentiment and her name, and shoved the note in her purse as he sat down across from her.

"Hi." At the sound of his voice, the knots in her gut tightened.

Abi looked up, knowing he'd see the remnants of her tears. She twisted the napkin in her hands and tried not the think about the weight she'd gained. And if he'd notice.

"Thanks for coming. I wanted to try to explain, but..." Abi shrugged. "After 9/11, after Mark..." The thoughts of her brother nearly overwhelmed her already overwrought emotions. "Daddy isn't going to pursue anything. I tried to tell him you weren't guilty, but he didn't believe me at first. He found your name in my journal on 9/11-before it was '9/11.' I'd left it lying out by accident." This time the shrug was a mere halfhearted lift of one shoulder.

"Mark?" he interrupted. "I read the list of firefighters a bunch of times to make sure he wasn't there."

"He wasn't on the lists. He was killed at a fire on 9/11. Not at the Trade Center. Another fire where they didn't have enough manpower because of everything else. They think he died right around the time the first tower fell."

Were those tears in his eyes? He and Mark hadn't spoken in months. "I'm so sorry."

Cassandra let out a cry. The disguised Brenda made a

shushing sound, but Abi didn't look. She couldn't. It was too much. She had to get out. "Can you excuse me for a minute?"

She didn't wait for a reply but motioned toward the back, leaving before he had a chance to stop her. Brenda went out the front door. Abi dug the paper out and waved the barista over. "Can you give this to that guy?"

The woman nodded. Abi fled to the other side of the street and collapsed in Brenda's arms.

Travis read the note three times before it began to sink in.

Dear Travis,

She had to have written it earlier. There hadn't been time since she excused herself.

I hate doing this to you, especially like this. I tried to handle it on my own. I thought I could, but this semester was so hard. Even more than just everything on 9/11 and Mark. I can't do it. I can't be a college student and a mom.

It took several minutes for that to really register.

A mom?

He read on, his disbelief growing with each word.

The baby in the stroller is yours. From that night. I hate that I haven't told you sooner, but I didn't know how. I couldn't tell my parents what happened, not all of it. They would blame you, and it wasn't your fault. I know this is the coward's way out, but I can't tell you to your face. Everything you need for a couple of days is in the diaper bag and the duffel on the bottom of the stroller. So is her birth certificate.

Her name is Cassandra. She's only a few days old. Please take good care of her for me. I won't be home for a while so you can't reach me. My parents left for vacation out of the country, so they wouldn't be here when she was born.

I wish things had worked out the way we planned. The way we talked about all those times. ~~I wish~~

Whatever she wished, she didn't finish the thought before scribbling through it. About like their relationship had been. A wish that was never finished. He went back to the letter.

Tell Cassandra I love her.

I'm sorry.

Abi

He read it two more times, starting to come to grips with what it meant.

And then the baby began to fuss.

Taking a deep, steadying breath to fortify himself, he turned to the blanket tented over the handle of the car seat. Lifting up one corner, he saw pink. Fuzzy bunnies on the toes of a sleeper. A tiny foot kicking those bunnies in the air. He looked further and saw the bluest eyes he'd ever seen staring back at him, almost as though she knew who he was.

Her father.

Her daddy.

The one responsible for her from here on out.

And in that moment, he fell helplessly in love.

December 25, 2001

Christmas night, the little gray Toyota turned off I-44, south towards Serenity Landing, as the wailing in the backseat reached a new level.

"I'm sorry, Cassandra. We're almost there. I'll get you something to eat in a ten minutes, I promise." Jennifer kicked him out the moment he tried to explain his arrival at the apartment with a baby. Instead, he'd boxed up all his worldly belongings along with the things Abi had left for the baby and packed it in his car. They headed for the only place he knew he could get the help he needed until he had a better handle on things.

Over twelve hundred miles. Stopping every two or three hours to feed his daughter or change her diaper. Sometimes more often than that. Always taking much longer than it should. Failing to take into account how many things would be closed on Christmas Day, he ran out of the bottled water when he needed to make one more meal for his daughter. He pressed the pedal a little closer to the floor in an effort to reach Serenity Landing a little faster.

The newborn squalling had quieted a bit when Travis finally pulled to a stop in front of the house where he'd grown up. In the front window, a Christmas tree stood, multi-colored lights twinkling. In the window next to it, he could see Mom and Dad sitting at the dining room table, though he knew they wouldn't be able to see him. His brother walked in with a platter, piled high with a turkey way too big for the three of them. They'd be eating leftovers for a month.

Another squeak came from the back. "Okay, baby. We're here."

Somehow, Travis managed to get the diaper bag and the baby seat out of the car and headed toward the door, snow crunching under his boots with each step. The smell of oak burning in the fireplace both comforted him and heightened his anxiety. What if they turned him away? Then what?

Should he knock?

He hadn't been home in two and a half years. Did he just walk in?

Even with his hands full, Travis managed to press the doorbell. He took a deep breath and blew it out slowly, finishing as the door opened.

Mom stood there, her jaw hanging down for a second before her hands covered her mouth. "Travis!"

He tried to smile but failed miserably. "Hi, Mom." In the space of a heartbeat, he saw what he needed to in her eyes. Forgiveness. Acceptance. Love. Grace. With a prayer tossed heavenward, he tried again to smile, this time successfully. "There's someone I want you to meet."

Available Now!

Travis Harders has been a single dad since the day he learned he had a daughter with his only one-night stand. Fifteen years later, he and Cassie are getting along just fine and he's even fallen in love. The last thing he expects to find on his doorstep one Tuesday morning is Cassie's mom - the one person he thought he'd never see again - and she's asking the impossible.

Circumstances, including her firefighter brother's death on 9/11, forced Abi Connealy into a decision she's spent years regretting and her daughter grew up without her. But now, a family crisis compels her to do the one thing she swore she never would: find the daughter she'd abandoned just a few days after birth.

Shocked when Travis doesn't send her packing, Abi prays to a God she doesn't believe in that her relationship with her daughter will be restored. Travis plans to propose to his girlfriend, but their relationship hits the rocks as he and Abi both struggle with the long-dormant feelings that never had the chance to develop.

When Cassie demonstrates incredible grace toward the grandfather who refuses to acknowledge her existence, Abi begins to learn the love of a Savior - a Savior who has more than enough Grace to Save.

Previews may not be in their final form and are subject to change.

When she's not writing about her imaginary friends, USA Today Bestselling Author Carol Moncado prefers binge watching pretty much anything to working out. She believes peanut butter M&Ms are the perfect food and Dr. Pepper should come in an IV. When not hanging out with her hubby, four kids, and two dogs who weigh less than most hard cover books, she's probably reading in her Southwest Missouri home.

Summers find her at the local aquatic center with her four fish-er, kids. Fall finds her doing the band mom thing. Winters find her snuggled into a blanket in front of a fire with the dogs. Spring finds her sneezing and recovering from the rest of the year.

She used to teach American Government at a community college, but her indie career, with nearly two dozen titles released in the first 2.5 years, has allowed her to write full time. She's a founding member and former President of MozArks ACFW, blogger at InspyRomance, and is represented by Tamela Hancock Murray of the Steve Laube Agency.

CANDID Romance

Finding Mr. Write
Finally Mr. Write
Falling for Mr. Write

Montevaro Monarchy

Good Enough for a Princess
Along Came a Prince
More than a Princess

Brides of Belles Montagnes

Hand-Me-Down Princess
Winning the Queen's Heart
Protecting the Prince (Novella)
Prince from her Past

Serenity Landing Lifeguards

The Lifeguard, the New Guy, & Frozen Custard
(previously titled: The Lifeguards, the Swim Team, & Frozen Custard)
The Lifeguard, the Abandoned Heiress, & Frozen Custard
(previously in the *Whispers of Love* collection)

Other Novellas

Gifts of Love

Carol Moncado

(also available as part of the *Snowflakes & Mistletoe* collection)
Manuscripts & Mistletoe
Ballots, Bargains, & the Bakery (also in the *Table for Two* collection)

Made in United States
Orlando, FL
26 May 2022

18211355R10221